Steel Victory

The Steel Empires Series BOOK ONE

J.L. Gribble

Published by Dog Star Books
Bowie, MD

Revised Edition

Cover Image: Bradley Sharp
Book Design: Jennifer Barnes

Printed in the United States of America

ISBN: 978-1-935738-73-2
Library of Congress Control Number: 2015943000

www.DogStarBooks.org

ACKNOWLEDGMENTS

Books should never be written in a vacuum. I could not have accomplished this without the support of many.

To my incredible writing community: Jennifer Brooks, Christe Callabro, Ron Edison, Judi Fleming, Vanessa Giunta, Kathleen Kollman, Chun Lee, Rhonda Mason, Jason Jack Miller, Erica Satifka, Deanna Sjolander, Shara White, K. Ceres Wright, Stephanie Wytovich, and everyone else from the Seton Hill University Writing Popular Fiction program (past, present, and future). Thank you for your support.

To everyone who read all or bits of this novel in its many incarnations: Sabrina Benulis, Matt Betts, Faryn Black, Greg Fisher, Glenn Garrabrant, Tristan Horrom, Adrienne Kapp, Michael Mehalek, Heidi Ruby Miller, Maryn Rosenberg, and Chris Stout. Thank you for pushing me to be a better writer.

To Jennifer Barnes and John Edward Lawson. Thank you for believing in Limani.

And to Jeffrey Coleman, Timons Esaias, Diane Turnshek, and Stacie Yuhasz. Thank you for being my mentors in literature, writing, and life.

Also from the Steel Empires Series

Steel Magic
Steel Blood
Steel Time
Steel Shadows

FOREWORD

It was a surprise and an honour to be asked to write the foreword to this revised edition of J.L. Gribble's *Steel Victory* by our shared publisher. It took me less than a heartbeat to agree. I absolutely love Gribble's epic alternative history chronicles with their trope-with-a-twist characterisations and Tolkien-esque world building, considering the *Steel Empires* series a must-read experience for any discerning speculative fiction lover.

Despite a passion for quirky fantasies, I discovered this series late, jumping in at book 3, *Steel Blood*, then book 4, *Steel Time*, before going back to the beginning to fill in the gaps. Happily, Gribble offers 'just enough and never too much' backstory and context, making the books equally satisfying when read as standalone episodes. It's hardly surprising; since graduating with a Masters in Popular Fiction from Seton Hill University, Gribble has been a professional medical writer by day and freelance fiction editor by night, so she knows her way around a sentence. In fact, she wields her words as deftly as her protagonists manipulate a rapier, conjure magic, and parlay themselves out of a procession of diplomatic disasters. Once hooked, the series is compulsive, and, like readers of GRR Martin's *Game of Thrones* waiting for that long-promised installment, I'm always impatient for Gribble to deliver up her next *Steel Empires* title. Okay, so I don't exactly lie awake at night worried that she will tire of her characters and go on to write other things—her *Steel Empires* universe is sufficiently complex and varied for another forty novels at least (someone should probably alert our publisher)—but I do sometimes wonder how she can possibly maintain the exceptional quality and unexpected variety of her narratives. She hasn't failed yet.

Whoops. I'm getting ahead of myself. I'm supposed to be writing a foreword to the *first* book, *Steel Victory*, not the entire series. In this foundation novel, which Gribble wrote as her thesis text and has subsequently revised, emboldened humanists have increased their attacks on the non-human minority of Limani, a neutral city-state which acts as a territorial buffer between the British and Roman colonies, where retired mercenary and Vampire Master of the City, Victory, is a ranking member of the city council. Casualties of the latest civil unrest include Victory's daywalker, Mikelos Connor, as well as two werewolves and a rather feisty young elf, all of whom are convalescing in the local hospital. But the council have another bigger problem to deal with: Victory's daughter, Toria, has stumbled upon a Roman military camp near Limani's southern border, and enemy scouts have captured Victory's sire, the vampire Asaron, and warrior-mage Kane Nalamas. Toria herself has escaped the ambush, but not without first being cursed. With Limani forces outnumbered and undermined, Victory and Toria—made vulnerable by the incapacity of their respective partners—must bring together the city's supernatural factions to face an imminent Roman invasion, mother and daughter trying not to kill each other in the process.

Steel Victory has it all: complex kick-ass female protagonists, high action battle scenes, betrayal, intrigue, identity politics, martial law…and *were-porpoises.* In lesser hands, this potent cross-genre mix of post-modern post-apocalyptic paranormal urban fantasy would be like a sandwich with too many fillings, but Gribble holds it all together with seamless ease to create a bold and coherent narrative that works. Part of the charm is Gribble's unabashed use of well-known tropes lifted from other worlds, a decision which allows her to hold back on the heavy-handed explanations. After all, we know about vampires and mages already; we've studied Roman history. Yet Gribble isn't afraid to tweak and twist those familiar notions to her own intent, either. For example, in the prequel novelette, *The Reluctant Master,* which appears in the back of this volume and tells of the events leading to Victory's bonding with Mikelos Connor, Victory defines 'daywalker' in her own words: "I've heard daywalkers referred to as 'human servants,' but I hate that term. While the daywalker gets the benefit of longer life and the vampire gets the benefit of a daytime guardian, which was much more important in ages past, it's not a one-way street. A daywalker has to be a partner, because the trust goes both ways. And while my partnership with Mikelos has grown out of love, it's a relationship that needs care and feeding like any other, whether romantic or otherwise." This quote by the character, published in a rare real-world interview, is an excellent example of how Gribble subverts the trope of the sun-intolerant vampire to her own device, creating a version which is original and fresh.

However, readers mustn't mistake *Steel Victory* for just an entertaining read about vampires, werewolves, and mages on the brink of a Roman invasion, because in each of her titles, Gribble underpins her work with a slew of highly relevant themes. At its simplest, *Steel Victory* is a coming of age story set around blended family and intergenerational relationships. It's also an examination of the myriad small events which can lead to full-blown warfare between neighbouring states. It takes a keen look at unbridled prejudice towards marginalised groups and its impact on a multicultural society, and it includes a discourse on the evolution of weaponry and the dangers therein. It highlights the importance of alliances in assuring global stability, reveals there is more than one way to approach a problem, and that history, even alternative history, tends to repeat itself. In reading *Steel Victory*, I was also pleased to learn that frequent imbibing of coffee is a vital ritual in any civilised society.

After several years of online acquaintance, I was delighted to finally met author J.L. Gribble in person at a convention in Grand Rapids in 2019, and I discovered a woman who is as complex and intriguing as her novels. She's warm, intelligent, informed, and funny. Sometimes assertive and outgoing, and sometimes a little shy. When she's not writing, she's a gamer, a reviewer, a movie critic and fanfiction lover, a blogger, a self-confessed geek, and slave to a court of Siamese cats. She's fond of cheese. Watches far too much Netflix. Drives a Tesla. She also takes gleeful pleasure in accelerating quickly to terrify unsuspecting passengers.

In short, I liked her as much as I liked her *Steel Empires* books.

If you haven't sampled this series yet, then you're in for a treat. I won't hold you up any longer.

Lee Murray
February 2020

In another lifetime, Victory spent her nights hustling for money in the fight ring, conning coin out of men who never believed a woman possessed skill with a blade. Finding a willing meal in one of those same men, then vanishing before the dawn.

In another lifetime, Victory spent her evenings in the greatest courts across two continents, leveraging her reputation as a dedicated bodyguard in the service of powerful women. Protecting ladies whose rivals would see them dead, and building a reputation as one of the most famed mercenaries in centuries. She never worried where her next meal came from.

In another lifetime, Victory spent her evenings praying to any mythical beings who might exist that she live through another day, another hour, as bombs rained down and destroyed all she vowed to protect. She didn't feed for days.

Tonight, in this new lifetime, she awaited a boat.

Victory tapped the fingers of her right hand against her thigh in a steady rhythm as a lone moth circle the overhead fluorescent light. Each beat counted the movement of a blade as she dueled an imaginary opponent in her mind's eye. Lunge, slash, parry—launch into a forward roll, hamstring her partner—reset, en garde. On the bench at her side, her daywalker Mikelos made another notation in pencil on the blank sheet music spread across his lap. To him, the beat of fingers against denim in the tempo he'd set for her represented the music of a full orchestra, a hundred instruments in his head as he worked on his latest symphony.

A dock worker in a battered coverall entered the customs house's sparse waiting area. She paused her tapping, which distracted Mikelos from his work.

"Ms. Connor?"

Victory jabbed a thumb toward Mikelos. "He's Mr. Connor. I'm just Victory." The only name she'd known in her long lifetime.

The dock worker scrunched a rag in his oil-stained dark hands. "Sorry. Master Rhaavi asked me to pass a message."

Fear and hesitation twisted from the man's skin, along with undertones of a scent Victory could not identify offhand. Forest and shadow. She forced herself to stay seated—the poor guy might bolt from the room otherwise. She checked the embroidered name patch at his chest. "Go ahead, Taba."

Taba opened his mouth, but hesitated. The rag twisted again in his grasp. Steeling himself, he said, "The, ah, river transport isn't stopping."

Visions of the two-hundred-foot-long riverboat careening into the docks to crush the Limani customs house—and them in it—with tumbling cargo containers flashed through her mind. Then Victory interpreted Taba's true meaning. The riverboat intended to pass them by.

Mikelos rolled his sheet music and shoved it into the pocket of his cargo pants as he rose. "Where's Rhaavi?"

Taba tucked the abused rag into his own pocket. "His office. Want me to take you?"

"Please," Victory said. She and Mikelos followed Taba along a hallway. "I guess he got the radio fixed?"

"Part came down from the Brits last week, and I supervised the elf who installed it. That's how he got word." Taba hesitated as they approached the glass door that separated the open waiting and processing area from the offices.

Mikelos and Taba's own visages reflected in the light, but Victory knew she appeared as a shadowy echo to Mikelos, and to Taba not at all. A startling sight no matter the circumstances, but Victory had neither the time nor the patience to explain the mystical physics of life as a vampire. She stalked between the men, pushing her way through the door. If Taba could see her reflection, it would appear no different than the evidence of his own eyes. A woman of average height, auburn hair pulled into a long braid. Paler than most, maybe, but not a distinguishing characteristic on its own.

Taba regained his equilibrium and led them through an open office area brimming with file cabinets but lacking any occupants in the late hour. Taba's coworkers waited for the riverboat outside in the warm night, leaving the room with an eerie abandoned air. The low fuzz of static emanated from one office.

After the destruction caused during the Last War, traditional wireless communication became impossible. The elves had found a way around it, but kept control of the necessary enchantments. Victory suspected they wanted to keep the pesky warmongering humans from getting out of hand again.

"Master Rhaavi?" Victory knocked at the doorframe before stepping into the cluttered office. "Everything okay?"

The customs master hunched over a small table covered in old electronics. He raised one hand for silence and twisted a knob on the radio unit. "Limani calling Roman One Three Nine. Come in, One Three Nine. Over."

The radio spurted more static. Rhaavi wheeled his chair away from the table. "Nothing but noise for the past ten minutes." He rubbed his bald head, shiny with sweat. "Guess you two should have a seat."

"What's going on?" Victory moved a stack of folders on one chair to the floor before sitting. "Taba said the boat wasn't stopping. How far away is it?"

"I got the first call maybe twenty minutes ago?" Rhaavi shuffled through the forms on his desk. He found the appropriate paper and handed it to Victory. "Captain told me he received conflicting orders and he might be late. He radioed again a few minutes later, saying something about his new orders to skip Limani and continue to his stop in Calverton."

The scrawled handwriting revealed no further detail, so Victory replaced the paper on the untidy desk. This made no sense. Why go straight to the British colonies to the north? Limani was a good trade customer, and the riverboat must have deliveries to make.

But it still had to sail past the city to continue along the Tranosari Bay toward Calverton. They had a chance. "We can't let that happen," Victory said. "We need to borrow a boat."

Rhaavi shifted in his chair, which creaked with his movement. "You two are nuts. Yeah, some deliveries might be missed, but that's the shipper's problem. People here'll complain and it'll get made up. Some British stockholder must've thrown his weight around."

"That boat is going to Calverton." Victory emphasized the destination. "My sire is onboard as a registered passenger. If it docks in the British colonies, he will be sought and killed." This time, she did bare fangs and suppress a growl.

Realization dawned for Rhaavi. "Asaron is coming. I'm sorry, I didn't know he was expected today."

"It's okay." Victory backed away. "But now we need your help. Keys to a boat, at least. And I don't suppose you have any sort of armory here?"

The customs master darted around his office, opening a safe in the corner and retrieving a revolver and a box of bullets. "Why would we need weapons here? But I've got this, and you're welcome to it if you think you might need it. Taba!"

The dockhand poked his head in the office from where he'd lurked outside. "Sir?"

"These two need to borrow a boat. Make sure the *Anchorless* is ready to go." Rhaavi handed the gun and ammunition to Mikelos. "My grandfather passed this on to me. I want it back, you hear?"

Mikelos tucked the box under his arm while he inspected the revolver. "You have my word." He popped a moon clip into the cylinder.

"You don't want to call anyone for backup?" Rhaavi asked. "Asaron is Mercenary Guild, right?"

"No time," Victory said. They accepted good wishes from Rhaavi as they followed Taba out of the customs house, but she veered toward the parking lot once outside.

So much for a simple evening, reuniting with her sire Asaron after his latest mercenary contract in the Roman holdings to the south. Perhaps catching up on news and gossip over dinner in town. Victory had relinquished her own mercenary career decades ago, retiring to the independent city of Limani after the Last War. Following the upheaval of the city's political system decades ago, her quiet life vanished when she accepted a permanent seat on the ruling council representing the city's vampires. However, those vampires consisted of her and Asaron, and her power was more titular than anything else. These days, she used her sword to stay in practice and train with Mercenary Guildmembers, not for defense.

She unlocked the trunk to withdraw her beloved hand-and-a-half bastard sword, sheathed in a battered leather scabbard. She'd wield it with pride to protect the vampire who'd saved her life for the first time eight hundred years ago.

Gripping the *Anchorless* after untying the small fishing boat, barely more than a dinghy, from its berth at the Limani docks, Taba looked caught behind words he couldn't express. Victory scooted to the other side of the prow. "What's wrong?"

"You, ah, want me to come? I might be able to help."

His scent of fear returned, crisp and dark, overlaying the boat's fishy aroma. "No, kid, we'll be okay," Victory said. She gave him a closer study. He had broader shoulders than the more common varieties of werepanther. "You're a, what?"

"Leopard, ma'am. Sinai Clan."

That explained both his dark skin and shoulders, and he hadn't even hit his full bulk yet. "You're also young, Taba, strong as I'm sure you are. Don't worry, we've done this sort of thing before. But thanks. And call me Victory."

"You're welcome, Victory. I'll be here when you get back." He shoved the boat away, setting them adrift.

Mikelos started the outboard engine, and with a low rumble, they skimmed out over the river. "We've never actually done something like this before." Her daywalker's low voice carried over the engine and wind. "Unless you've never told me about your time as a pirate. We should have brought the leopard."

"I've never been a pirate, but I've had cause to board a ship or two. And I'm not risking the leopard." Victory scanned the dark water for the slow-moving barge's lights. "The Sinai Clan is dying out over here, and no one knows how they're faring in Europa. Genevieve would have my head if the kid got hurt." The leader of the werepanthers in Limani defended her folk with all the passion of a mama cat. The wolves might have the reputation for being a close-knit pack, but the felines had their own protective instincts.

"True, very true. See anything?"

Brilliant summer stars and a waxing moon bathed the world in pale silver, reflected twice over by the undulating surface of the river. Victory caught a faint golden glow in the distance. "There! Cut the engine."

The low rumble faded into silence. "How're we going to reach them?" Mikelos asked.

"It's hugging this shore," Victory said. "We can drift to them. We're shielded by the front of the barge itself."

Using an oar to steer, Mikelos kept them head-on to the barge until it came within reach. The growl of the slow-revving diesel engine camouflaged any splashes they made.

Victory uncoiled a line of rope and lassoed one of the barge's cleats. The transport rode low in the water, laden to the maximum limit with dozens of massive shipping crates. After pulling the smaller boat toward the barge, she secured them together to prevent the sides from scraping and betraying their presence.

"I'm going up." She double-checked her weapon. "You coming, or do you want to stay here and guard our retreat?"

"No close-range weapons." Mikelos left the stern to give her a boost. "One shot from me, and the whole crew will be on us. I'll stay here and be ready to drive the getaway car. Give a shout if you need me."

"You'll hear more than shouting if I need you." Victory hauled herself over the edge and onto the barge's deck. Good thing she hadn't dressed up to welcome her sire home—grime from the side of the hull streaked the front of her jeans. With one last wave to Mikelos, Victory darted between the shipping containers stacked in the front of the barge. She made her way toward the rear of the vessel, where the working and living quarters for the crew should be.

The real question concerned Asaron's location. They neared Limani, but had not yet passed it. He might not even be aware of the change in his travel arrangements. If all else failed, she could sit tight in hiding and wait for the mayhem when her sire figured out his new destination. Even before the British colonies launched their crusade against vampires, echoing their homeland's long-held discrimination policies, Asaron refused to travel there. Something about a woman.

But she had no guarantee Asaron was still loose on the riverboat. The captain might have ordered him restrained at once upon learning his new orders in order to prevent harm to his crew. Either way, Victory needed to find him now.

Could it be possible to take over the boat and force it to dock at Limani? Rhaavi didn't seem too concerned. She paused, placing a hand against the side of a container damp with evening dew. But if Asaron landed in Calverton, as a registered passenger of this ship, his odds of escaping the city were slim.

She kept to the shadows when she neared the rear of the barge. Mythology and legend skewed reality to her detriment, and no psychic link connected her with her sire. Instead, hearing heartbeats warned her of anyone approaching, her one main advantage.

Speaking of which—the dull roar of blood echoing through a heart's chambers alerted her along with the gentle rhythm of a crewmember's footsteps. She crouched between two containers in the last row, sinking to her heels. Her right hand found its way to the hilt of her sword.

A shaggy-faced man in no apparent uniform wandered through the space between the cabin bulkhead and cargo, swathed in a cloud of dissipating cigarette smoke as an explanation for his evening stroll. Making a split-second decision when he passed by, Victory lunged from the shadows and grabbed his coat, then hauled him between the containers.

She pushed him against the sturdy metal, bracing her forearm across his throat. "Don't scream." She dug her arm into his neck, not enough to cut off air or circulation, but enough to show she meant business.

He didn't even try to open his mouth, and his face shone with fear. He dipped his chin in a short jerk.

"Good," Victory said. "I do not intend to hurt you. I'm only here for one thing on this boat. Understand?"

"Yes'm." A mere whisper, but the reek of too many days on the boat with not enough toothpaste washed over her. "You're here for the vampire?"

"Smart man." Victory loosened her hold a mere fraction, but stayed tense, ready to restrain him if needed. "You know what will happen if this boat continues to Calverton with him on it?"

"He'll die. Cap knows this, but made us lock him up anyway. Said we couldn't afford trouble. But Asaron don't deserve that. He's been a passenger on our route a few times, never done me wrong."

"Well, I'm here to relieve your captain of his problem. You can either take me to him, or tell me where he is."

"I'll tell you, but you better do something with me. So I can tell Cap I resisted."

"Fair enough," Victory said. He asked for it. It was obvious Asaron had made an impression, which surprised her not in the slightest.

The man gestured toward the aft of the boat, from the direction he'd come. "Follow the side all the way. It's the first door you come to. Asaron's locked in the second cabin." He paused, apologetic. "I don't have a key, and I don't know who's keeping it."

"Thank you, but that won't be an issue." Victory released the man. "Asaron and I are in your debt." He met her eyes for the single second she needed. "Sleep."

The crewman dropped like a stone at the mental push behind her command, and Victory grabbed him before he slid to the deck. She lowered him into a comfortable position, arranging his arms and legs enough akimbo to appear like he'd put up a fight before losing. Lying in the shadows, he'd be invisible to a casual glance between containers. She knelt next to him, centering herself. Messing with people's brains always made her uncomfortable.

She peered outside the cargo area once again. With no one in sight, she crept out of hiding. The crewman had given excellent directions, leading her through a deserted section of the riverboat crew quarters. The outside door proved unlocked, so Victory knelt low before pulling it open. She peeked around the corner, but the passageway stood empty. Without unloading to do in Limani, the other crewmembers enjoyed a quiet night before reaching Calverton around dawn.

Hugging the wall, Victory darted to the second door. She pressed her ear against it. Movement inside, footsteps pacing, no heartbeat. Asaron. She tried the knob despite the man's warning. Locked, and her without her lock picks. That was the problem with spur-of-the-moment adventures—no time to pack the essentials.

She rapped out a staccato beat on the door. The movement inside halted. She knocked a second time, repeating the code.

She sagged against the wall at the answering pattern, then stepped away from the door, ready to kick it in. Drastic, but she didn't have many other options unless she wanted to hunt down the captain for the keys. Mikelos would have to be ready to go when they came tearing back.

A door farther up the hall slammed opened.

"Hands on your head. Now! Back away from the door!"

She pivoted on her heels to confront the new arrival, raising her arms as she did.

He aimed a crossbow at her chest. Shot with any accuracy, the crossbow's wooden bolts threatened vampires as much as anyone else. He kept a handgun holstered at his waist.

The man dressed better than his more helpful crewmember, and when he shifted the crossbow for a better aim, Victory caught the glint of gold at his collar. She had the honor of meeting the captain.

A muffled shout echoed from on deck, as someone discovered her unconscious friend. Victory wasted no time when the captain's fierce attention broke, diving for his legs. They crashed into the wall. He cried out in pain when they landed in a heap, and the crossbow clattered to the floor. He made a quick grab for his handgun, but Victory drew faster, snatching the firearm and pressing it to his throat. He flinched away and raised his hand from the holster.

With slow movement, Victory untangled herself from the man's legs and crouched over him. Rising to her feet, aim never wavering, she favored her prisoner with a glare honed by centuries of proving herself against larger opponents. "I want the keys to this cabin."

The captain conceded defeat without a word. Careful not to make sudden movements, he withdrew a single key from his breast pocket.

"Slide it over to me."

He followed instructions, and Victory scooped up the key. She slid it into the doorknob, and with a small *snick*, the door swung inward. "Asaron?"

A deep voice answered. "Right here, girl."

Tension released in Victory's shoulders. "Grab your things, we're out."

"Way ahead of you." A hand touched her back for the briefest moment, and her sire darted past her into the passageway and to one of the other closed cabin doors. She focused on the captain at her feet but caught a glimpse of Asaron's tall form before he disappeared again.

More shouts from outside. They'd found Mikelos. "Asaron, we have to go!" Time to rescue the rescuer. She gestured with the pistol. "Into the cabin with you, my good sir."

The captain scooted across the floor on his rear into the small cabin Asaron had vacated. His mouth opened, but Victory pulled the door closed and locked it before any excuses or curses could pour forth. She had no time for either. That should help keep the barge off their tail for a short time once they made their escape.

Asaron emerged into the hallway from the other cabin. He wore his familiar long leather duster over jeans with his ever-present rucksack slung over one shoulder. He belted his Schiavona around his waist, with its distinctive iron hilt. A second sword peeked out the top of the rucksack, wrapped in canvas. She led him outside onto the deck. Asaron remained silent. They'd worked together for centuries—they didn't need words. But Asaron by her side increased her confidence exponentially. She had absolute faith Mikelos could hold his own, but Asaron's combat experience dwarfed even her own.

The rear of the ship was deserted, the deck railing and river spread out before them. She tossed the key into the water and listened for more shouts. "See anything?"

"Nope," Asaron said. "Got a boat?"

"How else do you think we got here? Mikelos is driving."

"Then let's get out of here."

Victory retraced her steps. All the noise came from where she'd left Mikelos. They ducked between cargo containers, dashing through the maze toward the opposite end of the boat.

The shouting resolved into distinct orders. "Move, and we'll cut your line. Where's your friend?"

At the voice ahead of her, she halted Asaron with an arm across his chest. She crouched to spy around one of the containers, not wanting to attract attention yet. Three men stood at the deck railing with their backs to her. She couldn't tell whether they were armed.

Mikelos' voice carried over the edge of the craft. "I don't know what you're talking about. Your captain made the arrangements for me to ferry a friend out here for him since you weren't stopping in Limani. Guess he didn't want to share."

Excellent stalling tactic. Victory approved. Straightening, she strolled out from between two of the metal containers wearing her best innocent expression. "What seems to be the problem here, gentlemen?" She sauntered toward the railing, all but batting her eyelashes.

The center sailor sneered at her, revealing few teeth. "Who're you?"

"A visitor. You can check with your captain. He should still be in his bunk." Ignoring the men, she peered over the edge of the deck to Mikelos. "Ready to go?"

In answer, Mikelos pulled loose the rope knot tied to their little fishing vessel.

When Victory swung one leg over the railing, the man of poor dental hygiene grabbed her arm. "Not so fast, girl."

She bared fang. He yelped and stumbled back. Taking advantage of the opening, she dropped to the waiting boat. It rocked with the impact, but she regained her balance and checked above her.

Asaron appeared next to the men at the railing. He tossed his rucksack to Victory, then pitched himself over the edge of the ship with a smooth dive into the water. The sailors gaped as Victory shoved the boat from the side of the barge and Mikelos revved the engine. One drew a pistol from his belt and aimed.

Victory dropped to the deck as a bullet whizzed by. "Get down!"

More bullets hit the water around them. Good thing Asaron didn't need to come up for air.

The fishing boat drew away at top speed, such as it was. The crew shouted, but the shots ceased. They weren't being paid to keep vampires prisoner.

Water lapped at Victory's fingers.

"This isn't good," Mikelos said.

The boat listed to the side when Asaron hauled himself onboard. He shook wet hair, red darkened to burgundy, out of his eyes and peeled off his long coat. "Thanks for the rescue, kids."

Mikelos stared at the bottom of the craft. "You might have been better off in the water." A bullet had cracked the hull, allowing water to flow in.

The fishing boat limped to the nearest river bank thanks to frantic bailing and a lot of luck.

Asaron might be safe, but they weren't out of the water yet. It had been a long day already if Victory had resorted to terrible puns, even in the safety of her own mind. When the hull scraped land, Mikelos cut the engine. Asaron and Victory jumped out, and their combined strength dragged the boat onto shore with ease. Asaron collapsed onto the grass, and Victory avoided the temptation to join him. "How are we doing on fuel?" she asked.

Mikelos examined the bottom of the boat as water drained out. "Not the problem. We have enough to get home, but the boat itself isn't going to make the trip. Looks like a bullet found a weak spot in the hull, and it's a long fracture rather than a leak we can stuff."

"Where are we?" Asaron propped himself on his elbows. "And I don't suppose either of you knows what time it is? I lost track, being locked up the past three days."

Victory studied the lay of the stars. "Not long till sunrise. As for where we are, I'm with you."

"Daywalker?"

Mikelos shrugged at Asaron. "We passed Limani while you two played around on the barge." He turned in a slow circle. "Nothing looks familiar. I'd estimate we're no more than a few miles from the city, but sunrise is too close to walk that far."

This grassy area of shoreline led to dense trees in the full leaves of summer, but held no familiar landmarks. Mikelos was right—they had no way to ensure they reached shelter in Limani before the sun. The boat sat lopsided on the beach. "Guess we're camping here."

"You, Asaron, and what shelter?" Mikelos asked.

Victory pulled off her wet boots and socks and padded to the boat on bare feet. "This."

"How to do you propose to manage that, daughter?"

This was not the worst time the rising sun caught the two of them over the years. "Toria told me about how your truck broke down last summer," Victory said. "Stranding you guys near the Wasteland. The farmhouse."

Some deity must have smiled upon her family that night. Victory had traveled her share of the edge of the Wasteland, the flat desolate plain stretching from west of Limani across the bulk of the continent. The permanent reminder of the Last War between the British and the Qin. Now the land was home to dust and scrub and lingering radiation, unable to support more than limited life. The burnt-out husk of an ancient farmhouse had saved Asaron's life. Now this boat provided the same gift.

Asaron pulled off his own boots. "Good idea."

They dragged the boat farther toward the trees while Mikelos scouted out two full-sized tree trunks close enough together. The three of them flipped the boat and braced it against the trees. While Asaron tied the arms of his coat around the boat's cleats to create a makeshift curtain, he said, "I'm still amazed we came across that house when we did. Talk about a godsend."

Victory stuffed brush in the open space between the boat and forest floor. Any extra cover would be useful, even under the dense summer branches. "I can't believe anyone used to live out there for you to find a house in the first place."

"Used to be a lot more subsistence farmers in the area. Like Toria's birth family."

Victory shifted back on her heels. "Family. Right."

"The elves told us her father might become an abuser. Doesn't mean it was set in stone," he said.

Victory shoved in the final handful of leaves Mikelos passed her. "Still good luck you found her when you did." Bandits had burned the farm and killed the parents, leaving the months-old baby to the elements. Not in any position to raise her himself, Asaron brought the child to his progeny and her daywalker. Years later, they learned the elves had marked Toria for eventual "rescue" from her birth parents. Pure coincidence led Asaron to the site first.

More memories of her last trip to the Wasteland surfaced as she rose to her feet and brushed dirt from her knees. Dirt and rocks, strange animals, a desolation where nothing proper grew or lived. "Thinking of Toria growing up out there is terrifying."

Mikelos finished tying a sheet of canvas he'd found stowed beneath one of the seats. It and the coat would protect them from direct sun. He stepped away from the boat, surveying their handiwork. "I suppose it will have to do."

Sire and progeny were both seasoned campaigners and had often traveled with humans or others immune to the sun's rays. Compared to worse spots in the past, this ranked right up with a luxury hotel. "Guess there's not much else we can do," Victory said.

Asaron check to the east. The stars had faded as the sky transitioned from black toward midnight blue. Dawn approached. "Guess not."

His voice had hitched. Liar. Asaron never could hide anything from her. "What's wrong?"

Asaron captured her hand and gripped it tight, tracing her fingers with his thumb. "They locked me in the cabin after we left port in New Carthage."

"What, for a three-day ride?" Mikelos asked.

"Closer to four, with all the stops." Asaron gazed past Victory, giving her daywalker a hungry stare.

Victory pulled her hand free. "Four days, with no food?"

"Three days, after they locked me up. Bottles were gone when I grabbed my stuff after you broke me out. I'll have to get Toria to charm me more when we get home."

No wonder he eyed Mikelos like the evening special. But this was an old conversation. Mikelos belonged to Victory. Sire or not, vampires did not share daywalkers. "Will you be okay?"

"Yes." Asaron said, shoving his hands in the pockets of his damp jeans. "Been through worse."

So had she, but it was never fun. If Asaron thought he could handle it, Victory wouldn't argue. "Let's get settled."

Asaron ducked under the canvas. Before Victory could follow, Mikelos grabbed her elbow. "I'm not sleeping under there with you. Not while he's like that."

"I know." They shared a kiss, taking advantage of the moment of privacy. Then, Victory followed Asaron under the boat and settled herself into a corner. Asaron had snagged the prime spot, lounging against one of the trees. She contented herself with hunching over for this conversation. Mikelos laid on his stomach, stretching his legs out of the covered area into the open air.

"So, why the sudden trip home?" Victory asked. Until Asaron's telegraph, he'd planned to work in the south through the season.

"I very much appreciate the rescue, daughter."

That was no answer. Victory met his gaze directly, aware of the unsettling intensity of her attention. Mikelos could meet a vampire's eyes, but Asaron didn't live with a companion who stared him down on a regular basis. No escape behind coyness this time. Not after dragging her who-knew-how-far away from the city on what was supposed to be a normal evening. "Don't even try to pull that. I want to know why I risked our lives to save your sorry old ass."

"Have some respect, girl. This sorry old ass can still whip yours."

Though he often goaded their verbal sparring, Mikelos interrupted them tonight. "We are allowed to worry about you, old man."

In answer, Asaron pulled the mystery sword from his pack and passed it to Victory.

She pulled away the canvas to reveal the hilt. "Toria's rapier! I wondered why I hadn't seen her with it recently."

"The blade shattered." Asaron lifted a hand before she demanded an explanation. "She asked me to get it fixed for her, and that's what I did. I'm friends with a good smith in the Grand Strand."

"But why wouldn't she tell me?"

"She didn't want you to be mad that she'd broken Jarimis' sword." Asaron rewrapped the blade when Victory handed it back. "I'd planned to head west to investigate some deaths when she sent me a panicked message. Something to do with science and alloys." The elder vampire made a face. "Since another merc offered to take the contract in my stead, I promised Toria I'd get it fixed and she shipped it down."

"I wouldn't have been angry." Accidents happened. Her own bastard sword had been repaired more than once.

"My fault," Mikelos said. "I flipped out once when she let a friend play Connor's cello. She is terrified of hurting the relics from those we loved. And Jarimis was your progeny."

A guarded look crossed Asaron's face. "There's more. I've had bad news from the south."

"Is there any other kind?" Victory said. "Let me guess—something about the secession of the new Emperor?"

"Politics." Mikelos snorted. "Romans are crazy, and I grew up in the capital."

"Things have changed, but not by much. The Emperor chose an heir from among his nephews," Asaron said. "Not my first choice, and I'm surprised the senators approved him."

"Why?" Victory asked. Who was less important than the motives behind the choice. Her sire paid more attention to global politics than she did these days, since he still made his living as part of the Mercenary Guild.

"Humans are beginning to forget about the realities of the Last War and the creation of the Wasteland. To them, it's always been there," Asaron said. "The Romans weren't involved, and the results don't affect the Senate in Roma except when their holdings in the colonies are involved. The imperialist faction holds a majority since the last common election."

"And the colonies have spread as much as they can," Mikelos said. "The southern Wasteland is even more uninhabitable than ours."

"There's still north," Asaron said.

Victory froze. "But north is Limani."

"North is the direction in which the Roman army currently marches."

Sun broke over the horizon. This was not the sort of news Victory needed when she wasn't safe at home. Asaron would have to meet with the city council to share this information, and they'd need to coordinate with Max Asher, master of the local branch of the Mercenary Guild.

"Is the army going to get here today?" Mikelos asked. At Asaron's negative, he continued, "Then both of you sleep, and we'll raise the alarm tonight." Mikelos might be Victory's best friend and lover, but daytime guardian was the daywalker's original job description. He ducked out of the shelter to settle against another nearby tree.

Victory curled next to Asaron in the small space, entwining her fingers with his. Asaron completed her family, and with them, Limani could stand up to anything.

Thunder rolled through the apartment, to Toria's dismay. That wasn't supposed to happen. When the glassware in her impromptu laboratory stopped rattling on its shelves, she peered at the beaker and dagger in her hands. The silver solution coating the bottom and sides of the beaker had transformed into a black chalky substance. The dagger blade didn't fare much better. Useless, now. She plunked both items on the counter and pulled off her safety glasses.

"What the hell?"

At her partner's query, the containment spell collapsed around her in sparkles of violet light. When the last vestiges faded, Toria waved her glasses at the open doorway. "Hey."

Kane stepped into her lab—also known as the corner kitchen of their apartment—with over-exaggerated hesitance. "Am I in danger of being blown up?"

"No more than usual." Toria inspected the charred stain on the countertop. Yet another sample proven a failure. She exchanged her glasses for the beaker and crossed to the other counter, making sure not to scuff the chalk lines on the tile floor with her feet.

Kane kept away from her work area, choosing a stool from the sitting area of their open-concept apartment. "What happened to 'I will not set things on fire without my partner present'?"

Toria washed and rinsed the beaker. "You had plans. With a boy. This is me entertaining myself while you're out on hot dates." She brought a damp sponge to the other counter, and a hard scrub removed most of the black soot mark.

"You could have gone with Mikelos and Victory last night and stayed at the house. Mikelos would have cooked for you this morning."

"The whole sword thing might have come up. It's embarrassing." Asking Asaron to get it fixed was one thing. The sword's original owner was her mother's vampire progeny, the vanished prodigal son. The last thing she wanted was her mother finding out. "You're home early. Date no good?"

"He was okay." Kane ran a hand over his face. "Old-country British, so he got twitchy when he figured out I was Victory's foster son. In the middle of brunch. Also embarrassing."

"Sorry, hon." She was, honest. Her partner was tall, dark, and drop-dead gorgeous. And still got more dates than she did, even considering his more limited dating pool. In a perfect world, she and Kane would have lived happily ever after together, but fate and biology had decided otherwise.

No time to dwell, she had work to do. "The day is still young. Want to help?"

Kane left his safe spot to come closer to her workspace, dragging the stool behind him. A nearby row of vials contained different variants on the silver goop she'd discarded. "What are you up to now?"

He wouldn't be able to resist her latest chemistry project, even if he often limited himself to note-taker and general observer. Still more interesting than hoity-toity British boys. "I figured out why my sword broke. Simple, in the end, and I should have realized it a long time ago." Any middle-school kid with a chemistry set knew the answer. Or hobbyist jeweler. Or self-taught metallurgist. All of which she was, to one degree or another. "Why is silver mixed with copper in most jewelry?"

"Umm..."

He did this, acted the dunce to bolster her self-confidence. Yet another reason she loved him. "It's mixed with copper to make the piece stronger. Silver on its own is too soft a metal to retain its shape against hard wear and tear." She rearranged the vials on the counter again, then pulled on her glasses and gestured for Kane to grab his own pair hanging on the wall. "So, what did I do that was so stupid?"

"I was never clear on what you did in the first place." After donning eye protection, he lifted one of the vials and watched the silver solution slide inside the glass like mercury. "You converted part of the metal in your sword to silver?"

Toria plucked the vial out of his hand and returned it to its original place. "Yeah, when we were young idiots, and I thought I knew what I was doing. Before I knew as much about chemistry and metallurgy as I do now. I analyzed one of the shards, and frankly, I'm surprised it lasted as long as it did."

"How so?"

She pointed to a spot on the floor. Kane moved his stool and parked himself as instructed. "Because I had the damned proportions wrong." It would be a long time before she stopped berating herself for this. "I thought I could mess with the steel and my magic would retain the strength of the blade. I was so stupid."

"No, you weren't. Just young. You said it yourself, you didn't know as much as you do now. I assume now you're trying to fix the problem?"

"Yeah." She unstopped the vial at the end of the row to pour the silver solution into the clean beaker. "Grandpa wrote that he'd bring the hilt to a smith he trusts for a new blade."

"Asaron'll bring it home good as new. We'll redo the spell we did in high school, but you'll get the proportions right this time, and it'll be your old sword again. No problem."

Another tension headache threatened, despite her partner's soothing presence. Toria scuffed both hands through her short hair. "You're right. I should have gone with them. What if the boat was late, and they got stranded during the day?"

"It's a good thing Mikelos is fine in the sun. It'll be okay, love."

Toria swirled the silver in the beaker. Damn his logic. "Yeah, I guess."

"They'll bring him home. And your sword. Now show me what we're going to do to make it even better than it was."

After being wrapped up in each other's souls for almost ten years, he knew how to manipulate her. Prompt her to talk about her true passion: mixing the two volatile sciences of chemistry and magic. She held up the new beaker. "This is a formula I'm still attempting to perfect." She gestured to the remaining vials. "Those are the latest variations I developed this morning."

"Do I want to know what's in them?"

Toria had banned him from helping her play with chemicals due to his incurable inability to measure with any precision. He was a terrible baker, too. "The new idea is that instead of weakening the steel of a blade by converting a percentage of it to silver, I should coat the blade with a microscopic layer of silver instead. Bond it to the steel so well it can't even be scraped away."

"And what are we doing here, exactly?"

Toria snagged another sacrificial blade from the counter—a broken throwing knife, this time. "I'm trying to figure out the best way to bond the silver alloy to the steel of a blade."

"Magic?"

"Of course." Toria held out the beaker to Kane. "I've gotten used to working with the extra magical properties the silver gives me. But pouring the alloy and getting it to cover evenly takes too much concentration. You pour, and I'll spread."

Uncertainty clouded his face. "If you say so."

Her fascination with mixing chemistry and magic always left him a bit puzzled, similar to the way his own passion for literature made no sense to her. "You'll be fine, hon. Help me set the containment spell, then pour when I tell you to."

He grasped the beaker between thumb and forefinger, as if unsure how tight to hold the vessel. She pushed a sense of encouragement through their link, and he relaxed.

What she and Kane formed was unique in Limani—a warrior-mage pair. Before Kane, Toria was a regular mage. A bit precocious for her age, but nothing special overall. Before Toria, Kane had zero magical ability, despite both of his parents being mages. But when they first grasped hands at age twelve, their energies meshed and the jolt of power activated Kane's latent magical ability. Together, their stable power meant they achieved control over their abilities that took other mages decades to master. Some bonded mages used this control to expand the potential of their power, becoming legends in magical circles. Toria and Kane, on the other hand, had decided on the more traditional road of warrior-mages after bonding, spending their extra time on martial arts, swordplay, and tactics and apprenticing themselves to Limani's Mercenary Guild.

With Kane helping her, she could place the load of the containment spell on him and concentrate on spreading the alloy. She shouldn't have juggled both magical processes at the same time. Her lapse of mental control over the containment circle had resulted in the earlier thunder as her power echoed through her affinity element of storm. She didn't have enough concentration for the circle while doing two other things requiring such physical dexterity.

They locked gazes. Toria nudged a mental switch and the world around her flared into real color. Every time she used her magesight to illuminate the world, she wondered how mundane humans stood such bland surroundings. Now, her silver vials glowed, and the beaker Kane held gained more depth of light and shadow than seemed possible. The knife in her open palms shimmered with electricity, the result of a charm she placed on all of their weapons to prevent rust.

Kane overshadowed every other magical object in the room. His fluid emerald aura enveloped him, shimmering over the cool clay tones of his skin and representing the powers of earth he aligned with. All mages affected the magical power inherent in the world to an extent, but Kane's true talents lay in growth and protection.

She tuned out her aura by habit but knew Kane saw her body encased in a delicate crystalline structure glinting deep violet, deceptive in its strength. The power of her own element of storm reacted with the leftover electrical charge in the room, and the hair on their arms stood on end. Her alignment with storm allowed her to manipulate the power flowing through all people and objects, from the electrical power of a storm or a wall outlet to the bioelectricity in all living beings.

Other mages aligned with air, water, and fire, rounding out the so-called circle of planetary life. Warrior-mages came in any combination of the five elements, but Toria and Kane counted themselves lucky. Storm and earth complemented each other well, from powerful workings to simple exchanges of energy.

Toria's personal shields fractured, then spread to form the framework of a sphere around them, guided by the power she'd infused in the chalk circle on the floor. Kane's fluid aura expanded to flow in and around the prismatic shapes of her shield.

Contentment reverberated through their link. Kane poured more of his energies into the shield and accepted the weight of powering it. She remained connected to the energy, but now it was Kane's responsibility to maintain the containment spell. When they shared magic, they were as close as two hemispheres of a brain, working in harmony to accomplish one goal.

Kane raised the beaker. "Ready."

Toria grasped the knife hilt, holding the blade horizontal. Kane tipped the beaker, and the thick silver formula oozed toward the edge of the glass.

Her entire being centered upon the point where liquid met metal. Toria's perception shifted in a way she had not expected. Her vision tunneled, and the blade of the dagger magnified hundreds of times in her sight, more precise than a microscope. But it had depth, not the flatness of a sample smashed between two glass slides. The blade wavered in her hands, making the world appear as though it vibrated in a violent earthquake. A wave of dizziness passed through her.

Everything stilled when the silver liquid touched the blade. A brilliant flash of pure white light left Toria blinking away shadowy negative images. Uncontrolled power surged through her, followed by the familiar sharp crack of thunder. The world went black.

Kane shouted her name in the distance. Her left shoulder ached where she'd crashed to the floor. Heat licked her face.

"*Toria!*"

Her partner tugged at her arms, dragging her across the kitchen floor. The strange warmth grew hotter, followed by an acrid odor. Had she mixed some compounds wrong?

The pieces fell together, and she wrenched herself from Kane's grip. She pushed herself up, banging the top of her head into Kane's chin. They both yelped.

Broken glass littered the tile floor amidst oozing silver alloy. Blue flames leapt from the substance, gushing thick white smoke. The knife lay discarded nearby, the blade charred and black.

"What the hell happened?"

"You tell me!" Panic sharpened Kane's voice. Screeching beeps drowned out the rest of his tirade when the professional grade smoke detector kicked in.

Toria ignored the complaints of her muscles and ringing in her ears as she staggered to her feet. She lurched across the kitchen for the fire extinguisher as Kane dove for cover on the other side of the kitchen island. With practiced actions, Toria pulled the pin and sprayed the unnatural flames with white foam. This was not her first incident.

The chemical mixture overwhelmed the magical fire, and Toria thanked her luck that she'd once again not burned down their apartment building.

Kane emerged from his hiding spot and, pitching his voice over the smoke detector, said, "You're developing a habit."

She didn't have the energy to shout back. She set the fire extinguisher on the counter with a metal clang, then rubbed her shoulder, sore from where she'd landed on it. Already, the noxious taste in the air faded.

They stared at the mess of evaporating foam and scorched stains on the tile floor. With a final disgruntled beep, the smoke detector ceased its screams of alarm.

Kane rolled up his shirtsleeves. "That's going to set if we don't clean it up immediately."

"'We'? My project, my mess. I'm not forcing menial labor on you on top of a bad date."

"Nah. I'd rather spend time with you anyway." Kane caught the roll of paper towels Toria tossed to him. "Let's pop open all the windows. We can take the afternoon off while the air clears."

They made short work of cleanup, mopping foam and soot and disposing broken glass into the recycling. Toria added the charred knife to the growing collection of metal scrap tucked away in her bedroom. When she returned to the apartment's common area, she asked, "Want to help me again tomorrow? Or do you have another date with what's-his-name?"

"I doubt there will be more dates with Duncan. We were asked to leave the first restaurant we went to, and then the awkwardness never let up when he learned about my family ties."

"Dress code?" Not likely, since Kane wore pressed slacks and his favorite green button-up.

"A sign that basically said 'no nonhumans.' A light flashed when I walked in, so I guess mages qualify. Ironic, using magic as a detector."

"Where the hell was this?"

"Café Lizzette. We ate at the new Castillian place instead."

"Doesn't Emily Fabbri run Café Lizzette?" Interesting. According to the numerous campaign posters that had plastered the restaurant on Main Street, Fabbri had been elected as a human representative to the city council in the last election cycle.

"Something stinks. I'm curious to find out which mage set that charm. Up for an adventure today?"

"Absolutely," Toria said. "Limani doesn't have enough mages for one of us to sell out." She and Kane might be college students, but few mages lived in Limani, and they were the only warrior-mage pair. That gave them some pull, and she was going to pull threads and see what unraveled.

What else was she going to do on summer break beside set fires in her kitchen?

In simple black script, the sign in front of Café Lizzette read: *Humans welcome. Patronage discouraged from all others.*

Toria read the sign a second time, not believing her eyes. "Isn't this illegal?" She turned to Kane. "Please tell me it's illegal."

He leaned against a lamppost. "It's not."

Toria itched to storm the café and demand an explanation. "The last census showed more than eighty-five percent of Limani's population were non-magical human. It's not like we're overrunning the place."

"To some people, even one is enough."

"And one of the new councilmembers owns this place. No wonder you were worried." They stared at the restaurant. Toria's skin crawled. The city had almost descended into civil war less than five years ago when the werepanthers sued for fair representation on the council. She may have grown up in the rose-tinted world of Limani, but this bordered on ridiculous. Scratch that. Insanity.

Worry for her mother also itched in the back of her skull. No one had answered at the house when she'd called before they left, which meant her parents hadn't returned home last night. She kept telling herself the boat had been late and the three had been stranded at the docks. She couldn't worry about that right now. Which meant she welcomed this distraction.

"This is so not cool." Toria marched to the restaurant's front door. Her partner didn't follow, though amusement at her antics pulsed through their link. When she checked over her shoulder, Kane still leaned against the lamppost. Fair enough. He could come to the rescue if this ended in tears.

The bell above the door rang when she entered, and as Kane had reported, a shimmer of blue light washed over her. She searched for a taste of the caster with her own magic, but a waitress pounced on her right away, breaking her concentration.

"Hi, I'm Paige, and I'll be your server today. How many in your party?" The young woman grabbed a handful of menus from a small rack.

"Actually, is Ms. Fabbri available?" Toria attempted to match the girl's bubbliness, wishing for Kane's better acting skills. The eclectic artwork on the restaurant walls sparked inspiration. "I'm a local artist and wanted to talk to her about displaying some of my work."

"That's so neat! She's in her office." Paige replaced the menus. "I'm sure she would love to talk with you! Wait just a sec." The waitress swept through the restaurant, weaving between tables.

Toria peered out the front window. Kane now lounged on a bench in front of the music shop Mikelos frequented. He slouched, but she knew her partner in and out. His attention hovered at the edge of their link, ready to spring to action at a hint of her summons.

"Can I help you?"

A blonde in her mid-thirties glared at her when Toria turned at the frosty voice. "Ms. Fabbri?" Toria held out her hand. "My name is—"

"I know what your name is." She ignored Toria's attempt at civility. "And I know who your mother is. I trust you noticed the sign on your way in?"

Straight to the point, bigotry on full display. Well, Toria could match her chill. "Your sign is what I'd like to speak with you about today, ma'am." Her parents raised a polite girl, even if this woman didn't deserve it.

"Good. We have nothing more to discuss, *mage*." The title sounded nasty spilling from Fabbri's lips.

Toria's voice rose, prompting stares from nearby diners. "What the hell is your problem, lady?"

"People like you." Fabbri's lip curled. "Freaks who lord their power over normal humans."

Toria scoffed, barely sure where to begin a response. "What power? When has a nonhuman ever affected your life in any drastic way?"

"I joined the council so I could prevent them from abusing their power. Turns out I was too late."

Her lack of answer did not escape Toria's notice. "Too late for what?" The woman made less and less sense. "How did you even get elected to the council when you obviously have no idea how it's run?"

"I know how it's run—by representatives of a minority of the population who hold a majority of the power."

The bell above the door jangled, but Toria ignored the new arrival. She didn't have the patience to remind Fabbri how those minority representatives cast votes worth half those of the human district representatives, among other restrictions that limited their positions to mostly advisory roles. Every high school civics student knew that. "The council is going to kick you out if you keep this nonsense up." Toria waved at the sign behind her, and a heavy hand landed on her right shoulder. She twisted to find one of Limani's finest frowning at her.

"This is the young lady you called about, Ms. Fabbri?"

She cataloged the unknown man as a potential opponent, a force of habit trained into her since the beginning of her apprenticeship to the Mercenary Guild. Paunch strained his uniform and his hairline receded with age, but he had at least a head of height on her and a decent amount of weight. Most of Limani's police belonged to the Mercenary Guild as adjunct members, but Toria didn't recognize this stern officer.

Fabbri definitely did. She beamed at him. "Thank goodness you arrived in time. As you heard, this young woman entered my establishment to threaten me."

Toria bit her tongue. She'd been set up. Fabbri must have called the police from her office, once the set spell recognized the presence of a mage.

The man's hand weighted her shoulder, fingers digging into her skin. "I did indeed hear. Perhaps the young lady and I need to have a talk about respect. Your name, Miss?"

Fabbri leapt to answer first. "She's Toria Connor. Daughter of the Master of the City."

The officer's frown deepened. "I see. The daughter of such an upstanding member of the city needs to set a better example for her peers."

"I leave her in your capable hands, sir," Fabbri said. "Unless you need anything else, I should attend to my customers."

Kane's concern intensified in the back of Toria's mind, but she sent reassurance back even as she fought every impulse to repel the policeman with a shield.

The officer's hand tightened another fraction on Toria's shoulder. "Of course, ma'am. I'll escort her outside for our conversation." The grip released, and he nudged her forward.

Toria held her head high as she preceded the cop toward the exit. Paige the waitress stood next to the menu rack, jaw hanging open. Toria ignored her.

This morning, she almost blew up her apartment. Now she might get arrested. At least Kane sat outside, not in here with her stupidity.

Mama is going to kill me.

Kane came to Toria's rescue with his usual aplomb, featuring surprising backup. Dr. Lena Joensen, dean of Jarimis University, where Toria and Kane had completed their sophomore term the month before. Dr. Joenson was the second dean of Limani's local university, following the disappearance and presumed death of the founder, Victory's progeny Jarimis. Since Jarimis University included students from both the British and Roman colonies, the dean maintained one of the unelected city council seats along with Victory. For better or worse, she'd taken a personal interest in the education of the warrior-mage pair, the first in the university's history.

When Kane arrived at the small police station with Dean Joensen in tow, the police officer released Toria into her care after a lecture on "appropriate public behavior" and "representing her mother in public."

Toria and Kane leaned against each other on a bench outside the station while the dean completed paperwork inside. It didn't matter that she hadn't been arrested—the damage was done. The few officers and visitors in the station now knew the Master of the City's daughter had been there. Rumors would spread.

Toria soaked in her partner's calming presence. "Thanks, hon."

He kissed her temple. "Couldn't reach Victory or Mikelos at the house. Figured the dean was a better option than Max."

A full body shudder followed Kane's suggestion that he might have called the Master of Limani's Mercenary Guild. Before she could offer profuse gratitude for his decision, Dean Joensen exited the station and sank onto the bench on Toria's other side. The older woman stared across the parking lot, her expression unreadable, as she brushed an errant silver lock behind her ear.

Another potential rumor: Dean Joensen bailed out a simple university student because she was the daughter of the Master of the City. Talk about favoritism. Toria straightened on the bench. "I'm sorry," she said. "I lost my temper."

"No harm done, Toria. You're not in any permanent trouble."

"People will talk."

"Let them talk. The smart ones will wonder what really happened when they see the sign on the restaurant." Dean Joensen patted Toria's knee. "Those same smart ones will rethink who they may have elected to Limani's ruling council."

The sun warmed the back of Toria's neck, but embarrassment caused the heat in her cheeks. "You don't like her either, do you? That's why you came when Kane called."

"I'm the voice on the city council for the university students who hold citizenship in the Roman and British Empires. It's another check on Limani's neutral position between the two colonies," Dean Joensen said. "My predecessor never sat on the council because Victory already had a seat, and many people couldn't distinguish Jarimis the dean from Jarimis the vampire. I've always followed your mother's example of quiet neutrality. But I wasn't about to ignore Kane's call for help. I suppose I've backed myself into a corner."

Toria compared her recent experience with scattered memories. "Because your spot on the council is permanent," she said. "Mama has complained about the same thing. It looks like you guys have a lot of power because you weren't elected, but at the same time, you can't make too many waves because otherwise you'll be accused of abusing your power."

"Exactly."

"You would have come for any student who called," Kane said.

Dean Joenson gifted them with a knowing grin. "Sure, we'll put it that way," she said. "But you both know why Limani is so important."

Limani's original settlers, Greek colonists, modeled the city after the multiple Greek city-states who funded the expedition. Less than ten years later, a major Roman expansion swallowed all vestiges of the independent Greek cities, leaving Limani abandoned and adrift on the other side of the world. Today, either empire to the north or south could use their colonial forces to take over the city by moving in a few battalions of soldiers. Limani's regular military defense consisted of the handful of civic police officers, the small branch of the local Mercenary Guild dedicated to Limani independence, and one former mercenary playing politics as the Master of the City.

The tiny city-state held fragile power as a neutral zone between the two territories. It sat at the bottle-neck where the Wasteland crept closer to the eastern coast, leaving a narrow expanse of farmable land. Any hostile act by either side could result in all-out destruction, with Limani at ground zero.

Instead of reciting this by rote, Toria compressed the info. "Limani acts as the barrier between the two sets of colonies. What does that have to do with you helping us?"

Dean Joensen rose to her feet and faced Toria and Kane. "Because you'll tell Victory what happened today. And she'll have a reason to come discuss her errant daughter with me."

"Oh, she'll know," Kane said.

"Anything in particular you want me to pass along?" Toria asked.

"Tell her what happened to you today. Tell her what type of person Limani has elected to rule it, and that we need to do something about it."

Now Toria wished she had paid more attention to Victory whenever her mother spoke of the council. Fabbri had been elected with two other new councilmembers. Did either of them also spread this hate through the city? "We're with you."

Victory wasn't sure what woke her first—the last of the sun's rays setting over the forest or Mikelos' shout from outside their makeshift shelter. She scrambled to her feet behind Asaron and ducked out from the tarp into the dim evening.

Asaron's warning about an impending Roman invasion echoed in her ears. As if he followed her thoughts, her sire drew his sword and readied himself in front of Mikelos. Her daywalker already braced himself, pistol in hand. As the underbrush nearby crackled with footsteps, Victory drew her own sword in time for a familiar shout.

"It's us!" her daughter called out. "Don't shoot!"

Victory and Asaron lowered their swords and Mikelos barked out a laugh. "Stealthy you are not, daughter!"

The tall form of her foster son, Kane Nalamas, ducked under a low branch and emerged into view, followed by her adopted daughter. "Kind of the point," Kane said. "Didn't feel like getting skewered today."

He staggered when Asaron clapped him on the shoulder. "Clever call, boy. A good skewering is never fun."

Victory embraced Toria. "How did you find us?"

"Tracking spell in the hilt of my sword." Toria pointed at the small shelter. "I can find it down to a three-square-foot radius."

"We swung by the house and found a message on your answering machine," Kane said. "Customs master wanted to know where his boat was."

"After we called him and got the full story, we borrowed Max's truck from Merc HQ and came to the rescue," Toria said. "It's back on the road, about a mile from here."

"That's my girl." Victory squeezed Toria's shoulders again. "I wasn't looking forward to the walk."

Asaron ducked into the makeshift shelter and emerged with his gear. He withdrew the canvas-wrapped sword from his pack and passed it to Toria. "I believe this is yours, Granddaughter."

Toria all but hugged the weapon when Asaron relinquished it. "Thanks, Grandpa. I owe you one. Speaking of." She flapped her hand at Kane, who pulled two canteens from his backpack and handed them to the vampires.

In a blur of movement, Asaron popped the cap of the charmed bottled and chugged the preserved blood. Once drained, Victory handed over her own open bottle and he repeated the process. She could wait for her own supply back at the house. Her sire had had a rough few days.

"Let's go home," Mikelos said, accepting a bottle of water from Toria. "Have to call Rhaavi and tell him we owe someone a boat."

"Indeed," Victory said. "Did we miss anything today?"

Toria did not hide a dramatic flinch.

Kane smirked at his partner. "You could say that."

"You did *what*?"

Her mother's demand echoed off the kitchen's tile floor. Next to Toria, Mikelos rubbed his ear. The family had gathered while Toria, Kane, and Mikelos ate a late pasta dinner and Victory and Asaron nursed mugs of blood.

Toria refused to be put out. "Can I ask which one you're most mad at before I defend myself?"

"Burning down your apartment, I can understand," Victory said. "You've done worse."

Even while Toria admitted to the havoc she wreaked, it still wasn't fair to claim any real damage. "Almost burning down the apartment."

"Okay, almost burning down the apartment," Victory said. "No, what concerns me more is your little stunt at the restaurant."

"It was a bit drastic, Toria," Mikelos said.

"It's not my fault the lady was a jerk to me. I had no idea she would call the cops the second I walked into the place."

"Ooh, scary mage alert!" Kane's quip caused a ripple of laughter, breaking the tension around the table.

"You do get some credit, love," Victory said. "The police involvement was not wholly your fault. But we've trained you to expect all possible outcomes."

"I wasn't arrested," Toria said. "So, no record. But by her actions, Emily Fabbri proved in front of everyone in her restaurant that she is prejudiced to the point of extremism."

Victory circled the rim of her mug with a finger. "Now we have to figure out how far she's willing to take this prejudice."

"When's your next council meeting?" Asaron asked.

"Two nights from now," Victory said. "Sounds like I should call on Dean Joensen tomorrow." She stole a sip of Mikelos' beer. "Afterward, perhaps some coffee at Café Lizzette might be nice."

After sunset the next evening, Victory drove out to the Jarimis University campus. She arrived a few minutes before her appointment with the dean, so she wandered from the administration building toward the Garden of Remembrance. The area of manicured greenery overlooked the Agios River, where starlight dappled the calm water.

A light breeze brushed Victory's bare arms as she wound her way through the garden. Water splashed in a central fountain, the stone spout in the shape of Toria's rapier. She knelt at the edge of the basin and ran one hand over the bronze plaque—Victory's personal contribution to the garden established by the school.

IN HONOR AND LOVING MEMORY OF JARIMIS
BELOVED PROGENY AND FRIEND

A sudden flash of memory. *Jarimis stood before her, arms wide to encompass the river and surrounding land. His tousled black hair made even wilder by the winter wind off the water. "It's time I stopped trying to be a mercenary like you."*

Laughter interrupted her reverie, and a trio of students wandered into the garden. A blanket hung over the young man's shoulder and the girls clutched paper bags that clinked to her vampiric hearing. They must be cutting over to the shore for the traditional student pastime.

They froze when she rose to her feet, then the man asked, "You're Victory, right?"

"Good to know some of you attend my orientation lecture." Victory hoped the teasing note in her voice lessened the sting of her words. Every fall, she gave the same brief speech Jarimis used to make about the importance of education in the post-Wasteland era.

Their nervousness at stumbling upon Limani's Master of the City seemed to fade. "I enjoyed your talk," the young man said. A light drawl marked his Roman heritage from one of the southern colonies. "I've been to some of your other lectures, too. You're a good storyteller."

Unexpected, but welcome, praise for her skill as a guest lecturer in the History Department. "Thanks. If you ever want to discuss anything specific, my daughter or the dean would be happy to put you in touch with me."

He flushed. "That would be awesome. Um, it was nice to meet you." His two companions fidgeted beside him, not as comfortable conversing with Victory.

Victory wished them a good evening as the girls dragged him away. Speaking of the dean—time for her meeting. After a final sweeping look over the now-deserted garden, she cut through the grass toward Lena's office.

The dean waited outside as she approached the building. Lena grasped the railing and rose from her seat on the main steps. "Victory!"

"Lovely to see you, Lena." After accepting a hug, Victory studied the woman at arm's length. "Arthritis acting up again?"

"Not as bad as it could be, at my age."

Victory matched Lena's slower pace as they strolled toward the parking lot. "Thank you for coming out with me so late tonight."

Lena paused as Victory unlocked the town-car and held open the passenger door. "The pleasure is mine, dear. It's been too long."

Years, in fact. Victory asked after Lena's son in Calverton during the drive into downtown, which prompted discussion about both their families the rest of the trip. Neither brought up the real reason for this overdue coffee date.

Victory pulled into a parking spot in front of Café Lizzette. Emily Fabbri might have gotten away with throwing a young warrior-mage out of her restaurant, regardless of the mage in question's parentage, but she could not risk pulling the same trick with fellow councilmembers. This late in the evening, many of the diners were university students. They knew their dean.

"Interesting." Lena pointed toward the music shop down the block. A handwritten sign leaned inside the window, printed in blocky script:

NO NONHUMANS PLEASE

Victory leaned forward and crossed her arms over the steering wheel as she compared the new sign with that in the café's front window. "Looks like this crazy idea of Fabbri's is spreading. Also, Mikelos is going to be pissed off. That's where he orders all his sheet music."

"I know you want to go marching in there like your daughter did," Lena said, "but please remember we must be the respectable side in this situation."

"I know how to be good."

"Yes, but please do." Lena patted her shoulder. "Ready to go in?"

"Not much point in putting it off, is there?"

As Toria had warned, they entered the restaurant accompanied by a blue flash of light, which prompted stares.

Hostility filled some of the faces, though not all. Victory's hackles raised in response, and she wished for the comforting weight of her sword though she'd intentionally made this visit unarmed. With the possible exception of the two werepanthers in a booth toward the rear, she was many times stronger and decades more experienced than anyone in the room. If this confrontation turned physical, a blade would cause more damage than necessary.

No host appeared to be on duty, but Lena handled the pleasantries with a waiter who greeted them. They crossed the first obstacle, getting into the restaurant at all, when the dean greeted the young man by name and asked how his finals had gone. Confronted with such familiar authority, he'd had no choice but to lead the two women toward a booth. It did not escape Victory's notice how he placed them right next to the werepanthers. Or the empty booths and tables surrounding them.

The waiter noted their coffee orders—cream and sugar for Victory, black for Lena—and handed them menus. Instead of the kitchen, however, he disappeared into a side office after promising to return for their orders.

"Off to warn Fabbri already," Victory said. "I'd hoped to enjoy dessert before things went to hell." Though her body gained no nutrients from regular food, she enjoyed a sweet on occasion.

Lena stared past Victory, her lips pursed. "We might not even get that coffee."

Victory twisted in her seat. Emily Fabbri marched across the floor between empty tables. Their fellow councilwoman stopped at their booth, chin held high. "Can I *help* you, ladies?"

Victory made a show of surveying her menu. After shutting it, she grinned at Fabbri, showing fang. The human woman hid a flinch, but Victory didn't miss the quiver of suppressed tension. "Yes, thank you. I'll have a slice of carrot cake. Cream cheese icing, I hope?"

Fabbri placed both hands flat on the table and drew forward. Victory's estimate of the human lowered another few notches. She never saw signs of intelligence in antagonizing a vampire. Fabbri's attempt at intimidation fell flat as her gaze slid across Victory's cheek.

Victory ignored Fabbri's animosity. "If not, I'll take an apple turnover."

"Look, corpse," Fabbri said. At her derogatory comment, the werepanthers at the next booth turned. "It's obvious where your 'daughter' gets her stupidity from if you couldn't read the sign at the door."

Victory lifted a finger, but Fabbri scurried back a step before Victory could push the woman out of her personal space. "Are you aware the two ladies at the next booth are panthers? Having trouble reading your own sign?" Her questions dripped with more sarcasm than she had intended, but goading the woman was too easy. Lena kicked her foot under the table.

A slight flush reddened Fabbri's cheeks. "They were seated while I ran an errand outside of the restaurant. I informed the hostess that her services would not be necessary after tonight, and the girl left mid-shift."

Lena's hand flew to her chest. "You fired her?"

"Of course." Fabbri sniffed her disdain. "The girl could not be trusted to keep the unsavory elements of Limani out of my restaurant. I run a respectable establishment."

Victory relaxed against the padded booth and crossed her arms, and even the nonthreatening gesture caused Fabbri to flinch away. "Then why are they still here?"

In a stiff voice, Fabbri said, "They were already halfway through their meal."

"So you could collect their bill at the end of their dinner," Lena said, her tone daring Fabbri to protest.

"At least be consistent in your prejudiced policies, Fabbri," Victory said. "Otherwise no one will respect you."

Fabbri pointed at the door. "Get the hell off my property." Her raised voice attracted the attention of most of the diners in the restaurant.

"Wait one second, ma'am!" Victory mimicked Lena's previous shock, placing a hand over her breastbone. "I expected more from you. You'd call the police on my daughter, a half-trained warrior-mage, but not on me, the vampire Master of the City. Lena, should I be insulted?"

"I would be insulted," Lena said. "I don't believe Ms. Fabbri has the proper respect for your position."

"Are you threatening me?" Fabbri asked. "Because I'm happy to call the authorities and have both of you arrested."

Victory slid out of the booth. "Don't bother. We'll be long gone before they arrive." She held a hand out to Lena, who levered herself to her feet. "Have a good evening, Ms. Fabbri. Next time, we'll be sure to return when you do have fresh carrot cake. I so looked forward to it."

She stepped around the tables toward the entrance. Victory imagined Fabbri smashing a chair and attacking her with one of the table legs, but dismissed the image as too direct for the human's subtle hatred. Evidenced by her call to the police when confronted with an angry Toria, she was much happier allowing others to do her dirty work.

Soon they were ensconced in the town-car, leaving Victory churning with frustration and no relief in sight. Maybe Asaron would be up for a good spar later. Or Mikelos for a different sort of exertion.

"That could have gone worse," Lena said. "You didn't even lose your temper."

"It was tempting." Victory scrubbed her face a few times. "I do not want to face her at council tomorrow."

"Neither do I. We need to warn the others beforehand, though." No need for Lena to specify which of their fellow councilmembers she referred to.

"If you can reach Daliana and Lorus, I'll get in touch with Max, Tristan, and Genevieve." Victory would deal with the Limani's Mercenary Guildmaster and the much higher-strung wolf and panther councilmembers if Lena handled the representatives of Limani's elves and other werecreatures. The panthers were still touchy regarding politics, terrified of losing their hard-won council position.

"Not a problem." Lena paused. "Do you want to find coffee somewhere else tonight, or drive me home?"

"The latter, please." Time to salvage this ruined date later. Victory wanted to go home and gather her family for a much-needed conference. Now she had firsthand evidence of Fabbri's behavior, and she wanted to compare notes with Toria and get Mikelos and Asaron's thoughts on the situation.

Perhaps it had been a blessing in disguise when the werepanthers had rallied years ago. No time to think then, only act. The conflict had been clear. Now, things were much more muddled.

The buildings of downtown Limani faded into dark trees, the gradual change from city limits to surrounding countryside marked by a lone sign indicating JARIMIS UNIVERSITY—3 MILES. Every time she and Mikelos considered downsizing to a smaller house within the city, this drive reminded her of why she could never leave the manor. Her traditional title might be Master of the City of Vampires, but she claimed all of Limani.

"Come on, kid." Fosca circled Toria's prone body. "What are you learning in that fancy school of yours?" The middle-aged woman worked as a traveling mercenary based out of Limani. She had accepted Max's request to work with Toria with unrestrained glee.

Only her family could call her "kid" without sting. Toria regretted her rash quip concerning their respective ages at their first bows. The bruises now decorating Toria's body from the flat of Fosca's practice blade drove home her error.

If the unexpected appearance of two of Maximillian Asher's more errant Guildmembers surprised him when they'd asked to borrow his truck the day before, he hadn't shown it. Instead, he had extracted a promise from them to return as soon as possible for training. When they had arrived, he'd set them to spar with a few older members hanging out at the Hall on this lazy summer afternoon. Max never let her spar with Kane, claiming they got enough practice together.

"Mostly chemistry last semester." She wished herself safe in a lab right now. Her muscles ached as she staggered to her feet. She was more out of practice than she liked to admit.

"You think you're gonna be a warrior?" Fosca launched into the attack.

"I. Already. Am." Toria retorted with each parry. But two blows later, Fosca knocked Toria's feet out from under her once again.

Fosca knelt next to her. "When I was your age, I earned a living with my sword. Not playing grown-up." She gripped Toria's wrist and helped haul her to her feet. With no formal end to the bout, Fosca turned on a dime and sauntered across the training floor toward the locker room.

Okay, so Toria's reaction times were slower than usual. She'd spent the last six months juggling four courses and an independent study. Some things slipped to the wayside, such as her regular practice spars with Kane, who also had an overloaded schedule. These days, they often sparred at the college's athletic center in time scraped together between classes. Neither had visited the Hall in months.

Toria replayed the disastrous sparring match in her mind during her cool-down routine. She and Kane had work to do. If trouble was coming for Limani, they needed to be ready. They might be in school now, but as part of Limani's Mercenary Guild, the city could call on them for defense at any time.

Victory had taught Toria the art of combat since she could string three steps together without falling, and had acted as their primary weapons teacher after Toria and Kane bonded. She had allowed Max to lure the coveted pair into a Mercenary Guild apprenticeship during high school. They completed the beginnings of their journeyman phase the summer after high school graduation when they accompanied Asaron through the edges of the British Colonies and into the Wasteland. Official Guild training was on hold while they attended Jarimis University, but after those four years, they'd be sent out on their own. Kane pushed for going south to the Roman Colonies, but Toria had her mind set on Europa and visiting Victory's old stomping grounds. The debate would probably continue until graduation.

Toria turned half an ear to the spontaneous hand-to-hand lesson Max gave Kane across the training room floor. The retired mercenary sent Kane to his knees with even less trouble than Fosca. Time to buckle down this summer.

The mini-lesson ended while Toria attempted to plan a summer training routine Kane wouldn't hate. She included magic-focused time to appease him, though the real reason was so she could continue work on her new sword. He could help recast all the offensive and defensive charms.

When she opened her eyes in the middle of a convoluted stretch, the partner in question stood over her. "Having fun?"

"Always."

"I wish I was as bendy as you are. How do you even do that?"

"Carefully." Rolling on her shoulders, Toria used her momentum to push off the ground and land on her feet. "I think I'm part cat."

"Explaining your love of naps, but not your fear of rodents," Kane said. They crossed the mats, giving a wide berth to the trio sparring with long staffs.

Toria rubbed at the bruise forming on her right shoulder. "Damn, she got through my guard a few times."

"What the hell happened?"

"Fosca was spoiling for a fight. Or Max wanted to teach me the evils of falling out of shape." Still didn't justify Fosca accusing her of being a spoiled child.

Kane rested a hand on her shoulder and pushed healing energy through his touch. He let go when she winced at the growing heat. "Poor girl. Max wants to see us after we shower."

"To talk about Mom's call last night?

"Do you even have to guess?"

They met in the front lounge after changing, then Toria followed her partner to a secluded flight of stairs to the administrative section of the building. They emerged in a hallway next to Max's office, where the retired merc who acted as his aide-de-camp held court.

Liliah waved them toward the door without looking up from her paperwork. "He's waiting for you."

"Thanks." Toria rapped her knuckles against the wood, Kane lurking behind her.

After a muffled welcome, the pair pushed the door open. The large desk that dominated the back half of the room sat empty.

"Over here." Max had also showered and changed into street clothes; his damp silver hair clung to his scalp, revealing the slightly pointed ear tips that signaled his mixed heritage. He stood at the picture window that gave him a view of the training room floor, studying a duo who sparred with wooden practice knives.

"You wanted to speak with us?" Toria asked.

Max turned away from the window and gestured to the facing couches on the other side of the room in favor of the more formal seating arrangement at his desk. "Have a seat. Either of you need a drink?"

Max plucked two bottles of water from a small refrigerator hidden in a sideboard. Kane accepted one with thanks and settled next to Toria, who promptly stole a sip. Max sat across from them. "Care to explain the fight with Fosca, Toria?"

"She started it!" Toria deflated under Max's smirk. "Neither of us started it. We were both being bitchy. She accused me of being a spoiled brat and not a real fighter."

"You're not a real fighter. You're a journeyman in name alone while you attend university."

"Yes, sir," Toria said. "We'll be here more this summer to train." Kane echoed his agreement.

"Good," Max said. "We also need to talk about your little incident at Emily Fabbri's restaurant the other night."

Toria groaned. "The stories have spread already?"

"Not stories, necessarily," Max said. "A few of the Guild were there eating a late lunch. They came straight to me afterward, to warn me both of the detestable sign out front and about your confrontation. They also made it clear whose side they'd have come down on if Fabbri or the police officer accosted you physically."

"Good to know," Toria said. "But I'm glad it didn't come to that."

"Aren't we all," Kane said. "And Victory called you last night?"

Max nodded. "She told me about her experience with Dean Joensen." He rolled his water bottle between his hands. "Now everyone's pissed off, and council tonight should be loads of fun. Do you know whether Asaron is at Victory's house today?"

"He should be, since he's not here," Toria said. Her adoptive grandfather kept a set of rooms in the manor's basement, but occasionally spent days at the Mercenary Guildhall to train and catch up with friends.

"Good. A few journeymen finished their rotation in the Roman Colonies and brought word of recent military activity," Max said. "It could be a response to one of the nasties that keep coming out of the southern Wasteland, but I wanted to speak with Asaron about it, get his opinion."

"What's going on?" Kane asked.

"I don't know," Max said. "The kids reported a few groups of soldiers marching north, but rumor only, and no actual numbers. I hoped Asaron might have heard more."

"Never hurts to ask," Toria said. "Come over for dinner tonight. You can talk with Mama before the council meeting, then arrive together. Really piss Fabbri off."

"And I'd hate to do that." Max grinned when Kane strangled a laugh. "Better call Mikelos and tell him to make extra for dinner."

Victory had braced for the meeting to begin with a bang. Instead, she rocked in her over-engineered ergonomic chair while everyone tiptoed around the issue at hand. With fifteen councilmembers, the tiptoeing resembled a herd of elephants in a crystal shop. Two of the elected human members hadn't been aware of the current situation. Genevieve and Tristan, pack leaders of the leopards and wolves, respectively, had heard rumblings but not the full picture until she called them earlier. Lena took control when the head of council requested a rational explanation of recent events, and Victory distracted herself from interrupting with irate commentary by seeing how far back she could balance without toppling to the floor and making a spectacle of herself.

As Lena finished, another councilmember presented his opening riposte. "This behavior is unacceptable," Lorus said. The barest hint of vibration, evidence of his other self, underlay Lorus' pronouncement. The council's representative of werecreatures other than wolves and panthers curled his hands into fists on the table.

Emily Fabbri sat opposite him, matching his icy fury. "I have received multiple complaints from my constituents. They demand action regarding blatant offenses against Limani's community."

Lorus split his glare between Fabbri across from him and the other humans arrayed on her side of the table. He didn't often move his eyes independently in mixed company, so this signal of his unease forced Victory back to attention. Soon, he might flash a mouthful of teeth even sharper than hers.

Time to look for an opening to interject, before she lost the bet made with Max over dinner. She had expected Tristan to lose his temper first. Limani's most powerful male werewolf did not get his position in pack hierarchy by being a pushover. Of course, Max had bet Victory would be the first to lash out, so perhaps now she could keep her twenty bucks.

Fabbri muttered a retort under her breath, as if forgetting about the enhanced senses of multiple councilmembers around her. Tristan's deep voice resonated off the council room's walls. "You are a lying bitch!"

Tristan's apparent insult roused the meeker human councilmembers. Lucia Stein, the eldest member of the council, leaned to whisper in Fabbri's ear.

Fabbri waved her off. "My restaurant is private property. I have the right to deny service to anyone I choose."

Max radiated a veneer of unconcern. "What, like 'No shirt, no shoes, no service'? But now it's 'No humanity, no pure blood, no service'?"

"Humanity has nothing to do with it," Fabbri said. "I don't see what your concern is. My policy doesn't affect you."

"You keep thinking that, ma'am." Max toasted her with his glass of water.

She blanched. "Don't we have better things to discuss tonight, Alex?"

Alexander Sethri, human head of the Limani city council, sat in impartial silence with steepled fingers. "While there is such dissent amongst our ranks, anything else we review tonight will be tainted by our strong emotions. And believe me, Emily—they are very strong." He lapsed into quiet calm, his disapproval made known.

"What is your goal here, Fabbri?" Soren Abramson, one of her fellow human representatives, spoke up. "For us to support your idiotic notions simply because you're afraid of anything different?"

"I am not afraid of them."

Victory's opening presented itself. "You called the police on my daughter instead of confronting her yourself. The only reason you didn't do the same to me was because it's bad politics to have councilmembers fighting in public."

"I didn't call the police on you because you didn't storm in looking for a fight," Fabbri said. "You at least have a reputation for civility. I couldn't be sure about your daughter." A biting emphasis on her last word showed her true opinion of their relationship.

"What makes you so sure Torialanthas would cause trouble?" Toria's given name rolled off the lips of another heretofore-silent observer. Daliana, this decade's representative of Limani's elven population, had watched the debate with the same aloofness she possessed during more routine discussions regarding traffic laws and residential zoning.

"You mean besides her history of violence? The girl was a killer before she even graduated from high school!" Fabbri lit with success, the pleasure at being able to pull this trump card evident in her voice.

With surprising defensiveness, Tristan beat Victory to the punch. "You go too far, Fabbri."

Victory would never have a better chance to defend her daughter without seeming too biased. "Toria killed a criminal." She kept her voice even, but her short nails dug into her thighs under the table. "She acted in order to protect her family. You wouldn't know the full story—you were elected to council less than six months ago."

"Elected is the key word there," Fabbri said. "I earned my place on this council. What have you done besides live for a long time?"

"You mean besides doing her job keeping Limani safe from vampires who see humans as snack food free for the taking?" Lorus said. "What, exactly, have you done for this city, Fabbri?"

"My position on the council is not under debate here," Victory said. "Your decision to discriminate against other citizens of Limani is, Ms. Fabbri."

"Emily, your actions do contradict the oath you swore when you joined the council to uphold the values that make Limani a peaceful community," Soren said. "We have grounds to impeach you."

"You wouldn't dare," Fabbri said.

"I would," Max said. "I would impeach you. Kick you out of the city on top of it. While I don't think the others would agree to exile you, I might have backup for the impeachment."

"Seconded," chorused Victory and Tristan.

Max held out his hands in a "what can you do?" shrug. "There we go. The proposal is on the table."

"The council has not impeached a member in over fifty years," Lena said. "Victory, were you serving then?"

A logical question, based on her long experience with Limani's city council. "Quinn murdered another councilmember. It wasn't a hard decision to make, so I don't remember the details. Alexander, you've reviewed those council procedures most recently."

"I don't know the exact procedures offhand," Sethri said. "I do know impeachment cannot occur during the same meeting as the proposal in order to prevent us from being ruled by our emotions instead of common sense."

"Then we break to review the policy," Soren said. "I propose an emergency session tomorrow night."

"Seconded," Lena said.

"Two councilmembers have spoken, one elected and one appointed," Sethri said. "It's settled. I hereby call an official council session tomorrow night led by Dr. Joensen in order to follow proper impeachment procedure." He made a note in the book in front of him without waiting for any argument.

Victory sent silent gratitude toward Max for his support. She had already resolved to raise the issue of impeachment that evening. However, if no one had seconded the idea, her place on the council could have become tenuous indeed. She and Asaron traded the titular position of vampire Master of the City if she had to travel outside of Limani, but her sire refused to have anything to do with the politics of the city council. Max had a stronghold on his leadership of the local Mercenary Guild, but she knew he would have no regrets if forced to move on, to follow through with his occasional threats to retire and live out the rest of his life with his sister's family in the north.

No drastic steps needed. Instead, she noted her strongest backers. Now the problem would be to make the impeachment stick. Fabbri's humanist superiority would be more difficult to argue than Quinn's murder.

Fabbri's elitist tone dragged Victory's attention back to the table. "Now that we've settled this nasty business," she said, "what are we going to do about the Roman army marching toward Limani?"

Asaron rapped on the doorframe to the den soon after Victory and Max left for the council meeting. "Travel gear. We've got work to do."

Roused from the book on tactics she'd snagged from Max's office, Toria blinked at Asaron. "What?"

"Max gave me a mission."

She slipped paper in the book to mark her place. "Does this have to do with the Roman troop movements?"

As Asaron escorted her through the kitchen and to the bottom of the stairs, he explained, "I hope its simple training maneuvers. But I'm not inclined to make assumptions now."

Toria paused. "Kane coming with us?"

"You do come as a matched set. I'll grab him from the library. You've got ten minutes."

"I outgrew my gear here at the house. My new set is at the apartment."

"You're a smart girl. Figure something out."

Halfway up the staircase, Toria halted and turned to Asaron again. "Does Mama know we're going?" Mikelos had gone into town after Victory left with Max, muttering about a replacement C string. Once he and the proprietor of the local music supply store got to gossiping, her father might be gone for hours.

"You think your mother would let me take you anywhere near an army? Why do you think we're leaving while she's at council?"

"Good point. We'll leave a note." She didn't prefer to launch an expedition by night, but she'd grown used to it during her previous journeyman stint with her grandfather.

Toria ransacked the closet in her former bedroom for something suitable to wear, since her current gear sat in a storage trunk back at the apartment. She and Kane hadn't lived in this house since high school. Old jeans replaced her cutoff shorts, and she pulled a black long-sleeved shirt over her tank top. After buckling on a worn leather belt, she snagged her old duster from the hook behind her bedroom door.

Toria met Kane in the hall coming out of his old bedroom. He wore similar attire, with the addition of an armored leather vest that still fit. He trailed after her downstairs, where Toria pushed through the grand double doors off the foyer. Since Victory's occupancy, the ballroom dance floor sported more martial forms of footwork. She and Kane had spent half of high school here, when not in the attic's magic workroom.

Kane pulled their swords—her returned rapier and his own elegant, curved shamshir—from the bags they'd left in the corner while Toria rummaged in a chest for sword harnesses. Next came the knives.

Asaron leaned in. "You two set?"

Kane sheathed his shamshir. "Ready for a night on the town."

"Hey," Toria said, "are we going to need guns?" Never hurt to be prepared, even if she could already anticipate Asaron's answer.

Her grandfather still found firearms a modern novelty. Victory had to pry his crossbow out of his fingers to get him to try a musket.

Then again, Asaron also viewed the weaponry as a passing fad. Part of the massive spell the elves cast over the world after the Last War prevented the creation of new firearms. Bullets were easy enough to manufacture—lead, steel, silver, whatever form needed for whatever creature needed fighting. But these days, irreplaceable guns failed from normal wear and tear.

Her mother wasn't a huge fan of them either, but she kept some in a locked cabinet in a discreet corner of the training room. A few small pistols Toria and Kane had trained on, along with a rifle and antique shotgun. Even a peculiar submachine gun acquired by Asaron in his travels and "forgotten" at the manor.

"It's just a scouting run on the Roman army," Asaron said. He plucked his own duster from the coatrack at the front door. "We won't need guns because they'll never see us coming."

On occasion, Mikelos imagined that music flowed through his blood and soul the way his daughter manipulated magic. But unlike the unknown heritage that provided his Toria with such a gift, he had not been born to music. Instead, it had rescued him from a short life before he burned out into obscurity.

After being expelled from the Roman orphanage upon reaching his majority, Mikelos earned a scant living singing on street corners. One night, a young man swept out of the darkness to give him so much more. The vampire Connor welcomed him into the world of music and night, teaching him the art of the violin and transforming his life. The vampire and daywalker string duo dazzled Europa's society elite for almost two centuries. Mikelos evolved from homeless orphan to pampered musician. He had a family, albeit an unconventional one. He was happy.

Then Connor disappeared, leaving Mikelos adrift. Mortal once again, in a world changing faster each day. After the war, he crossed the sea and settled in Limani, hoping to live out the rest of his days in anonymity. No longer known as half of the famous concert pair, long vanished across the ocean in a different world.

For a while, Mikelos lost his music. A few years passed, and another vampire blew into his life. Once again, Mikelos found himself a daywalker, a human for whom time stood still. But now he was a true partner, and Victory cherished him for bringing intimacy to her cold life while he treasured her for returning meaning to his.

Violin case thumping against his thigh, Mikelos pulled the strap of his messenger bag higher onto his shoulder to balance the weight of the two bags. Hans had escorted him out of his music shop a few minutes before, claiming his old bones needed sleep. He'd also promised to pull the offensive sign from the window, which Mikelos considered a win. Mikelos left the High Note with one C string and several books of new music from the British colonies. Overall, a successful visit.

He wandered toward the center of Limani, the night warm despite the late hour. He encountered a few pedestrians, people on their way home from evening jobs of their own. Light shone from the upper windows of City Hall, showing the council session still in full swing. Mikelos fretted about the results of the meeting, but he would have to wait until Victory finished inside. He couldn't help but hope Victory and Max put that awful woman through the wringer.

In the parking lot beside City Hall, he secured his gear in the car. With time to kill before Victory would be ready for him to drive her home, it wouldn't hurt to visit an old haunt. She'd find him if the meeting let out earlier than expected.

Limani called itself a city, but with such a small population, districts bled into each other within blocks. Thus, it was a short jaunt to the Twilight Mists nightclub, one of the few havens for the younger adults of Limani. Strolling toward the club, he imagined decades past. He would walk the same route after work to join a friend's band before returning to his empty apartment. Victory opened the Twilight Mists decades ago, trying her hand at a civilized business after the constant stress of the mercenary lifestyle. She first found him in the club, changing both their lives forever.

The front door opened and a group spilled out, laughing and shouting into the night. Loud music washed across the street.

"Mikelos!" The doorman greeted him by name and clasped his hand.

"Hey, Radek. Busy night?"

"Not too bad. School is out for the summer, so every night will be busy. Might be too crowded for you." Another group of customers arrived behind Mikelos, diverting Radek's attention.

Dancing would keep Mikelos' mind off the council session, including the random visions of Victory lunging across the table and throttling Emily Fabbri. Entertaining though it was, that particular scenario wouldn't end well.

The half-moon cast deep shadows over the forest. "Hey, how far are we going tonight?" Toria asked.

In the lead, Asaron's mount picked its way along the worn dirt road. His low laugh carried to her, but her grandfather did not turn in his saddle. It's not like she'd asked, *Are we there yet?*

Kane pulled his horse abreast of hers. "What's wrong?"

Toria nudged her own mount around a stone in the road. "We're only a few miles from the Agios River. We can camp in the old tollhouse by the ford during the day, but any further south is out of our usual range if we keep going."

They'd borrowed horses from the stables kept by Limani's Mercenary Guild. This mode of travel traded speed for distance and stealth in lieu of Asaron's diesel truck, with its engine loud enough to wake the dead.

Now Asaron deigned to answer. "I did survive before trucks, child. Modern times have corrupted the youth. It's a shame."

"I have no problem being corrupted," Kane said.

"I'm sure you'll muddle through. You're—" Asaron broke off, reining his horse to a halt.

Toria and Kane followed suit. Rather than question Asaron's action, Toria cast out with her own special senses.

Keeping her permanent physical shields intact, she lowered the mental blocks preventing the magic she saw flowing through the world from overwhelming her. She tuned out the brilliant emerald shields surrounding Kane and ignored the uncomfortable black hole Asaron's presence created.

"Anything?" Kane peered into the underbrush at the side of the road, then glanced at her. "Oh, you're going weak in the rear."

"Thanks." Toria caught the loop of power her partner threw and reinforced her shielding.

"Hush." They stilled at Asaron's command, until the elder vampire relaxed his alert stance. "Odd."

Toria banished her magesight. "What's going on?"

"Anything out of the ordinary?" Asaron asked.

Both partners answered in the negative. But if Asaron already saw bad signs on home ground, it didn't bode well for the mission.

"I must be getting old. Let's get out of here," Asaron said. "The night's not getting any younger, and we've still got a river to cross."

They resumed their progress. The darkness made Toria sleepy, so she set passive scans that echoed through the surrounding woodland. Within moments, Kane bolstered her power and set his own complementary scans. Power simmered between them.

After another mile, Kane interrupted her reverie. "Penny for your thoughts?"

"Just trying not to fall asleep. Hoping we won't have a close call at dawn."

Asaron's chuckle echoed out of the darkness. "Victory and I have had our share of close calls. They don't happen as often as you think."

"Often for us or often for you?" Toria asked. "Your definition of time can get a bit warped, Grandpa. You talk about events three centuries ago like they happened last week."

"Time is strange for those who live for centuries," Asaron said. "Vampires are forced to realize current events can echo decades in the future while also living in the here and now."

Kane swigged water from his canteen and tossed it to Toria. "Must be even stranger for Mikelos."

"Indeed," Asaron said. "My daughter's daywalker does not live in a life ruled by the change of the light."

"But he does live by his connection to Mama," Toria said. "He told me once the three years he wasn't bonded to a vampire were the hardest of his life. How sometimes he worries about me growing up. I think he's afraid of change."

"He wouldn't be the first daywalker with such a phobia," Asaron said.

Toria nudged her chestnut mare to the forward position when the conversation turned more philosophical, leaving her partner and grandfather behind. The more intangible aspects of life were Kane's specialty. The chemist in Toria lived in the physical. The others' low voices retreated behind her.

Soon she scented water in the air, as they neared the point where the Agios River could be forded on horseback. The original colonists chose their settlement site on a defensible peninsula, though it made transit more difficult in this modern era.

The wide expanse of the Agios River ran next to the university, after various other water sources had merged with it. Here, however, a wide creek masqueraded as a river, with water shallow enough to ford on horseback with no risk beyond damp boots. Springtime's rushing torrent had faded to a firm, steady current.

Returning to the lead of their trio, Asaron urged his mount into the water. "Let's go."

Kane's gelding followed suit without a problem, but Toria's mare exhibited an immediate dislike of the situation. At the point where the water met the narrow band of sand and mud alongside it, the mare planted her hooves and snorted in derision.

"Oh, come on, girl." Toria nudged the horse's flanks with her heels. "I'm not going to get off and push you."

But any effort to press the horse forward resulted in her skittering to either side instead of forward progress. Her companions laughed at her from across the river. "Enjoying this, are you?"

"Of course!" Asaron called back. "But we don't have all night, Toria!"

"I promise I'll feed you an apple when we get across." Another loud exhalation of air met Toria's bribe. "Carrots?"

A mixture of amusement and urgency slipped from Kane to Toria through their link. "Tor!"

"I'm working on it!" The hydrophobic horse was not her fault.

She swung out of the saddle and glared at the horse as a rush of displaced air stirred her hair. A crossbow bolt thudded into a tree trunk beyond her. She yelped and lunged away, grabbing the mare's reins to haul her into the woods. The horse jerked with a grunt, displaying her clear annoyance. But the mare wasn't panicking. A second bolt followed the first, sailing farther into the woods before snapping against a tree.

Toria's brain dredged up worst-case scenarios as she scrambled toward cover. Now the horse followed without protest, away from the dreaded water. Pulling the mare farther into the trees, Toria threw the reins over a low branch.

Shouts registered, frantic male voices sharing warnings. The bolts had come from the opposite side of the river—Kane and Asaron faced far more danger. She wanted to dive into the river herself and help them out, but such a lack of common sense would appall Asaron. She paused for half a beat to draw power from the ambient energy in the air to reinforce her shields, then crept toward the edge of the tree line in a low crouch.

Across the river, Asaron slashed with his sword, keeping three attackers at bay while astride his mount. Safe enough for the moment. But Kane?

"Bastards! Get off! Ow!"

Not faring as well as Asaron. He must have dismounted for a better connection with the source of his magical energy, and now he writhed on the ground beneath two figures in dark clothing. A final nearby stranger held the reins of Kane's horse, a crossbow slung over one shoulder.

In her crouch, Toria slapped a palm to the ground. She pushed a tendril of power through her bare skin and into the earth, threading beneath the water. Nature provided the current, and the water surged through her magical net.

She had never tried this before. The spontaneous backwash of energy through her line of power pummeled her with all the force of a raging maelstrom. She drained the overload into the earth, a quick and dirty way to discharge power.

A holler of pain interrupted Kane's steady stream of insults. On instinct, Toria pushed energy through her link with Kane, helping the only way she knew from this distance, without a clear shot at her partner's foes.

Physics didn't fail her. The sudden influx of pure electricity caused a negative reaction with Kane's shields and shocked his attackers off him with a few hundred volts.

Except the river's energy shunted back into her own body, and the last of the power overloaded Kane's shields and rebounded to Toria. She passed out before she hit the ground.

Mikelos paused at the edge of the Twilight Mists' dance floor, as bass reverberated through the soles of his feet. He savored the scent of an old building filled with half a century of sweat and smoke and music. The new owners of the club had updated the décor, but the place still held many fond memories.

He first trained in classical music three hundred years ago, but time had broadened his tastes. His younger street-rat self sang anything for a penny or bread crust. His famous self once refused to play accompaniment for an operatic soprano who might be more popular than he. Now, he appreciated the modern beats and synthetic sounds not possible from a classical orchestra. In his old age, he had relaxed and learned how to have fun.

Youth and nocturnal standards meant the night had barely begun at ten o'clock. Many of the patrons were students from the high school and university enjoying summer break. Toria knew more of the current crop who frequented the club, but he did receive waves from the group of young werewolves in human form lounging on couches in a corner. A lone elf already spun across the dance floor. A beautiful woman should never dance alone.

The elven girl paused at his approach, though her hips still swayed in time to the subtle beat.

Mikelos put on his best court manners, with a sweeping bow. "May I join you, your ladyship?"

She examined him, bright green eyes hooded beneath a suspicious squint. She appeared to be about Toria's age, not much older than twenty. In reality, a human would be close to retirement age. Decision reached, her posture eased, and she accepted his hand. "My pleasure, daywalker."

With a cascade of harsh drumbeats, the music launched into a faster rhythm. Mikelos spun the girl around to the whistles of the wolves. Other dancers cleared the floor, leaving them plenty of room.

He'd relaxed into the rhythm when the speakers cut out, creating a ringing silence after the loud music. Mikelos and the girl froze. The burly Twilight Mists bouncer approached, Radek trailing behind with a helpless expression.

The bouncer stopped short of invading Mikelos' personal space. "We need to ask you and your friend to leave."

"I'm sorry?" Mikelos asked.

"New company policy."

Next to Mikelos, the girl huffed. "You've got to be kidding. Here, too?"

It seemed Fabbri's ridiculous prejudice had spread. Mikelos hated to play this card, but— "You do know who I am, right?"

"You're not human."

"I'm sorry, Mikelos, Syri," Radek said, "but there's nothing I can do. You need to leave."

The tableau froze under the eyes of all others in the club. When the wolves rose to their feet in unison, someone had to make the first move. Mikelos decided to err on the side of caution. He offered his elbow to Syri. "Shall we?"

She ignored his gesture. "You're giving in? Can't you call Victory? I know what she'd have to say about this happening in her club."

This could get ugly, and Mikelos was in no mood for a fight. "It's not her club anymore. C'mon." He snagged her elbow and guided her toward the door.

When he passed them, one of the werewolves grabbed his shoulder. "We can't tolerate this."

"We can and we will, at least for tonight," Mikelos said. "You know he's going to order you guys out next."

The young wolf, barely out of high school, bared his teeth in the bouncer's direction. "Only two of them."

"I can't order you to leave with me, but I can tell you fighting is a bad idea." Mikelos pulled out of his grip. "Victory's in council right now, figuring out how to put an end to this. Beating the crap out of some humans tonight will only hurt what she's trying to do." He added the last bit through gritted teeth.

"Fine," the wolf said. "We're with you, for now. Let's go."

Under the stares of all in the silent club, Mikelos led the wolves and elf to the exit. Radek and the bouncer followed the group all the way to the doors, shutting them out with a resounding *bang*.

Mikelos didn't stop to loiter outside, and the others followed him without a word. Once they rounded the corner toward the center of town, the elven girl stopped in her tracks. "Why would they let us in just to toss us out? I'm going back." She turned, but two of the wolves barred her way.

"No," Mikelos said, voice firm, "you're not. I was serious when I said Victory was working on this right now."

She whirled on him. "You'd better be right, daywalker. The elves won't stand for this."

"You think the wolves will, girl?" The lone female werewolf in the group sniffed in disdain. "Tristan in on this with Victory?"

"As far as I know, they're all working the issue," Mikelos said. "I'm sure the results of tonight's council meeting will be spread. If the problem isn't dealt with, we can consider more drastic measures."

"I should hope so." At that, the elven girl stalked away.

"Syri got dumped right before you got to the club," the female wolf told Mikelos. "She's having a crappy night. Otherwise she wouldn't have agreed to dance with you."

His evening grew stranger by the minute. "I guess I'll go camp out by the council building and wait for Victory. Take care, all."

The werewolves said their goodbyes, and Mikelos watched them fade into the darkness before making his own way through the deserted Limani night.

Since they met after normal business hours and the rest of City Hall cleared out, the council locked the front door. Mikelos didn't mind waiting outside in the pleasant evening. He settled onto the wide stone steps below the Grecian building, but the silence grated on him. A little music wouldn't hurt anyone in the quiet business district. He retrieved his violin from the nearby car, drawing the instrument from its case with reverence before returning to the front steps.

Fingering drills bored him after a few minutes, so he switched to a reel. But a reel could not be played while sitting, and soon Mikelos stood at the top of the steps. After the reel, he launched into a more classical piece, one of the first he had ever played in concert. Lit by City Hall's spotlights, the building behind him transformed into a full orchestra, the street became an adoring audience. He imagined the flashing bow of Connor's cello in the corner of his field of vision.

"Hey, freak."

His bow skittered across the strings with a harsh shriek. Mikelos lowered the violin to his side before facing his unwelcome visitor. The unfamiliar bouncer from the Twilight Mists strode up the steps, sporting a pronounced sneer.

"Can I help you?" Had the guy followed him here? Mikelos didn't want a confrontation while this tired. Not on the council steps.

At the top, the bouncer once again invaded Mikelos space, forcing him to back down a step to lower ground. Not his first choice of action, but the guy had horrid breath tinged with alcohol. Drinking on the job and leaving early. What were the new owners of the club letting their employees get away with these days?

"Didn't appreciate the way you talked to me back there." The bouncer glared down his nose at Mikelos. "You need to learn some respect for your superiors."

Mikelos stifled his laugh. "Thanks for the advice."

Meaty hands shoved at his chest in response. Mikelos pin-wheeled his arms for balance and staggered down another few steps. The other man followed, too close for comfort.

Not good. "That was uncalled for, sir." Mikelos couldn't fight with his violin in hand, but leaving the instrument unprotected seemed a bad idea.

"'Sir' is right. I'll teach you some manners yet."

"Fine, lesson learned. Let's agree you've made your point and both go home."

"I don't think so, you freak."

He couldn't come up with another derogatory name? "No, I don't—"

Instead of grabbing Mikelos, the bouncer snatched the violin away. He hurled it in the same movement, where it crashed into the steps behind him. The fragile antique wood shattered on contact with the concrete.

Mikelos' heart broke. It wasn't his first instrument, but it was his oldest. Connor had given him that violin. Mikelos dropped the bow from nerveless fingers and lunged for the other man.

The man met his attack with a ready fist, bashing his knuckles into Mikelos' jaw. Mikelos' forward momentum carried him into the bouncer's chest, and they both tumbled onto the stairs.

Mikelos rolled to his feet first, spreading his weight across two steps. He licked his lips and tasted blood. He'd done his best to avoid a physical fight with the guy, but now all bets were off. The vampire-daywalker bond with Victory increased his strength and speed. This man had destroyed one of the things most precious to him. He could kill the guy, if he wanted.

He wanted.

The other man also got to his feet, rubbing his head where it had bounced against the edge of the stone steps. His fingers retracted, turning claw-like, as a vein throbbed at his temple.

Oh, Mikelos wanted. But it would destroy what little ground the nonhumans of Limani had against this new crusade. Mikelos would be banished for murder, or worse.

Damn it, he had to pull his punches.

Mikelos shot out with his own fist, catching the bouncer in the solar plexus. At full strength, he could have cracked the man's sternum. Instead, the man yelped in pain and fell.

The bouncer kicked out a foot amidst his tumble, catching Mikelos' leg and pulling him off balance. Mikelos' knee bounced off the edge of a step with a sickening crack. His leg wouldn't hold him when he tried to rise, and Mikelos staggered. But he missed the last step and crashed to the sidewalk.

He landed with all his weight on his arm and hip, his knee screaming in pain. Before he compensated with the opposite leg, a shoe met his forehead, snapping his body to the ground.

A second kick connected with Mikelos' chest. This time the pop came from a rib, and the next shot landed at his stomach.

He shouldn't have pulled his first punch. He couldn't get to his feet while the blows kept coming. Mikelos covered his head with his arms and curled around his torso, pulling his legs to his chest. He pushed lung strength past battered ribs. "*Victory!*"

Mikelos braced his uninjured hand on the ground to rise and renew the attack. A mistake. The man's boot heel smashed again, followed by the sickening sound of the bones in his fingers breaking. He had encountered worse in three hundred years. This human, this single human, couldn't kill him.

He hoped.

The council chamber erupted into chaos.

Councilmembers demanded explanations or protested, per their nature. Gloating, Fabbri sat back in her chair. Max pitched his voice over the others. "Hey!"

Next to him, Lorus quieted, but the others paid no attention. Daliana snapped her fingers once. Everyone silenced when a brilliant white light flashed. She gestured toward Max, giving him control of the room once again.

"Thank you, Dal." Max stared at Fabbri. "Now what the hell are you talking about, woman? My source said standard troop rotations."

"I do hope you planned on sharing this with us, Max." Sethri's dry voice held a hint of rebuke.

The mercenary mimed shock. "Of course!"

Victory came to his rescue. "Max consulted with me before the meeting. We already have someone investigating the situation." Her ears picked out the strains of violin music. She relaxed with Mikelos' presence, even if outside the building.

"Who?" Soren asked.

"My sire Asaron graciously volunteered to be Limani's eyes," Victory said.

Fabbri snorted. "Because he can be trusted."

"He is accompanied by the warrior-mages Toria Connor and Kane Nalamas." Max paused. "You can't claim they're not full Limani citizens."

Victory kept her mouth shut despite her surprise. It seemed he and Asaron had laid plans in addition to those they'd let her in on. But she needed to portray solidarity instead of the role of worried mother. "Both Toria and Kane are journeymen of Limani's Mercenary Guild. They are obligated to return with a proper report."

This time, even Fabbri couldn't argue. The devotion of Limani's mercs to their home was legendary. Not only because they were on the payroll as a reserve battalion—one of the first lessons new trainees learned was the history of the Wasteland and the importance of Limani's location between the Roman and British colonies.

Victory also trusted Asaron. He had worked as a mercenary or soldier for most of the two millennia of his life, and while she had mostly kept to mercenary work for private citizens instead of armies, he had forgotten more about combat than she ever learned. Including tactics and camp life, two things that would tell him what the Romans planned, depending on how large the group was, how they were provisioned, and which direction they marched. A few small parties meant they had set out to kill Wasteland beasties plaguing a western town. A company or two could indeed be the field maneuvers Max suspected.

A large force marching straight for Limani meant only one thing. Victory didn't need her own years of mercenary work to tell her it wasn't the Emperor coming for a visit.

"They are on a covert information-gathering expedition," Max said. "An unknown number of soldiers are on our border for an unknown reason. That's what the mission is for. They're not planning on contacting the Romans or even letting their presence be discovered at all. They'll return within twenty-four hours. We can even have an emergency session to hear their—"

The door at the end of the council chamber slammed open, and the lone city clerk left on duty downstairs during council sessions rushed into the room. "Mr. Sethri!" He scurried to Sethri to whisper in his ear.

A scream came from outside. Her name. Victory leapt to her feet. No time to make excuses. She dashed for the door as Sethri spoke to the rest of the room. "A man attacked Mikelos Connor outside our doors."

Victory burst from the council building—Tristan, Max, and Lorus on her heels—as a strange man kicked a prone figure at the bottom of the steps. She tackled the man to the ground. The force of her blow knocked them clear into the street. His body fell limp when his head connected with the pavement.

Victory untangled herself and shot to her feet. Lorus and Tristan joined her, ready to restrain the attacker. Max knelt by Mikelos, and Victory rushed to his side, then dropped to cradle Mikelos' unconscious head in her lap. Blood smeared his face, his left hand was a mess, and his right leg bent at an unnatural angle.

Daliana knelt next to Victory and placed her hands on Mikelos' chest. Her gentle touch shimmered with golden light. "He's hurt, but he'll live. Some broken ribs, but no serious internal injuries." She gave Victory an apologetic expression. "I'm sorry, physical healing isn't my strong suit. I can feed him power, but not much more."

Max crouched next to Victory. "Lena's calling the ambulance. We shouldn't move him."

"I know." She bit her bottom lip, tasting blood. Wounds were nothing new to her. She smoothed Mikelos' lank hair around a patch sticky with blood. He was her daywalker; he could survive anything. They would get him to the hospital, the doctors would diagnose and treat him, and she would get some of her own blood into him to strengthen their bond and speed his healing. But right now, numbness spread through her. She stared at Daliana's hands, willing her own strength into them.

The other councilmembers gathered atop the steps. Victory wanted to demand information from Fabbri, but she couldn't jump to conclusions yet. Maybe Mikelos had just been mugged. Right, a likely theory.

A groan of pain caught her attention when Lorus and Tristan hauled the stranger to his feet. "Let go of me, freaks!" He struggled in their grasp. "Did I kill the bastard?"

No, not a random act of violence. Victory almost jumped at him again, but Max snatched her wrist and held her firm. His low voice spoke into her ear. "He's not worth your time or effort."

She sank to her knees. Attacking this man would invalidate everything she said in council.

The man laughed. "Too afraid to take me on without your little bitch?" He tried to shake off his captors, but the werewolf and wereporpoise kept their hands wrapped around his arms.

"Shut up or I'll hit you myself." At the feral growl underlying Tristan's warning, the man's struggles ceased.

Lena pushed her way through the crowd of councilmembers. "The ambulance is on its way." She spared a nasty glare for Mikelos' assailant. "I gave the police a ring, too, and they should be right behind. How's Mikelos?"

"Banged up pretty bad," Max said, "but he'll live. Daliana's doing what she can, but we'll need the hospital."

"This can't be a coincidence," Lena said. "Has the man said anything incriminating?"

Almost on cue, the attacker pulled against his captor again. Tristan growled, then the man yelped. "He threatened to bite me!"

Max smirked, but said, "Don't let Tristan bite the asshole, Lorus."

"Um, Victory?" Genevieve stood near them at the bottom of the steps. Splintered wood, broken strings curling like whiskers, lay in the werepanther's hands. "I couldn't find the bow," she said, stricken.

"It's here," Sethri said. He brought the unharmed bow to Victory. She gathered the fractured pieces under one arm and collected the bow. The weight in her arms tugged at her heart. This needless destruction would hurt Mikelos more than his own injuries.

"Ow!" Lorus elbowed his prisoner. "Tristan, put your claws away and stop being a jerk. What should we do with him, Alex?"

Sirens echoed in the distance, and Sethri studied the man in silence. "Fabbri!"

The crowd of human councilmembers shifted to reveal the woman in question. Fabbri remained where she was, arms crossed and hip tilted. "What? You think I had something to do with this?"

"Do you know this man?" Sethri kept his tone level.

Impressive. Victory would not have been so polite.

"I've never seen him before in my life," Fabbri said.

"You told me not to let that freak or his daughter into the club!" the man said from the street. "I got rid of some wolves and an elf slut, too."

The glow from Daliana's hands stuttered as she let out a hiss.

"I didn't tell you to beat him bloody, you idiot."

Fabbri damned herself. Victory smothered a humorless laugh.

"This doesn't look good, Emily," Sethri said, rubbing the back of his neck. "I should—"

The blaring siren cracked the air as the ambulance turned the corner. Max waved the vehicle in. Like Lena promised, a police cruiser followed close behind. The ambulance screeched to a halt and spit out two paramedics. The women shooed Victory, Max, and Lena out of the way, but didn't interfere with Daliana's flow of healing power. Victory let go of Mikelos with reluctance and stood, but continued to hover over the activity. They checked his vital signs and splinted his hand and leg, preparing to transfer him to a gurney. The medics would care for her daywalker well, as befitted the partner of Limani Central's best benefactor. Her self-assurance rang hollow when Mikelos groaned, even in unconsciousness, at the jostling to his injured leg.

More shouting from the attacker distracted her. Tristan and Lorus handed him over to the two police officers, who exchanged the werecreatures' vice grips for steel handcuffs.

"You can't let them do this, Fabbri!" His head hit the edge of the cruiser's roof with a muffled thump. The cops weren't being too careful with this one. Good. He shouldn't get consideration. "Those freaks deserve—!" The door slammed shut on any further complaints.

"Quite the imagination for insults," Max said. "Practically a sailor. He almost made me blush."

His sarcasm did little to cheer her, but she appreciated the effort. The paramedics loaded Mikelos' gurney into the ambulance. Daliana climbed in back beside one while the other took the driver's seat up front.

Mixed loyalties tore at Victory. The council meeting would continue, now that they knew Fabbri had influence beyond the sign on her restaurant's door. "Lena?"

"Go." The dean flicked her fingers. "Take care of Mikelos."

"We can deal with Fabbri," Max said. "I'll let you know what happens as soon as the meeting's over."

"Thank you."

Lena hugged her, and Max slapped her back. The ambulance's lights flashed, and she dashed to the passenger side. Right now, her place was with Mikelos.

A heavy object bludgeoned Toria's skull. Again. Again. And again. It didn't stop when she brought her hands over her head. The pain came from within, the fiercest headache she'd ever had. Her eyeballs were on fire, and her brain throbbed.

She risked cracking open her eyes. Darkness met them, and she fought momentary panic. It's still nighttime. Chill out. Dirt cushioned her cheek, and a rock dug into her side.

Kane! She had to help Kane. Toria scrambled to her feet when memory rushed back. Her head screeched in pain at the hasty action, and she listed to one side, struggling for balance. If the Romans were still nearby, they were done for. She fell to a knee, then staggered to her feet once more, trying not to retch from the roiling in her stomach. She peered across the river, but the haze of pain impeded her view. Her hand sought the rapier at her side, but met empty air.

She fell to her knees again, clutching her stomach in her arms. She made a prime target and couldn't do a thing about it.

But no attack came. Her stomach calmed, but the headache did not ease.

"Ugh." The inside of her mouth tasted like cotton, but the urge to faint had passed.

The river spread before her. No signs of a skirmish remained other than footprints in the river mud.

No Romans. No horses. Nothing.

Of course, any Romans still around would have shot her while she flailed around like a maniac.

"Kane!" Her voice echoed across the water. "Asaron!"

No response. A testy owl hooted from the trees behind her, and the river flowed on.

She pushed herself to her feet and turned in a slow circle, squinting into the darkness. The moon had set, indicating a few hours of unconsciousness. Now, faint starlight lit the night. She dug a glass bauble from one of her belt pouches and held it in her palm.

Focusing her intentions on the charm, she nudged it with her mind. Pain lanced between her temples. Toria doubled over, but managed to remain on her feet.

The spell infused in the glass activated. Purple light sputtered. It dimmed almost to nonexistence before steadying to its set brightness. A cool amethyst glow bathed the area around her.

Concentrating on the comforting familiar light persuaded the pain behind her eyes to fade to a manageable pulse. Now Toria examined her situation in a more rational frame of mind. No bodies across the river—they must have taken Kane and Asaron. Deep within herself, she found the bond in her soul that connected her with her partner. She would be able to tell if he died. Though faint with distance, the bond retained Kane's unmistakable trace. Kane's survival boded well for Asaron's.

Unless her partner had done something stupid. No. She wouldn't go there.

Now for supplies. No sign of her horse, even after she paced the edge of the woods and whistled for a few minutes. Either the Romans had stolen the mare, or she'd abandoned her crazy mistress and gone home.

Weapons? The horse hadn't disarmed her before wandering off, so the Romans must have searched her. They'd stolen her knives, along with the small amount of cash in her duster pocket.

And no sword.

"Bastards!" She hurled a rock from the edge of the river through the air. It landed with an ineffectual splash. Why hadn't they taken her with them? Maybe she'd managed to disable a few of them and they hadn't had the manpower. Not much of a consolation.

Toria glared across the river, trying to ignore the tap dancers in her skull. Her instincts urged her to track the damn Romans, to rescue Kane. Yes, he still lived, but for how long?

She reached the edge of the water, waves lapping at her boots, before thought surpassed action. "No, Toria." She didn't even have a water bottle, much less weaponry. Despite her strong magic, a rescue attempt would be a lot easier with supplies and a blade in her hand.

With great reluctance, she pulled herself away from the river's edge. She had to return to Limani for aid. And painkillers. At least she'd accomplished their mission. The Romans were close to the city, and she had to bring the warning.

Toria gripped the glowing glass even tighter in her hand. The power in the bauble strained, and the light guttered like a candle before fading. When she attempted to reactivate the spell, sharp pain lanced through her skull and she doubled over again.

She hoped dawn came soon. It would be a long, agonizing journey, but daylight at least meant she wouldn't trip over everything.

The second Mikelos' eyelids twitched, Victory shot out of her seat at the window and across the hospital room to his side.

"Victory?" His voice grated.

"Hush, love, you're safe." She pushed the call button by the side of his hospital bed. "We're at Limani Central, you're okay now." As okay as he could be with a leg brace, a splinted hand, bandages around his ribs, and a nasty bump on his head. Victory still seethed inside, but right now she needed to stay calm for Mikelos, not have a temper tantrum and throw furniture.

A nurse leaned into the room. Victory gestured toward the waking Mikelos, and the nurse disappeared again. The doctor would come soon—her continuous flow of money to the hospital in return for a steady supply of blood played to her advantage tonight.

Mikelos focused, and she brushed his hair off his forehead. He managed to raise his head a few inches. The sheet covering him did little to hide the thick leg brace. "My hand—?"

"Ah, awake?" The doctor handling Mikelos' case bustled into the room and nudged Victory out of the way to check on his patient. "Hello, Mr. Connor, my name is Dr. Preston. May I call you Mikelos?"

Mikelos attempted a nod, then pressed pale lips together. He fell against the pillows.

Victory tensed, but the doctor had things well in hand. "Easy, Mikelos," he said. "You've had quite a night."

She stared in fascination while he did mysterious medical things involving shining a light at Mikelos' pupils. Visions of doctors from centuries past haunted her, wielding saws to "fix" knee injuries like the one Mikelos had suffered. Mikelos would receive special treatment due to his connection with the hospital's best patron, but battlefield experiences of spilled blood and severed limbs still lived in her vivid memories. She'd confessed these to Daliana earlier when Mikelos was being patched up, but the elven woman patted her hand and told her memories were potent things. Truer words were never spoken, especially when spoken by the city's lead psychiatrist.

She ran her hands through her hair, pulling it into a messy bun. Dawn approached, and between the council meeting and Mikelos' attack, it had been a long day.

Dr. Preston finished probing at Mikelos' side, then included Victory when he spoke to her daywalker. "The good news is your ribs are bruised, but none of them are broken. Three bones in your hand are broken, but those are splinted and will heal with time. We've also ruled out a concussion. However, you also tore the anterior cruciate ligament in your knee, so we're going to have you pretty happy on pain medication until we can schedule surgery. Ms., erm, Victory has assured me you will heal faster than a normal human, but we're still going to take every precaution against further aggravation of your wounds." He flipped through the chart from the end of Mikelos' bed, making a few notations.

Mikelos traced the small bandage decorated with blue stars on the inside of her wrist where she had made the tiny incision with a scalpel snagged from a closet. The night nurse had balked at Victory's request for the medical supplies, but calling Daliana upstairs had bypassed the issue. "How much blood?"

"A few teaspoons." She entwined her fingers in his. "You'll be on your feet in no time. We'll reevaluate in a few hours and see whether we can avoid the surgery." She repeated it to herself: Her daywalker was strong. He was not a normal human. Mikelos would heal even faster than Toria had when she broke her leg a few years ago.

"There will be the matter of some necessary physical rehabilitation, but, um, yes." Dr. Preston's discomfort rose, as it had earlier when Daliana helped Victory cut her wrist to collect the blood. Victory pitied him, but there wasn't much choice. It wasn't like any of the doctors here knew anything beyond the basics about vampire or daywalker physiology. Since they were the only two permanent residents of the sort in Limani, it wasn't a specialization in much demand. He cleared his throat. "Until then, we will take excellent care of you." From the hallway, a loudspeaker requested his presence on another floor, saving him from further awkwardness. Dr. Preston mumbled his excuses.

"Thank you, Doctor," Victory said, but he had already fled the room. "Poor guy. But he's a good doctor. Or so Dal assures me."

"That's my girl." Mikelos slurred his words.

He was crashing, hard. No surprise, between the combination of pain medication and work of her shared blood. Accelerated healing used a lot of energy. Victory tried to lighten the mood. "You didn't put up a very good fight. I'll have to put you in training with the kids when you're better."

"The guy?"

"In police custody. He's got his own set of bruises. I tackled him halfway across the street to get him off you. Tristan and Lorus got to manhandle him a bit. A bit more than necessary, but I wasn't about to stop them." She rambled with nerves. Gods, she must be tired.

"Good. Love you." Mikelos drifted off, and his grip on Victory's hand relaxed.

"I love you, too." Victory placed a gentle hand over his heart for the steady, reassuring beat in his chest. The door to the hospital room opened, and she raised a hand to silence the visitor. She pecked a kiss to Mikelos' forehead before standing to greet the newcomer.

"How's he doing?" Max asked, his voice low.

"About as well as can be expected." Victory gestured for the mercenary to join her on the other side of the room. She reclaimed her perch on the windowsill, and Max sat in the uncomfortable plastic chair she had ignored. He was welcome to the hideous thing. "He didn't ask about his violin."

"He might not remember. It'll hit him pretty hard later, but now he needs to concentrate on healing." Max shifted in his seat, already uncomfortable, but he would never give in and move like she had. He was more stubborn.

"You're right." Victory rested her temple against the glass and stared out across the mostly empty hospital parking lot. "What's the news?"

"This guy who attacked Mikelos, Ed MacClellan, has been charged with assault and destruction of property. Unfortunately, no one can prove whether he intended to kill Mikelos, and MacClellan isn't talking until he gets a lawyer."

"How did the rest of the meeting go? Since it looks like Fabbri's nonsense has spread."

"She's just the most vocal. Being on the council might make her the de facto leader."

"The vibe I'm getting isn't so much a desire for more power, but a desire to take power out of our hands." Victory spoke in general terms, speaking for all of the nonelected councilmembers. "She doesn't seem fond of you, either. Even though you're human. Well, mostly."

"Mostly." Max made an aborted gesture toward one ear. "But it's not surprising. Politically, Lena and I are on your side."

"But does she want the power to be in the hands of only elected councilmembers rather than sharing with those appointed to special positions? Or does she want it only for humans?" Things didn't make sense. Maybe Fabbri was plain nuts. But an argument against the woman's sanity based on whom she let in her restaurant wasn't good enough.

Max studied Mikelos' still form. "MacClellan implicated Fabbri in Mikelos' attack. It's safe to say she's pro-human, not pro-elections. When I left the station, the police were about to call the new owner of the Twilight Mists for questioning. This might be even bigger than we think."

"It is bigger," Victory said. Another soft tap came from the half-open door where Daliana had appeared. Victory waved her in, and the elven woman ghosted across the floor to join them.

Max shifted to the side of his chair, and Daliana perched on the arm. "Ain't this a regular party?" Max asked.

Daliana ignored him. "How is Mikelos doing?"

"Okay," Victory said. "He woke enough to talk to the doctor, but conked out again. I thought you were going home?"

"I took a quick consult in the emergency department for an elven patient." She hesitated, her face grave.

"Spit it out, girl," Max said.

"Things are getting bad. Three more people have been brought in within the past few hours. Two werewolves and an elven girl," Daliana said, voice stilted with suppressed anger. "All beaten like Mikelos. One of the wolves even more so, his back might be broken." She pulled a flier out of her pocket and smoothed it flat. "He had this."

The crumpled paper had almost ripped in half. One corner had soaked in blood, now dried to a flaky brownish tint. A simple flier, with an advertisement for a meeting.

TOWN HALL MEETING

REGARDING: STATE OF THE LIMANI CITY COUNCIL AND ITS MEMBERS. ALSO FEATURED WILL BE A Q&A SESSION REGARDING CURRENT PUBLIC POLICIES AND THEIR EFFECTS ON LIMANI CITIZENS.

JUNE 27th—6:00 PM—TWILIGHT MISTS

SPONSORED BY: LIMANI HUMANISTS

REFRESHMENTS WILL BE PROVIDED!

"Okay," Victory said. "That bad vibe went from worse to horrible." The location of the meeting outraged her more than what it planned to discuss. When she'd sold the club after over fifty years of ownership, she never expected it would be used like this.

"Damn." Max studied the flier. "This comes off as a civil gripe meeting, but if they're already attacking people, this is going to get a lot worse before it gets better. Impeaching Fabbri and getting her off the council might not fix this."

"We can't assume these Humanists are responsible for the attacks." Victory hated to play devil's advocate. Mikelos filled that role under normal circumstances, but right now he was in no position to do it. "These could be more punks operating on their own."

Daliana rose to pace the room. "One can hope."

The elven woman was one of the calmest people in Victory's social circle, able to handle anything with aplomb. She had never seen Daliana so worked up. Again, these weren't normal circumstances. "Well, you said MacClellan was charged. Have they questioned Fabbri?"

"That's the other problem," Max said.

Daliana stopped pacing, and both women stared at the mercenary.

"She didn't," Victory said.

"She did."

Victory rubbed her face as she cursed the woman. "Hell."

"Did what?" Daliana asked. "Explain. Or is this some sort of merc code I'm not privy to?"

"She disappeared," Victory said. "When?"

"We don't know. We were busy controlling MacClellan," Max said. "He tried to kick the glass out of the cruiser window. You two left in the ambulance. By the time both vehicles left, half the council had wandered inside, and I figured she'd gone with them. Lena thought she was still outside with me."

"Perfect." Victory groaned in exasperation. "Is there going to be an arrest?"

"I asked the cops to stay on the lookout since MacClellan implicated her," Max said, "but once he shut up, they decided there wasn't enough evidence. Never mind the whole council heard what she said to him."

"No arrest warrant?" Daliana asked.

"Nope."

Daliana's lips pulled back, baring her teeth. "But you do believe Fabbri arranged the attacks?"

Victory didn't want to know what Daliana found in the ER to rouse such fury.

"Hell, yeah," Max said. "MacClellan didn't strike me as the type to be imaginative enough to pin this on anyone else. The bastard is proud of what he did."

Victory resisted her immediate urge to go on the hunt. "What do we do now?"

The three stared at each other. Max spoke first. "I'd say it's time to call a meeting."

Toria learned in junior high geography class that the southern portion of Limani's territory remained wild compared to the civilized enclave the original Greek settlers had carved out for themselves on this New Continent. The farms and ranches and fisheries that surrounded the city and provided much of the population's primary food staples eventually gave way to the Ocean of Atlantika to the east, unclaimed British colonial territory to the north, and the Wasteland to the west. But south of the city, beyond the Agios River, lay untamed wilderness where even the werecreatures only roamed on the rarest occasion. The reality of this had never sunk in until this walk home, the sunlight fading around her. Her head still ached, her feet felt like she walked on hot pokers, and she'd last drunk from a small stream at least five miles back.

But power called to power, and she and Kane maintained a magical workroom in the attic of her childhood home. Even without access to her magical abilities, it shone like a beacon through the forests, guiding her home as a perfect compass.

She cut through the last bit of woods to get from the road to the manor, and her spirits lifted when the house came into view. Tears moistened her cheeks, and Toria raised her hands to her face.

She laughed—and cried—in relief. Exhaustion and dehydration made for a dangerous combination. She might not know Kane and Asaron's current location, but her parents would be home, and they would make everything better. A childish sentiment, but one Toria clung to as she entered the security code to unlock the back door. The Romans had even snatched her keys.

"Mama!" Toria clutched the doorframe when air-conditioned coolness washed over her in an artificial breeze.

No answer. A louder yell, for her father's weaker senses: "*Dad!*"

Still, no one came running. Maybe they were out? The original plan had called for Max to tell Mama of their mission at the council meeting last night. No one had reason to expect them home this soon. But what kept Mama out last night that she had to shelter elsewhere for the day?

The kitchen wavered in front of her. Toria used the counter to pull herself over to the kitchen phone, where she dialed Max's direct number at the Guildhall.

The line rang for what seemed forever. Then, in a businesslike tone not often heard from her mentor, "Hello, you've reached the office of Maximilian Asher, Mercenary Guildmaster of Limani. I'm not in right now—" Directions to call the Guildhall's front desk or leave a direct message for Max followed, then a long beep.

"Max! I had to walk home. Kane and Asaron got kidnapped by the Romans. They left me by the river and I don't know where they are. I lost your horse, I'm so sorry." The words battled with the sobs that threatened to escape. "I don't know where Dad or Mama are, I don't know what to do." The phone cord stretched long when Toria slid into a heap on the floor. In a whisper, she repeated, "I don't know what to do."

With no energy to hang up the phone, she let it drop into her lap. The voice mail registered the silence and listed her options, then the call disconnected with another beep. The dial tone joined her in the otherwise empty kitchen.

The cool of the tile floor beneath her seeped into her limbs. She should tug off her boots, get some water, have a shower, go to bed, wait for her parents to come home.

In a minute. She could rest for a minute.

Victory woke to a stiff spine and foul-tasting tongue. But the familiar fingers running through her long hair soothed her. She hummed in bliss.

Mikelos' clear eyes glinted in the dim room when she raised her head from the edge of the bed. Her back let loose a loud protest, which she supplemented with a groan as she switched on the bedside lamp. Her daywalker's good hand dropped to his stomach. "I can't believe you fell asleep like that."

"I've slept through worse. How do you feel, love?"

"Okay. What time is it?"

"No idea." The night before, Max sat vigil with her until dawn, leaving after he helped her scrounge the hospital ward for blankets to supplement the window's thin curtains for protection against the daylight. The direction of the faint glow that shone through the edges showed the day had almost come to a close. She pulled herself out of the wretched plastic chair and stretched, arching her arms up and out to the sides. Her spine complained one more time before settling into its proper alignment. She checked the clock above the door. "A little before seven. You've slept for over twelve hours. You needed it."

"I'm sure I did." Despite the renewed energy, his voice remained soft and listless, bereft of its usual lilt.

She wanted her old Mikelos back. "Are you hungry?" *Don't ask about the violin,* she prayed. *I can't deal with that right now. Neither can you.*

"Starved."

"I'll be right back." At the nurse's station, she found a nursing assistant filling in a crossword, who was more than happy to find Mikelos a replacement for the dinner he'd missed during the earlier meal rounds. His eagerness verged on manic;

she'd earned herself a bit of a reputation earlier when she'd told off a nurse for trying to remove the blankets from the window.

The nursing assistant returned with a tray twenty minutes later, along with the cup of steaming coffee and newspaper Victory had slipped him change for. After they maneuvered Mikelos into the least painful sitting position, her daywalker fell on the meal with gusto. He must be hungry if the stuff the hospital called food appealed to him.

Victory shoved the horrid chair into the far corner of the room and settled herself cross-legged at the foot of the bed, clutching her mug in both hands.

Coffee made the world seem more manageable. Later she would call the blood donation office and ask for a proper breakfast, but this would do for now. Victory spread the newspaper over the lump of Mikelos' cast, flipping through each page. She wasn't sure what she'd expected to find, but finding absolutely nothing was bad news. "Ah, hell."

Mikelos paused in his eating, soup spoon hovering near his mouth. "What?"

"There's nothing in here about the attacks last night."

"Attacks? Plural?"

Victory sketched out what Daliana had shared the night before, along with her own efforts to find the other victims before dawn and get more information about their attackers. "We're pretty sure they were attacked by these 'Humanists' like you were."

"Why me, though?" Mikelos stared at her coffee until she relented and handed the cup over. "I'm practically human."

"Because they're stupid, but not that stupid. An elven girl doesn't look like much. Enough humans can overcome a werewolf, at least one of the younger ones. An elder wolf would rip them to shreds. But no one in their right mind would go after me."

She retrieved her coffee before he drank all of it and studied the paper spread before her. "Werewolves, and the panthers, have an ancient reputation of stealing livestock. The elves steal human children and leave changelings, but they've managed to twist the legends in their favor, convincing the public they steal children destined for horrible lives." Like the life Toria would have had, in the middle of nowhere at the edge of the Wasteland. "But vampires have always preyed on healthy humans as their preferred target. These Humanists will assume I'll eat them if they go after me."

Mikelos laughed at her obvious expression of distaste, then put his hand to his ribs and groaned. He gasped a mixture of laughter and pain. "Please don't make me do that." He shifted in the bed again. "What are we going to do about these Humanists?"

"I have no idea, yet. We need to implicate them in the attacks. Max said he would stop by the police station and get an update after he got some sleep." Victory traded her coffee again for a bite of applesauce. "Ugh. I'm finding you some proper food."

Dr. Preston flipped on the overhead light as he entered the hospital room. "I don't think so. And I hope that's not coffee."

Mikelos returned the cup to Victory. "Course not, Doc."

Victory slid off the bed to give Dr. Preston room to examine Mikelos. She perused the newspaper again, but found nothing upon a second search. The biggest news story featured the triumph of the university sailing team over a college in the British colonies.

The doctor finished his exam. "Everything looks good here. Surgery might not be necessary if you continue to improve at this rate." He made notes on Mikelos' chart. "How are you feeling? Need any changes to your current pain management?"

"I'm hanging in there."

"Good. No need to suffer now, there'll be plenty once you start physical therapy."

His joke fell flat. "Right," Mikelos said.

"I'm off on to continue my rounds, then. I'll drop in on you before I leave in the morning."

With no further attempts at small talk, Dr. Preston left the hospital room. Once she heard him conversing with a nurse farther down the hall, Victory said, "I don't think I like him too much. Maybe he's one of the Humanists." She didn't mean it. Really.

"Now you're being paranoid." Mikelos interrupted himself with a yawn.

She placed a hand on Mikelos' cheek. "Rest, love. I'm going to try to poke around some more." Different nurses were on duty now, and she might be able to speak with the other attack victims. She hoped the morning shift hadn't given them too much warning. Victory helped Mikelos lay flat again, then smoothed his hair away from his face. His breath evened out in sleep by the time she left his room.

According to gossip overheard in her slow meander by the nurses' station, the two werewolves remained in intensive care. But hospital staff had transferred the elven girl from the emergency room direct to a recovery ward. Either she'd escaped with light wounds, or she sported a strong healing ability.

None of the nurses, doctors, aides, or other evening visitors paid attention to Victory wandering the third-floor hallway, admiring the bland hospital décor that adorned the pastel yellow walls. Watercolor landscapes seemed to be the rule of the day, though a few random pieces consisted of strange geometric shapes. The majority of patients in this unit were human, but she caught the earthy scent of a werepanther before the brightness of the elven girl she sought. Not her primary target, but now any injury to a nonhuman roused her suspicion.

After a gentle tap on the doorjamb, she slipped into the room. The young panther slept with his cast-covered leg held above the bed in traction. Victory stared at the contraption for a few moments, thanking whoever or whatever listened that Mikelos hadn't been so injured.

The teenager mumbled in his sleep. When he didn't wake at her presence, she crossed the room and examined his chart.

A brief skim showed an accident during afternoon rugby practice. A werepanther had the innate speed and grace of an excellent athlete, which hadn't saved him from a bad tangle with a teammate. Poor kid.

So, not another Humanist attack. At least at first glance. But she couldn't dismiss anything out of hand, regardless of the age of the victim or apparent circumstance. For all she knew, the younger nonhumans might be a more tempting target for the Humanists. Victory would interview him when he woke.

"Can I help you?"

Victory slipped the chart into its holder before facing the nurse who'd entered the room. "Nope, I'm good."

"This is a private room," the nurse said. "Do you know the patient?"

"Yes, of course," Victory said. The nurse didn't mention Victory's perusal of the chart. How did they manage to be so intimidating in purple pants and shirts decorated with cartoon cats? "Tyrone is a friend of my daughter. I was in the hospital on business so I thought I'd check in."

The nurse held the door open wider, her expression expectant. Not wanting to press her luck just yet, Victory accepted the unspoken invitation and exited the boy's room. The nurse shut the door on her heels.

Part of her hesitated at the idea of leaving the kid alone with an unknown human, but she squashed the sudden irrational paranoia. After a quick survey of the quiet hall, ensuring no one else had noticed her interaction with the nurse, Victory continued in her original direction.

She passed the nurses' station on one side, and two more rooms containing human patients on the other. Then she found her target: The light scent of Other, of fresh-cut grass and tangible sunlight signaling "elf" to Victory's vampiric senses. A relief after the harsh antiseptic smell permeating the hospital.

And it was obvious this patient did not sleep.

"No fucking way! I said I'm fine!"

The girl had a set of lungs on her. Victory resisted the urge to cover her sensitive ears at the shriek that emanated from the next room. She peeked around the door frame.

Three harried nurses clustered around the hospital bed, one holding a glass of water and cup of pills out to the elven girl. "But you'll feel so much better," she said. "If you take the painkillers, you'll be able to eat. You need to keep your energy up so you can heal."

"Yeah, I need to eat real food! Not mess myself up with your crazy drugs." The girl slouched forward and pouted, and Victory caught the flinch of pain the girl almost hid. A possible injury to her ribs, to accompany the butterfly bandages holding together a long cut on her left cheek and temple. "That shit is not food. And your so-called medicine already made me puke once. Fuck that."

Victory stifled a laugh at the elven girl's coarse language. This girl would horrify Daliana.

The nurse set the items on the bedside table by the untouched tray of hospital food, slowing her movement in time to avoid slamming it and scattering the contents. "Fine. Do what you will. Let's go, ladies."

Victory ducked out of the doorway and studied more art, hoping she retained her air of inconspicuousness. It must have worked—when the three nurses left, they passed her without comment. Victory slipped into the hospital room.

"I *told* you—oh," the girl said, cutting off her attitude midsentence. "You're not one of those vultures."

Victory gestured to the chair in the corner. "Mind if I have a seat and talk with you for a bit?"

The girl released her arms from across her chest, relief visible on her face. "Can I bribe you to get me real food from the cafeteria?"

Taking her question as agreement, Victory pushed the door closed behind her and dragged the chair closer to the bed. "You don't even have to bribe me. I know how bad the patient food is here." Different style of chair, even more uncomfortable. What was it about hospitals? "I'd like to ask you a few questions, and I'll go pick up whatever you want."

"Deal. You're my hero for the evening."

Victory held out her hand. "I'm Victory, by the way."

"I know who you are, vampire." They exchanged handshakes. "I'm Syrisinia, Syri. Sorry I'm grumpy. I've had a crappy couple of days."

"I don't blame you. My daywalker is under care here as well, and he's not the greatest patient either."

Syri sat straight up in the bed. "Shit. They got him, too?"

All of Victory's attention now hung on Syri's every word. "Tell me what you know." If her version of events resembled Mikelos', she would have serious evidence against the Humanists.

"I don't know much. I danced with Mikelos at the Twilight Mists last night before we got kicked out of the club with the wolves. I wanted to go back in, and the wolves were gonna support me, but Mikelos convinced us not to, said the council had things under control."

Victory answered her unspoken question. "The bouncer who kicked you guys out attacked him. Right in front of the council hall."

"While council was in session? Bloody idiot."

"Indeed, not the brightest idea. Where did you go after Mikelos left?"

Pain creased Syri's forehead. "The wolves left to go do whatever werewolves do. I stuck around for a bit, tempted to sneak back into the Twilight Mists. Two other elves came up to the club, and I warned them off. I might be stubborn, but I wasn't going to let them get into trouble, too." She plucked a spoon from her meal tray and toyed with the utensil, but ignored the food. "Then, I heard shouting a couple blocks away. When I heard the howl, I figured it was the wolves in trouble. So, I ran to the rescue."

Victory hadn't heard anything so ridiculous since the time Toria declared her serious intentions to create a flying carpet—at age eleven. She studied the girl. Since she appeared Toria's age, Syri was still not more than a child by the standards of elves, who lived thousands of years. And despite whatever magic she possessed, the girl resembled a twig, and not a sturdy one.

As if understanding Victory's appraisal, Syri said, "I may be stupid, but I'm stronger than I look. Sort of."

Victory laughed at Syri's admission. "Did you rescue them?"

"Hey, they're in the intensive care unit, and I'm not." Syri's smug voice matched her attitude. "What do you think?"

"I am suitably impressed, and one day I'd like to know how you managed it."

"I ain't going anywhere," Syri said. Her voice lost its bantering tone when she continued. "Six humans, all men, cornered Mal and Gregory in an alley. One had a gun. I can't remember the last time I saw a person—not a merc—in this city with a gun."

Victory tensed at the girl's words. Daliana had cited patient confidentiality regarding the extent of the two werewolves' injuries. She'd had no idea firearms were involved.

"They'd already shot Gregory in the stomach, still in human form. Mal hadn't shifted to wolf-form. He just growled at them."

"Both of them would have been unprotected if he'd shifted."

"Yeah, I figured. So…I kind of jumped into the fray. Got knocked around with the wooden clubs a few of them had before the cops ran them off. Hence the forehead and cracked rib."

"And you're lucky you didn't get shot, too." Victory took Syri's hand. "When I was young, the world was different. I saw the empires move from swords, to guns, to missiles, to nuclear weapons. After the Last War, your people forced us to return to the past, to a world of blades.

"Antique firearms still float around, pistols and rifles. My sire told me he's run into a few old automatic machine guns. But there are always going to be those who want a better gun, one to shoot farther and make bigger holes, even despite the world-altering spell. Elves and werecreatures and even vampires have to remember we're still vulnerable to what the humans can create. The world isn't safe anymore for those like you and I. Immortality can only take us so far. We've lost our edge, and now they can kill us as easily as they kill each other." Had Syri learned anything about the Humanists? One way to find out. "It looks like they've started again."

"What is going on in here?" a voice snapped.

Victory twisted in her lumpy chair. One of the ever-present nurses glowered from the entrance to the room, another nursing assistant hulking behind her. "Can I help you, ma'am?"

"You are disturbing my patient," the nurse said, sneering. "What's wrong with you? Filling a girl's head with such ideas when she's already hurt."

"I'm old enough to be your grandmother, lady—" Syri cut off this newest rant when Victory squeezed her hand in warning.

After checking the nurse's nametag, Victory again asked, "Can I help you, Ms. Sjolander?" No point in being indignant over the woman's spying.

"Visiting hours are over. Sully will escort you from the hospital now so Syri can get her rest."

"Well, regular visiting hours are rather outside my travel ability, aren't they?" Never hurt to try reason. "I'm almost done speaking with Syri, I'll be happy to leave right after."

Syri contributed her own opinion on the subject. "Yeah, she's fine. It's not like I sleep much. Victory can stay as long as she wants."

Ms. Sjolander stiffened at the mention of Victory's name. How long had the nurse been spying on them?

"You're the vampire?" Ms. Sjolander's hands clenched at her sides.

Victory rose to her feet. She stood shorter than the nurse, but attitude countered more than inches. "I am."

Without a word, the nurse spun on her heel, grabbing the elbow of the confused assistant on her way out.

"What the hell was that about?"

Victory resumed her seat next to Syri. "Hell if I know." The elven girl's language was catching. "But now we have to talk fast."

"You said something about someone starting again."

"Right. The reason you and the others were kicked out of the club? Why you were all attacked? There's a group forming, the Humanists, who—"

Heavy footsteps clunked in the hall, along with a distant voice. "She's in room 302."

Syri perked up, her pointed elven ears even more sensitive than Victory's. "I'm room 302."

Victory shot out of her chair as three hospital security staff appeared in the doorway.

"Ms. Victory," the lead guard said, "you need to come with us."

A fight in the middle of Syri's hospital room would not be a smart idea, even though Victory's hands itched for a nonexistent weapon. "I'm not finished talking to my friend yet."

"Hospital policy is immediate family only outside of visiting hours. You can either return to Mr. Connor's room or leave the hospital."

Ms. Sjolander appeared behind the security guards. "No, she needs to leave the hospital. She has harassed the patients and staff since last night."

"It's true, sir," the youngest guard said. "Lots of complaints."

What complaints? She'd gotten chewed out by the one intensive care nurse earlier, but no one called security on her. Victory straightened further, drawing on the poise acquired over centuries. "Syri, I'll call you tomorrow."

"Not going anywhere."

Time for Victory to play nice. "Would one of you kind young men like to escort me to my car?" She pushed a beat of mental influence through her words, and the lead guard leaned toward her before catching himself. If they wanted to throw her out for being a vampire, they got the full treatment.

"Ellis, Wim, go with her," the leader said.

"Thank you so much." Victory brushed past them toward the exit. The guards hastened to fall in place on either side of her. "It is best if I leave," she said, "since I haven't eaten in hours."

Now she left the hospital room, on her own terms. To Ms. Sjolander's sputtering, the guards' pale faces, and Syri's hysterical laughter.

Getting thrown out of a hospital by a nurse had to be almost as humiliating as getting thrown out of a bar by a bouncer. And Victory had been thrown out of a lot of bars in her long life, for one reason or another. Once or twice she had even deserved it.

Despite Victory's levity while the guards escorted her out of the hospital, a lump in her throat formed the second she got in her town-car and grew larger the entire drive home. If she stopped moving, she might burst into tears and be worthless to everyone. She knew better than to exhaust herself, but she had to stay awake long enough to make phone calls to Max and Daliana and the other nonhuman councilmembers. Then back to the hospital, and this time she would try to make it home again before dawn. She could sleep then.

Victory kicked off her sandals in the foyer. Once in the kitchen, she flicked on the overhead lights. The telephone dangled off its hook by the cord.

Huh. She hadn't touched the kitchen phone in a few days. Maybe one of the others forgot to hang it up before leaving last night—Asaron, perhaps, since he and technology did not mix well. Victory circled the island to return the phone to its rightful spot, hoping no one had called during her day stuck in the hospital.

Toria lay on the kitchen floor beyond the island, curled up on the hard tile. Not her usual napping location.

Victory crouched next to her daughter, placing a hand on her shoulder. No obvious signs of injury. No telltale tang of blood. "Toria! Wake up, sweetie."

Toria groaned in response. One of pain, rather than her usual grumbling displeasure of being woken.

"Mom?" Toria allowed Victory to pull her into a sitting position. She stared around the kitchen. "Oh, man, I didn't mean to pass out here." Dryness cracked her voice.

Victory hung up the phone and fetched a glass of cool water. Toria accepted it with two shaking hands and an expression of utter gratitude.

"Are you okay?" Victory kneeled next to her again while Toria drank. "What happened?" He daughter sported a grimy and sweat-stained sports bra and jeans, her shirt and duster lying in a pile on the counter above them. "Where are the guys? I didn't expect you until tomorrow at the earliest." She dreaded more bad news. She dreaded sharing her own much more.

Toria set the empty glass on the floor and scrubbed at her face with her hands. "We weren't supposed to be. Things got bad fast, Mama."

Victory clasped her daughter's tremoring hand in her own. "Where are Kane and Asaron?" She braced for the worst.

Toria stared into space over Victory's shoulder while she gave her report. "We ran into a Roman patrol right after the guys crossed the Agios River. I was still trying to get my horse to ford the water. I funneled my power to Kane to help him fight them off, but a backlash knocked me out." With obvious effort, she brought her eyes to Victory's nose, her daughter's equivalent of staring her straight on. Tear marks stained Toria's ashen face. "When I came to, they were gone. So was my horse, and the patrol had searched me."

Mikelos lying in front of the council hall—unconscious, bleeding—had been a blow to the stomach. The news of her captured sire and foster son was almost a knife to the heart. She unclenched her fist before she drew blood. "But why—"

"I don't know why they left me. Maybe they didn't have room for another prisoner. They should have taken me."

"No!" Victory lowered her voice and said, "More likely they left you in warning."

"For who?" Toria laughed without humor, staring at the white ceiling. "It's the army of the Roman-fucking-Empire. They declared hostile intent when they took Kane and Asaron. Limani doesn't stand a chance."

"For someone with such a grasp of tactics, it's a wonder you're so terrible at chess." Victory's quip fell flat. Mother and daughter shared expressions of despair.

"How can you joke about this, Mama?"

Because if she didn't, she might put a fist through the wall. "I'm sorry. Asaron has survived worse situations over the years. He'll watch over Kane."

Toria braced a hand on the floor and pushed herself to her feet. "Hey, where's Dad?"

"He's in the hospital."

"Oh no, what happened?"

"He was attacked. The Roman army's not the only thing we have to deal with right now. The Humanists have also made their move."

At Victory's news, Toria staggered to one side, catching herself on the island in the middle of the kitchen. Victory grabbed her elbow before she fell.

"Gah, Mom," Toria said. "Don't do that. Dad will be okay, right?"

Pain and fear filled the look Toria gave her. The fear for her family was obvious, but the pain concerned Victory more, so she ignored her daughter's query. "When they knocked you out last night, what exactly happened?"

"Mama. Is Dad okay?"

"He'll be fine. He just hurt his knee and ribs." She wouldn't mention the hand. Victory grabbed Toria's chin and peered into her face. Pupils of equal size, not dilated. But Toria's storm-gray eyes seemed large in her pale face. "Now, what happened to you? How did you get hurt if the Romans were across the river?"

Toria pulled out of Victory's grasp. "Power backlash. I've never had one this bad before, but using a river for power is kind of a rush. Can't expect anything less."

"You need to see someone about this."

"Who? A doctor?" Toria crossed the kitchen with halting steps, using the counter for balance. "This isn't anything physical. I just need sleep."

The phone rang. Her daughter waved her off, and Victory answered, then followed Toria into the family room as the long cord trailed behind her. "Hello?"

"Toria! I got your message. What's going on?" Max's concerned voice poured out of the phone, his volume piercing.

Victory pulled the phone a few inches away from her ear, but not fast enough. "I don't sound that much like my daughter, do I?"

Without apology, Max said, "Have you seen her? She left a panicked message on my private line a few hours ago."

"I just got home. She's fine." Victory tried to hand the phone over to her daughter, but Toria grabbed a pillow and curled around it on her side. Victory settled next to her and related the events of Toria's past day and night to Max. "She's passing out here on the couch next to me. I want to pass out with her, but we have work to do. I was about to call you. We need to figure out what we're going to do."

"On two fronts, now. With these idiots here, and now with an army. Toria's sure that Kane and Asaron are okay?"

"Her link with Kane is still strong, but it tells her nothing about Asaron," Victory said. Toria wasn't asleep—she grunted in affirmation, and Victory rubbed her shoulder.

"Can you tell whether he's okay? He is your sire."

"You know it doesn't work like that."

"Worth a shot. So. Meeting?"

"Meeting. With whom?" Victory wished for a better way to get things done, but that was her mercenary days speaking, when she could grab a sword and fix things her own way. Now, too many lives were at stake. She wasn't about to try to fight an army by herself. Contrary to Asaron's stories of her wild youth, she had never been that stupid.

"The usual suspects. Daliana, Tristan, Genevieve, Lorus."

"And Lena." Victory's hand stilled on Toria's shoulder, her complete attention on Max. "Did you know one of the wolves attacked last night was Tristan's Second in the werewolf pack? This is a pack matter now, as well."

"It became a pack matter when they got kicked out of the Twilight Mists with Mikelos. I haven't spoken with Tristan, but I'm sure he's furious."

"Fun, fun."

"What was that?" Max asked. "You mean you don't want to deal with an enraged werewolf? I hear they're almost as obnoxious as enraged vampires."

"Shush. He'll have calmed down since last night. Won't hold things up when we meet."

"A man can wish. Get your ass over here. Since this is going to be on my territory, I'll make the calls."

"No problem." Victory studied her daughter. "I'm bringing Toria. Do you have any other mages in the Guild right now?"

Silence from the other end of the line for a few seconds. "Victory, why do you think I want your pair so badly?"

"There's no one?"

"Aside from those two, there are maybe a dozen mages in Limani. None of them come close to matching our two for power. What's wrong?"

"Toria suffered some sort of power backlash last night—"

"I'm fine," Toria said, not moving other than to speak.

"—and I wanted someone to examine her," Victory continued over her daughter.

"I can ask Daliana whether she knows of any elves who have experience with mages when I call her," Max said. "Otherwise, I've got nothing."

"Thank you. See you in a few."

"Take care."

She dropped the phone on the cushion next to her, ignoring the static of the empty line. "Let's go, sweetie."

"I'm staying here and sleeping." The pillow muffled Toria's words. "Tell me how it goes in the morning."

"I'm getting you checked out. Come on."

With a groan, her daughter pushed herself up. "Can I at least get a shower first? I feel gross."

"You look gross. Promise not to pass out in the shower?"

Toria held out her hands, and Victory stood to pull her off the couch. "Bang on the door after five minutes, just in case."

Victory slung Toria's arm across her shoulders and supported her around the waist, assisting her out of the family room and through the kitchen and hanging up the phone on the way. "I bet Max will let you crash on one of the couches in his office."

"Like he'll have much choice."

Victory helped Toria toward the front entrance to the Guildhall. Raucous laughter erupted from the outdoor training area, and she scented barbeque on the breeze. In the warm summer night, Max must have ordered those mercs who congregated at the Hall most evenings to take it outside. This would give their meeting privacy—and hopefully keep Toria from sneaking down to the usual bar area to join them.

"I can walk, Mama." When they neared the front steps, Toria pulled away from the arm around her waist.

But Victory held her daughter tight. Relief washed over her when Max opened the front door to greet them.

"Here, let me help," he said, coming forward. "Give your mum a rest." With one swift movement, he hooked his arms behind Toria and swept her up like a baby. "I'm glad you're okay, girl."

Toria chuckled and relaxed against Max's shoulder. "Thanks."

More than exhaustion plagued Toria if she didn't fight her mentor's coddling. Victory held the door for Max while he carried Toria inside. "Have you heard from Daliana?"

"She's on her way with someone who may be able to help." Then, to Toria, "Do you want one of the guestrooms or a couch in my office?"

Max's shirt muffled Toria's reply. "Couch. Better than those things you call beds."

"I'll take her," Max said. "Genevieve and Tristan are in the common room. Lorus brought a friend. And the coffee's on."

Victory pressed a kiss to Toria's cheek. "I love you. Rest."

"Love you, too."

Victory remained at the bottom of the stairs while Max carried her up. Once he disappeared around the corner at the top landing, the low chatter and the aroma of fresh-brewed coffee drew Victory to the gathering room. She pushed open one of the frosted glass doors. A handful of people clustered on the room's four couches drawn together into a lopsided square.

"—Is why they will ultimately fail." The speaker noted Victory's arrival but dismissed the vampire to return to her conversation. "Fabbri doesn't have the charisma needed to lead this kind of revolution. She has the drive, but no finesse."

Victory lurked at the entrance, identifying the other guests before making her own presence official. Lorus stood by the coffeepots, spooning sugar into a mug. The other two werecreature representatives shared one couch, opposite an unfamiliar elderly woman lecturing them on revolutionary theory. Tristan had gone unshaven and wore the same clothing as the previous night. In contrast, Genevieve's usual immaculateness shone.

Lorus waved Victory over and handed her a full mug. "Lots of sugar, right?"

Victory accepted the drink and savored the harsh burn of the scalding liquid. The caffeine and calories might be useless to her, but the experience soothed something in her soul. "Thanks, Lorus."

"My pleasure. Max told us what he knew. How's Toria?"

His concern piqued Victory's interest. She wasn't aware Lorus even knew her daughter except by reputation. "Not sure. She seems fine on the outside, if tired. I think something went wrong magically. Toria's trying to brush it off, but I can tell she's not herself."

"Mother's intuition," Lorus said.

"I guess." Victory curled both hands around the warm mug. "Who's your friend? I don't believe I've had the pleasure."

Lorus toyed with the spoon in his own coffee cup. "Oh. Yes. The other werecreatures of Limani don't have a proper hierarchy like the wolves and panthers. You know I'm on council because I'm the only one willing to take the job. Since I don't have a proper Second, I brought Bethany."

"I'm sensing regret here."

"I thought it would be a good idea. Any plan we get her to agree with should get the support of the rest of the other weres. But I always forget she's kind of cranky. She's gotten worse with age."

Almost on cue, Bethany's voice rose against a response from Genevieve. "I don't care what right Fabbri has! She's acting like an upstart little cub with this group of hers. I say we go in and clean them all out."

Victory studied the woman, noting the gray-streaked black hair, the plain clothing, the slight plumpness around the waist. "She's not terribly intimidating. More like someone's old aunt. What type of creature is she?"

"A badger," Lorus said.

"They make werebadgers?"

Lorus laughed, stuttering clicks emerging deep from his chest. "They make wereporpoises."

"Point taken."

"Shall we sit?" Lorus gestured toward an empty couch. The seat in the room farthest from Bethany.

"Let's." Victory curled in the corner of the couch with a pillow in her lap. Had Lorus heard about Kane and Asaron or just about Toria's injury? "Do you—"

The doors opened again, and Max escorted Daliana and Lena into the room. "Good, everyone's here," he said. "Have a seat, ladies."

Daliana settled herself between Victory and Lorus. "I brought Zerandan, one of our more powerful mages. He's talking with Toria now."

But before Victory could tender her gratitude, Tristan bounded to his feet and pointed to Lena. "What is she doing here?"

Genevieve put a hand on Tristan's arm, tugging him back, but Lorus spoke first. "She shares our status as a nonelected council member. Isn't that the problem Fabbri has with us?"

"But she's a human. And we're dealing with the Humanist problem."

"Perhaps you weren't aware," Lena said, her polite tone blade-sharp, "but I was thrown out of Fabbri's restaurant right beside Victory. I may be a pureblood human, but I've thrown my lot in with the monsters, which makes me even worse." She settled into position on a couch as if it were a throne.

"Monsters?" Genevieve asked, a note of challenge in her voice.

"I wandered around the farmers' market this morning," Lena said. "The Humanists are recruiting. 'Monster' was one of the nicer terms I heard."

"Then we are glad to have you on our side," Genevieve said, gripping one of Tristan's belt loops with a yank.

The conversation halted when Max reentered the room. This was the Guildmaster's territory, and werecreatures respected territory and dominance more than anything else. Tristan caved and slumped in his seat. He must worry for his Second, Gregory, the same way she did for Mikelos. Victory's aggravation at his combative attitude drained away in acknowledgement of their shared concerns.

Max claimed the empty seat next to Bethany, a notebook and pen in hand. He began without preamble. "The current situation. Victory's daywalker Mikelos is in the hospital, along with an elf and two werewolves." He raised the crumpled flier Daliana brought them the night before. "The Humanists have declared themselves an active organization and are not likely to stop with these attacks. In addition, the Roman military forces camp just beyond our southern border. They took the vampire Asaron and warrior-mage Kane Nalamas prisoner. For reasons unknown, they left behind the warrior-mage Toria Connor, but she might be suffering from some kind of magical attack."

Genevieve interrupted when Max paused for breath. "Poor Victory. Your family has come out the worst from all this."

"Might that be intentional?" Lena studied the Humanist flier, then passed it to Lorus. "It wouldn't be the first time grand events have been orchestrated to enact personal revenge against you."

"I can't say for certain either way," Victory said, "and it's just as likely for Asaron to have major enemies. But they might not have even known who they captured."

"Who with a grudge against Asaron would go after the whole city?" Genevieve asked. "He's not even a permanent resident."

"The Humanists can't have predicted Mikelos would go dancing," Victory said. "And the Romans can't have known Max would send anyone on recon so soon."

Max consulted his notebook. "Then we take it all at face value for right now. Humanists on one side, Romans on the other, and Victory stuck in the middle out of sheer coincidence. First question—how the hell are we going to deal with all this?"

Since she'd already read the flier and had no urge to see the bloodstains a second time, Victory handed it off to Daliana, who also passed it to Tristan without further study.

"Shouldn't the Romans be a problem of the complete city council?" Daliana asked.

Lorus scoffed. "Right now, the council doesn't have the solidarity to fight its way out of a paper bag."

"I'd still like to know how Emily Fabbri knew about them last night," Max said. "We can't assume there's no connection."

He had something there. Another thought occurred to Victory, almost lost in the madness of the night before. "Fabbri wanted to use the Romans to distract us from moving to impeach her."

The Humanist flier reached Bethany, and the woman spoke in outrage. "I have an easy solution to one of your problems. We don't have time to fuck around. We know where these Humanists are going to be and when. We go in and wipe them out. Then we deal with the Romans without any of this internal nonsense."

Everyone in the room gaped at her. Next to her, Lorus sank into the couch.

"Sure, brilliant," Genevieve said. "If we want a civil war, allowing the Romans to waltz in and kill everyone while we're too busy fighting each other."

"Isn't that the point?" Max asked. "The Romans are camped on our border. The easiest invasion is when you can walk in and claim territory without bloodshed. Victory?"

He needed agreement from the one person in the room ever involved in a large-scale war. Victory was more than happy to provide one. "It's true. I've experienced both ends, and even if the city shows no resistance, it's not pretty. Keep in mind all of us would be marked for death because we're political figures. This is Limani. Even if the council surrenders, the city's not going peacefully."

"Rioting in the streets, then looting and executions when the Romans pour in," Max said.

If Victory closed her eyes, memories of scenes Max described would be all too vivid.

"Maybe the Humanists aren't a coincidence," Lorus said. "Does Emily Fabbri have any Roman blood in her?"

"Fabbri is a Roman name," Lena said. "Evidence points to it."

Victory had lived in this city for decades. Even after brushing aside those memories of battle, the enormous weight of age still settled on her shoulders. "Let's not travel that road, condemning people because of their heritage or something as flimsy as a name. Limani has welcomed settlers from either empire for hundreds of years, and the families are so intermingled it would be pointless. We're not going to start discriminating now."

"Regardless of what they're doing to us?" Tristan asked.

"There's a difference between taking the higher moral ground and getting anything done," Max said. "Much as I'd like for both to be possible."

"We need to figure out how far we're willing to go," Victory said.

Lorus toasted the room with his coffee mug. "And how far we'll have to push everyone else along with us."

Toria may have made the wrong decision to stay in Max's office instead of resting in one of the Hall guestrooms. The couch might be comfortable enough for sitting or lounging, but the lack of back support made real sleep impossible.

The guestrooms had lumpy mattresses. She once accused Max of getting them from a trash bin, and he never did dispute her.

But tonight, Max gave her a pillow and tucked her under a warm blanket with orders to yell if she needed anything. The level of his concern almost shocked her, but she and Kane were Limani's treasured warrior-mage pair. Max had itched to declare them official mercenaries since high school, but Victory forbade it, claiming they needed more experience first. Maybe he didn't have ulterior motives—in his own way, he did care for them.

Toria reached for Kane's presence with her mind. She could do nothing more than verify his spark of life continued to burn before the wave of black washed across her field of view and painful spikes jolted through her brain.

She pressed her face into the pillow, riding out the throbbing in her head. When it receded, she consciously relaxed her tensed muscles. "Damn it all to hell."

"That's no way for a lady to speak."

An elderly gentleman stood in the open doorway to Max's office, hands resting on the head of a cane. He dressed like he came straight from the stage, in old-fashioned black breeches and a green tunic. His unlined face radiated age and power.

The man gestured toward a seat opposite Toria. "May I come in?"

"Yeah, please." Recognition sparked at his pale hands and long, tapered fingers. He kept his hair cropped close, covering the ears that would have otherwise given him away. Toria braced an arm beneath her, ready to rise. "Sorry, I'm not usually this rude."

"Please, remain comfortable. You've experienced an ordeal." He held his hand out. "I am Zerandan. My granddaughter Daliana asked me to meet with you."

If Daliana was his granddaughter, Zerandan was one of the oldest elves Toria had ever met, making her previous rudeness even more inexcusable. She dredged her elven manners from the recesses of her brain, where she stored them with old piano lessons and how to write in cursive. While she shook his hand, she said, "It is my pleasure to meet you, Zerandan, grandfather of Daliana, friend of my mother. I am Torialanthas Connor, daughter of Victory, friend of your granddaughter." A more difficult connection would have been tough to wade through right now.

Humor glinted in his eyes as he settled across from her. "Well done, child. You go by Toria, I believe?"

"Yes, sir."

"The foundling child of the Wastcland. Your adoption caused quite the scandal. That was, what, fifteen years ago?"

"Yes, sir." She hoped he hadn't come to reminisce about a past of which she only had sketchy memories. She sensed magic around him, almost leaking from his pores. But when she opened her senses to investigate further, the spikes drove into her head again.

When she managed to open her eyes after this latest wave of pain and nausea, she found Zerandan's face mere inches from her own. He knelt before her, cane discarded, two of his fingers resting feather-light on her cheek. "Don't do that again." Concern had chased the amusement from his voice. "At least not until I tell you to."

This time she couldn't even manage a "Yes, sir." She rubbed away new tears.

"How often does this happen?" A mage who must equal Asaron in years of experience replaced the paternal figure.

"Every time I try to use magic. No, every time I even try to actively sense magic."

"Which were you doing now?"

His fingers remained on her cheek, and his power pressed against her own. She shied away from it but didn't try to block him out. "You felt like magic. It's habit to check. One of those things you do."

"One of those things." Zerandan closed his eyes, though his voice echoed her attempt at humor. "Yes, I see. Tell me in precise terms what you were doing when this feeling first occurred."

Toria sketched out the events of the brief battle with the Roman soldiers, concluding with the backlash of the power she'd poured into Kane and passing out on the riverbank. "But I don't think this is a backlash headache. I've had them before, and this is different."

"You tried to harness the power of a river, child." His eyes opened again, settling into a milieu of cautious curiosity. "You thought this would be a normal backlash headache?"

"But those are constant pain for a few hours. When I woke, I had a bad headache, but it passed. Right now, I'm fine unless I try to do something."

"Like contact your partner?"

"Exactly." Wait a second. "How did you know I'm trying to do that?"

"I could see it." Without bothering to explain this particular insight, Zerandan continued, "I have had some experience with warrior-mage pairs over the years. They don't do well apart."

"We manage okay."

"Since you've bonded, what's the longest time the two of you have separated? Distance and time."

Toria avoided Zerandan's stare in favor of Max's office ceiling. Water damage splotched a section of old plaster. "Three days? Well, a weekend, I guess, when I went camping with Dad, and Kane couldn't miss play rehearsal. We did almost break the partnership in high school, but we were still in school together all day, so the distance bit doesn't count."

"Do you know what happens when warrior-mages are separated for too long?" Zerandan removed his fingers and retrieved his cane.

That didn't sound good. "We've never had a problem. And no other warrior-mages have lived in Limani for so long. The only other person I know who's met a pair is Mama, and she never mentioned anything to me." Toria braced herself for the worst.

Zerandan dropped onto the couch behind him. "Then nothing bad, I hope."

Age must make you crazy. The man reminded Toria of Asaron at his most contrary. "Do you know what's wrong with me?"

"I've scanned you lightly, but I wanted to warn you before I went deeper. This might not be a purely internal problem."

Magical theory was more Kane's department, but Toria put the pieces together. "You think they might have cursed me?"

"You said you didn't know why the Romans left you behind?"

"Mama thinks it was a warning. It makes sense they would leave behind the useless girl and take the two men who are more valuable hostages, who they might get ransom for."

"Were mages part of the group who attacked you?"

"I don't know. I ducked crossbow bolts, and they fought Kane and Asaron with blades and hand-to-hand. Wouldn't any mages have used magic against us? They were the aggressors and would have had time to plan spells or effects against us."

"This is a moot point, with no way to know for sure. The real question becomes, will the proximity of someone else's magic inflict the same pain?"

"Unless I've developed an allergy to magic, I guess that would be a good test of whether I've been cursed or whether this is some insanely strong form of backlash headache."

"Will you allow me to do a deeper scan of your magic?" Zerandan balanced the cane against the couch, resting his elbows on his knees. "It can be a personal experience for the person at the receiving end. You'll have to lower your shields."

She couldn't remember the last time she'd done that. Could she bring herself to do it for a strange mage, even Daliana's grandfather?

The priority right now was finding out what was wrong with her. It might not be an easy fix, but the sooner she learned what was going on, the better. "Do it."

If the strident tones and circular debate were any indication, Victory was not alone in her lack of sleep. She'd taken a break to refill her coffee but didn't have the energy to disrupt the current string of arguments.

"I vote to be rid of the Humanists." Bethany raised her chin. "Be free of one problem so we can focus on who might actually wipe us all out."

Genevieve inched to the edge of the couch, as if ready to launch out of her seat but restrained by Tristan's gentle touch. Wolf and leopard seemed to alternate as the silent voice of reason tonight. "I cannot believe you would advocate such a thing, lady."

Bethany opened her mouth to retort, but Lorus beat her to it, waving her silent with a slice of his hand. "Bethany, I did not invite you here so you could tell us to kill people."

Someone needed to step up and shut this down before it escalated further. After a fortifying sip of coffee, Victory said, "Bethany's idea is sound. It's her method that's flawed."

"What are you talking about?" Tristan asked. "The woman's crazy." He'd managed to pull Genevieve onto the couch, and now both sat with hands gripped tight. Victory would have found it charming except for the white knuckles indicating the death grip each had on the other.

"Question." Max's turn to prevent an outburst from Bethany. "How many of us here have actual military experience?"

Victory raised her hand, along with Max. To her surprise, Lorus did, too.

When everyone stared askance, Lorus said, "Depends on what you consider military experience. I served one term in the British Naval Service out of Calaitum before I immigrated to Limani. Never saw combat."

"But you were still trained, and you must know the basic goal behind every fight," Max said. "Victory, you're in a swordfight. What do you watch? Your opponent's blade?"

She responded at once. "Their eyes. A sword can feint in any direction. The eyes never lie."

"Good." Max entered teaching mode. "What do we need to do to the Humanists?"

Tristan's feral grin showed hunger. "Cut out their eyes?"

"We need subtlety here," Max said. "Can't let them know we're on to them, despite how they haven't hidden their intent."

"We can't let them hold this meeting," said Lena. "We can't afford to let them become any more organized than they already are."

"Find an excuse to close the Twilight Mists," Genevieve said.

"And every other major gathering place in Limani? The theater, the high school auditorium?" Lorus asked. "Perhaps cutting off the head instead of removing the eyes might be a better allegory."

"We need to find Emily Fabbri," Victory said. "Find her, get her under control."

"Our control," Tristan said. "Somewhere the other Humanists won't go looking for her."

"She's been implicated in the attacks last night, and the police are already searching," Max said. "I can set the mercenaries on the chase in the morning."

"Consider my panthers at your disposal," Genevieve said.

"The wolves are already on the hunt," Tristan said. "After this is over, I'll put out the word they're not allowed to kill her if they find her."

The idea obviously displeased him, but Victory knew he would bow to the wishes of the council majority. At least this part of the council. "We should still do something about a few of the meeting places," she said. "I can manufacture a reason to shut down the Twilight Mists." Shouldn't be too hard to find an old file that warned of hazardous insulation material and turn it over without the accompanying documentation proving she'd already had it replaced.

"What about everywhere else?" Bethany asked.

"The owner of the theater is a werebear," Lorus said. "He won't let them hold a meeting there."

"I'll talk to the high school principal," Lena said. "Convince him not to let them move there. If he argues, I can get Sethri to remind him the school is public property and under the command of this council. They won't get the auditorium at the university without my approval."

Max made a few notes on his pad. "Speaking of Sethri, you presume that he's on our side. I didn't invite him tonight because I wasn't sure how you all would feel about it. His is an elected position."

"I've known the man for decades," Lena said. "He firmly believes in Limani's founding tenets of equality."

Victory first met Alexander Sethri during his initial campaign for city council almost thirty years ago. The man had never once wavered in his convictions, and she shared Lena's high opinion of him. "I'll second that."

"I'll be sure to invite him next time," Max said. "That takes care of our first step in the Humanist problem, that stupid meeting. Now what are we going to do about the Romans?"

Toria dragged a couch cushion to the floor and sat on it cross-legged, wrapping the blanket around her shoulders. Zerandan knelt a few feet in front of her with his cane resting across his thighs. Something told her it wasn't a simple cane—maybe it was the emerald orb that appeared, replacing the original wooden handle. A neat trick, one she filed under the mental folder labeled "Things to experiment with later."

Zerandan rolled up his shirt cuffs. "Are you comfortable, child?"

Toria tugged the warm blanket closer. "I was more concerned for you, sir."

"I'm not so old I can't sit on a floor. I'm a mere lad of two thousand or so!"

She wouldn't reward him with the expected shock and awe. "You know I hang out with Asaron on a regular basis, right? He might actually be older."

"Ah, the cynicism of youth." They shared a grin, then Zerandan got down to business as he surveyed Max's study. "I'll shield us both, and you can drop yours underneath. If it's magic itself you've acquired an allergy to, at least you'll only sense mine. You know our host better. Is there anything in particular nearby I should be worried about?"

Toria pointed to one bookcase. "Three talismans in a chest on the third shelf that Kane and I created. Anything more powerful he keeps in a safe under the desk, already warded and shielded. They won't be a problem."

"I suppose I'll have to take your word for it."

"You have to. I helped to ward and shield it."

"A good reason indeed." Zerandan rolled the cane over his knees, wrapping his fingers around the emerald orb. "Ready, child? Give me to the count of ten heartbeats after I drop my hand, then release your shields."

She braced herself. "Okay."

Zerandan lifted his right hand, reminding Toria of her father pretending to direct orchestras from the record player. Like a conductor, his hand dropped, and Toria counted.

At four heartbeats, the white shimmer that distorted the room almost jolted her concentration. By seven, it encased them in a wide dome.

Eight brought Toria on task, and she laid a mental finger on the invisible button she hadn't used in years, the one that lowered all of her protections in one fell swoop. Kane was the only other person with access, and he helped her craft many of the protections around it.

At nine, she braced herself.

On ten, she imagined a cartoonish red button labeled "Off." And pressed it.

The light from the shimmering white shield exploded into prismatic starbursts, and Toria squinted against the double brilliance of the physical and magical sight of Zerandan's power. Her shields no longer offered shelter from every spark of magic in the world being visible to her sensitive mind.

She risked a peek at Zerandan's dazzling power. Kane's powerful aura of earthen magic paled in comparison to the ancient viridian power flowing across and within Zerandan's kneeling form. Motes of electric energy danced around her even without her own prismatic purple shields. Her eyes adjusted to the brilliance, and she let the sparks entrance her, keeping her distracted from the eerie mental "rummaging." Zerandan kept his touch light, but the trace of his power moved under her skin, searching out the problem.

After no more than a minute, the touch receded and Zerandan gestured a second time. She gave him a few more seconds to fully retreat from her mind before rebuilding her shields. First, the walls around her mind itself, and the blinding lights around her paled. Then she reconstructed her familiar crystalline shields.

Once again protected in mind and body from the onslaught of the world of magic around her, Toria forced herself to release the tension in her neck, twisting her head to either side. "Anything?"

"I'm sorry, child." Zerandan's calm never wavered. "You felt no pain? I kept my probe mental, but I worried my shield or other items in the room might have an adverse effect on you."

"I'm still tired, but nothing hurt." She dug deep for a shred of optimism. "At least I'm not allergic to other magic. And I still have control over my shields."

"Shielding is not active magic to the experienced mage. Over the years, it has become an innate part of you. Similar to how you sense the link between yourself and your partner."

"Then we know the limits to all this. Active attempts at magic equal horrible headaches. Got it."

"Since you are still able to manipulate your passive magic," Zerandan said, "we can safely say you've been cursed."

"The Romans haven't contacted us," Lena said. "Did we ever establish this was indeed an invading force?"

"The attack and kidnapping made it pretty clear," Victory said. The conversation circled once again. If possible, this half of the council might be more ineffectual than the whole at making a decision on such a grand scale. With their initial plan against the Humanist problem established, everyone seemed reluctant to commit to further action. She drained the last vestiges of her coffee.

"Has anyone tried to communicate with them?" Bethany asked. She caught everyone's attention with her wild suggestion. "What if they wanted to expand their border to the river, and they took the two because they invaded their territory. They left Toria because she never crossed the river."

"And ransacked all of her possessions and stole her horse for the hell of it?" Genevieve asked.

Victory smothered her impulse to second Genevieve's retort. But Bethany did have an idea there. Pulling herself a few mental feet away from the emotional situation, she acknowledged the sound theory when examined with a more rational and experienced mindset.

"Soldiers are soldiers," Lorus said, speaking aloud her unvoiced thoughts.

His voice stony, Max said, "We're lucky they didn't do worse to Toria."

Victory's daughter had escaped a horrible experience by the narrowest margin. Soldiers were soldiers, but her daughter told her that while they stole the gear from her belt, no evidence pointed to anything worse occurring during her stint of unconsciousness.

"Perhaps we should speak with the Romans?" Daliana said. "Approach them as a diplomatic group instead of potential spies?"

"Might be the only option now," Victory said. "Anyone else who crosses the river risks the same fate as Kane and Asaron."

"Any volunteers?" Lorus said.

Victory shot her hand up, followed half a moment later by Max. She wouldn't let this potential opportunity pass her by. She bet Max had the same idea. Kane considered the Mercenary Guildmaster his mentor, a responsibility Max treated with the utmost seriousness. And once upon a time, Asaron had trained a brash young Max the same way. The man might as well be family.

"No surprises there," Lorus said. "You're our best fighters if everything goes to hell and you have to retreat under fire."

"We have to take Sethri along, as well," Max said. "He's the real leader of the council. We are representing the city. If Victory and I go alone, it's easy to stonewall us if they think we're a rescue mission in disguise."

Victory couldn't dismiss that option until they learned more about the whole situation. She checked her watch. Already past midnight, and exhaustion tugged at her despite the psychosomatic infusion of caffeine. "We'll leave tomorrow night at sundown."

"Armed? Unarmed?" Max asked.

He posed the question to the entire group, but Victory was well aware he deferred to her experience. "And risk being taken along with the others? Armed, of course," she said. "But not too blatantly. We are trying to be polite."

"They're the ones invading our territory," Bethany said. "We have every right to drive them off."

"Our neighbors have always outnumbered us," Tristan said. "Despite the treaties establishing a neutral zone, Limani exists on their sufferance."

"We have to see what the Romans intend and hope for the best," Max said. He rose and shoved his notepad in his back pocket, signaling the end to the meeting.

Victory remained curled in on the couch, wrapping her arms around the pillow in her lap, while Max showed everyone out. She longed for her home and bed, even an empty one, but couldn't leave until she discussed logistics with Max about the following evening's plans.

She jolted out of a light doze when a weight settled next to her on the couch. "Everyone gone?"

"Yep," Max said. He braced his elbows on his knees and stared unseeing at the far wall. "You think this is going to work?"

"Which part? Controlling the Humanists or having a rational discussion with the Romans?"

"I'm not laying bets on either."

"Tristan was right, Limani is the neutral zone. The British won't be happy about the Romans destroying Limani. What's stopping us from calling them for aid?"

"You talk like our doom is inevitable." Max rubbed the back of his neck. "On the one hand, offering aid to us might be seen as breaking the treaty. On the other, they might do it so we can stay neutral, their own personal buffer zone."

"Damned if we do, damned if we don't. They help us, the Romans attack for the violation of the treaty. They stay out, the Romans attack anyway, and we get taken over or wiped out."

"Our silver lining is that this can't turn into another Wasteland. Not with the world spell in place." Max's tone suggested the words were more of a prayer than a statement of fact.

"We won't be around to appreciate it if they do invade. We're the government," Victory said. "Even if they take the city with minimum bloodshed, we can't be allowed to live." She loosened her hold on the pillow before she squeezed out the stuffing. The new power-hungry Roman Emperor didn't have enough to deal with on his continent, so he had to be greedy with hers. "What a mess. Fabbri couldn't have picked a better time to cause trouble."

"On the positive side, she'll be executed with the rest of us when we lose," Max said.

"Fatalist. Pick me up tomorrow with Sethri?"

"In my truck, even. We can ride in style."

"You spoil me." Victory and Max were not often physically demonstrative with each other, but she leaned against his shoulder for a moment.

He shared stoic comfort with her for a few beats, then pushed himself to his feet. "I'll grab Toria from upstairs. You both need real rest."

Max did not hide his frank appraisal of her, and she hated to imagine the bags under her eyes. Coffee couldn't cure all. Once he left, Victory hauled herself to her own feet. They all needed rest before the real work began.

Toria allowed Zerandan to conduct further experiments once they established her cursed state. She experienced no ill effects when Zerandan cast a glamour over her, or when he levitated her off the floor. But any attempt on Toria's part to cast the tiniest charm sent a stampede of agony through her skull. Zerandan called a halt to the proceedings once he figured out Toria was choking down sobs of pain. But he remained with her after these brief trials, investigating the books on Max's shelves, while Toria dozed on the couch. He did promise to continue research into her conditions once back home, to help attempt to reverse whatever curse the Romans cast.

None of his assurances repelled the encroaching helplessness. They'd stolen her sword—again—and now she couldn't even use her magic. Some warrior-mage she was. This made a rescue attempt more difficult, but at least Victory had plenty of spare weapons at the manor. None replaced her rapier, but she could still be lethal against the Roman bastards who captured her partner.

With plans circling, her efforts to keep the despair at bay, she drifted on the verge of sleep. She roused at once when Max entered his office, struggling to push herself up, the warm blanket falling away. "Meeting over already?"

"More or less," Max said. "Ready to head home?"

"Oh, yes." A real bed, where she could sleep in safety behind layers and layers of shields she'd established over her childhood home. Convincing Victory to drop Toria off at her city apartment would be an exercise in futility, not worth the effort. Her mother wanted her close, and she couldn't face the apartment with Kane's absence haunting her.

Zerandan snapped closed the book he held. "I shall be off, then." He placed more weight on his cane than Toria suspected he needed as he crossed the room. "I will contact you when I learn anything, my dear."

"Thanks, Zerandan." Toria nodded in respect to the elder elf, who returned a slight bow before wishing Max goodnight and exiting the office.

"Let's get you downstairs," Max said. "Victory's waiting, and she needs to get you to the manor before she passes out herself."

Toria needed a moment to banish her drowsiness before she moved. And one other thing. "I need a favor."

Ever fastidious in his own space, Max grabbed the book Zerandan left on the corner of his desk and searched for its correct home on the bookshelves. "Yes?"

"In the morning, you have to help me to rescue Kane and Asaron." She held her breath. He had to say yes. If nothing else, leaving Kane in the hands of the Romans for any longer than necessary risked the survival of his treasured warrior-mage pair. No better bribe existed.

Max found the book's correct spot and slid it into place. "No."

"You have to!" Why was he being an idiot? "Do you want Kane to die?"

"He's still alive right now, is he not?"

Toria checked again, grateful this small act didn't fall under the "hot iron poker through an eye socket" category of magic use. "For now."

"If they didn't kill him right away, he's likely to live for the foreseeable future." Despite his refusal to participate in her rescue scheme, Max dropped onto the couch and wrapped a comforting arm about her shoulders.

Not wanting to, and still cranky, she couldn't resist the hug after a difficult day. Even from a jerk.

Gentler, Max said, "I want to get Kane back, too. I've had friends captured before. I know what you're going through."

No one had been part of his soul the way Kane fit hers. Petulant words sprang forth. "No, you don't."

His shoulders sank in a silent sigh. "Toria, you're in no shape to go running off."

She considered and disregarded multiple arguments before settling on compromise. "I'll sleep for a few hours. I'll be okay by dawn." But a yawn welled up inside of her, hurting her case when she couldn't suppress its escape.

"Can't go with you anyway," Max said. "I'm accompanying Victory and Alexander Sethri to attempt a diplomatic meeting with the Romans tomorrow night."

She let her shoulders slump and a tinge of relief suffuse her voice. "Promise you'll ask after him?" Let Max believe she would be a good little girl, and allow her partner to remain in hostile hands for another twenty-four hours.

"Hell, we have every right to ransom their release under Guild law." He patted her shoulder and stood. "Victory's waiting downstairs."

Toria gripped both of Max's hands, and he hauled her up. She shivered in the air conditioning when the blanket slid off her shoulders, then the world tilted around her while a strange darkness encroached on her peripheral vision.

"Whoa!" Max swept her up again before she fell. "Yep, home for you, now."

"Sounds good." She yawned again as he carried her out of the office.

Toria would sleep, for at least a couple of hours. A rescue attempt in her current state would be fruitless. But plans coalesced, regarding weaponry and transportation. A sharpened saber hung between the ballroom windows back at the manor. And she could finagle a mount from the Guildhall stables.

She would get Kane back.

Toria's alarm beeped away at dawn, never knowing how close it came to flight amidst the bright sunlight that streamed through her bedroom windows at the manor. More than anything, she wanted to burrow underneath the summer-weight quilt and sleep until Kane dragged her out of bed for breakfast and a workout.

But Kane wasn't getting her up this morning. At the cold reminder, Toria shoved aside the blanket and sat up. Her head came alive in fiery pain, the tap dancers returning for an encore. Groaning, Toria collapsed onto her pillows until the pain receded to a manageable level, then rose with more care. Her leg muscles protested the miles walked the day before, in counterpoint to the headache.

She had more important things to do than bemoan the hour, so Toria crawled out of bed—careful not to revive the headache with sudden movement. Five solid hours of sleep renewed much of her energy, though she didn't have any reserves to speak of. Adrenaline would carry her today.

She dressed in clean clothes and opened a window to beat the dust from her long coat. A quick stop in the bathroom to run a brush through her hair and clean her teeth. Now, to raid the kitchen pantry for a high-energy breakfast and the ballroom for a blade.

As water for her oatmeal warmed in a pan, Toria contemplated her options in the ballroom. She considered and dismissed the Roman gladius on display. But she'd made the correct choice the night before, and she grasped the hilt of the old saber below it. A few practice swings warmed up her limbs, then she found its scabbard in a chest to the side of the room. She completed her ensemble with extra knives and a small pistol.

All the stops were out. She would get Kane back no matter the cost.

Back in the kitchen, Toria stared at the phone while she devoured her oatmeal and considered additional support options. Max had already declined with prejudice. Any of her fellow mercenaries might alert the Guildmaster to her plans. None of her school friends had the requisite training for such an excursion.

She was on her own, supported by her own wits and what she could carry. As a final step, she put together a pack with water bottles and food. Nothing else remained to hold her back as she stepped out of the manor house into the rising sun.

Toria drove toward the Guildhall in Limani's city proper, but passed the grounds and instead pulled into the rear parking lot of the high school campus. She parked in a far corner, leaving the town-car in the shade of a large oak. With classes out for the summer, no one should notice it for a day or two.

Between the high school campus and the grounds owned by the Mercenary Guild stood a small copse of trees. She left her backpack in the crook of two branches before continuing through to the stable behind the Hall. She climbed the split rail fence and cut across an empty paddock, crossing mental fingers Max hadn't decided to take an early ride after his own late night.

"Toria!" Senac, the Guild's compact stable master, rose from his desk when she entered the small office attached to the main stable. "You've come to check on Greenstar?" The retired mercenary regularly trounced those half his age in mounted combat, and Max allowed him to rule his equine domain without interference.

Toria stopped in front of the desk, jolted by Senac's question. "Greenstar?"

"All three horses returned on their own yesterday!" Senac gestured her to follow from his musty office into the spotless stable.

Belated recognition stirred. Greenstar—the horse she'd borrowed from the Guild with Kane and Asaron. "Great! That's why I'm here. To find out whether they came home okay."

Senac did not register her hesitation as his concern remained on his beloved horses, and he continued to chatter while she followed him past the rows of stalls. "All three still had their tack. Whatever the Romans wanted with your friends, they didn't have interest in much else. Good for you, I guess," he added with a sideways look.

Time to implement the next stage of "Operation: Rescue Kane and Asaron" before Senac questioned her presence. "Do you mind if I exercise Greenstar this morning? To make up for her misadventure the other night?"

"That'd be right sweet of you, girl." Senac beamed, any potential curiosity sated.

No time to question the ease of her success. She'd much rather acquire a mount with the stable master's misguided blessing than "borrow" one without. "My pleasure. She's a good horse, a joy to ride." Yep, keep talking up the horse.

"I have coffee brewing. Why don't you help yourself to a cup while I saddle her for you?"

"Thanks, I'd love some coffee." She allowed him to shoo her in the direction of his office.

Phase one complete. Too bad she had no idea what the rest of this rescue attempt might throw her way.

The sun rode high in the sky three hours later, the day burning hotter than the one previous. Toria twisted in the saddle to dig her bandana out of the backpack strapped behind her. After wiping sweat from her face and neck, she tied it over her head.

But no complaints here, as she sipped from her canteen. Compared with yesterday's forced march, today bordered on luxurious. She even felt spoiled enough to long for the sunglasses back at her apartment.

She paused at a crossroads in the wooded trail to check the map again. She'd chosen a different route than Asaron, aiming for a different sort of river crossing. An old bridge still spanned the river there, built from sturdy concrete. Toria hoped Greenstar had fewer issues about going over water than through it.

Senac must have realized ages ago Toria never intended to return with Greenstar after a short jaunt through the back fields. She'd be in for hell when she got home. But Max hadn't come with her, so the Guildmaster could blame himself. By the time Senac figured out she'd vanished, Toria had ridden too far to worry about pursuit. With any luck, Kane and Asaron would accompany her home, and celebration would outweigh horse theft.

Toria stuffed the map in the outer pocket of her backpack, exchanging it for a handful of dried fruit. She needed to keep up her energy, stave off the crash that was sure to come once her adrenaline-fueled reserves ran out. Despite her lack of hunger, she forced herself to eat every bite of the snack, ignoring the leathery texture.

On the up side, Greenstar didn't appear to connect her misadventure two nights ago with her current rider. Toria gave the horse her head, relaxing in the saddle while Greenstar plodded through the trees. "Good girl." She patted the mare on the neck and trusted this particular brand of luck to hold out once they sighted the river.

While the sun rose higher in the sky, sporadic beams of light through the branches warming her neck, Toria resisted the urge to hook a knee on the saddle horn and nap. The single cup of coffee at the stable hadn't been enough, but brewing a full pot at the manor house would have tempted fate. Despite her mother's enhanced senses, she could sleep through fireworks. The scent of coffee, on the other hand, would be sure to rouse the vampire and ruin Toria's plan.

She resorted to identifying the different species of plants along the path, dredging up memories from freshman-level botany. She remembered more than she'd thought from the required biology class, a nice surprise despite her resentment at being forced to take the course when she'd much rather have progressed with her chemistry studies.

The immediate problem with her magic hung over her head like a boulder. To steal her family back from the Romans, she'd have to rely on physical skills instead of magical tricks. Figuring out ideas that didn't involve magic were good thought problems in and of themselves. Mama and Max often barred her and Kane from using their magical ability while passing various tests in their training—Victory never hesitated to tell them stories about foolish mages who fell into the trap of believing magic solved all the world's problems.

In almost simultaneous succession, a gunshot echoed through the trees and her violet shields flared to life around her. Greenstar pranced to one side, and all exhaustion forgotten, Toria had her hands full with the frightened horse.

The bullet's speed had activated the physical shields that laid dormant until needed. She summoned them to full force again, settling the comforting amethyst prisms around herself as the horse calmed. She dismounted to present a smaller target and drew the saber at her waist, sparing one more wish for her familiar rapier.

A second attack should have followed by now. Perhaps the shot's intention had been to warn rather than disable. She was miles from the city at this point, enough distance to be unsurprised by nearby Roman activity.

"Come out, come out, wherever you are!" Toria circled Greenstar and peered through the trees. She refused to be frightened off by one hidden soldier. It might not even be an enemy soldier, but a local hunter who'd mistaken her for game. Larger than usual game, but she'd give the benefit of the doubt.

No one emerged from the underbrush at her summons. She returned the saber to its scabbard and mounted Greenstar again, ready to continue down the path undeterred. Then, her shields flared again, fractal angles deflecting another bullet. This time the horse had no patience for such excitement.

Toria bent low over the saddle, ducking branches as Greenstar veered toward the edge of the path. She resisted the urge to jerk the reins even as she hung on for dear life. The horse didn't even have the sense to retreat, instead carrying them both toward any number of unseen enemies. "Slow the hell down!"

Greenstar ignored her pleas. At least no more gunshots barked behind them, and once the path curved to the left, perhaps they were out of sight from the mysterious attacker. The mare's burst of manic speed tapered as fast as it had emerged, and finally Toria calmed her to a restless stop.

Silence reigned from the trees around them, under the mare's nervous grumbles. Like Greenstar, the gunshot frightened the local wildlife into safety. Smart animals. Stupid horse. Hesitant to dismount a second time and risk losing the horse to another panicked dash, Toria drew the pistol from the holster at the small of her back.

She spared a brief wish for her magic. The limits of normal eyesight to scope out danger frustrated her, without the ability to switch to magesight and scan for human—or werecreature or elven—auras amidst the emerald glow of the trees. And bolts of lightning were much more effective than tiny bullets.

"Okay, Greenstar. What now?"

The mare swiveled a curious ear at Toria's question but did not deign to comment.

"Can't go back the way we came or we'll get shot at again." With a gentle touch, lest she set off another mind-boggling headache, Toria tested the strength of her shields. Both gunshot blows had glanced, no major reconstruction necessary. She remained protected for the time being.

Toria nudged Greenstar into a walk. "We might be screwed. You ran us into the direction they didn't want us to go." Without Kane by her side, she'd resorted to conversing with her horse.

A branch snapped. Toria twisted in the saddle and raised her weapon. A Roman legionnaire in scouting gear emerged from the woods. Toria did not appreciate his full-blown smirk. "Got that right, kid." Not the same shooter from earlier, but he did carry a pistol at his waist to accompany the standard-issue gladius. Perhaps an accomplice, urging her into this trap. But two soldiers with guns? These were no ordinary foot soldiers, to be trusted with such valuable equipment.

"You're in Limani territory, sir," she said, in the most level voice she could manage. "State your name and business."

"Julius Octavian at your service, miss. Scout for the Eighth Legion, investigating the state of this road."

Something in his relaxed posture raised her hackles. "Why the hell would you need to know that?"

"Scoping out possible supply routes," Octavian said. "Or escape routes."

"Why would you need either?" Their veneer of civility wore thin. Toria searched for signs of rank on his uniform, finding nothing on his worn gear. But Octavian appeared in his mid-forties, much too old for a simple recruit.

"One never knows what one will need."

No rank, too old, and way too comfortable in her gun sight. Hints of long-healed scarring crept up the side of his neck. Special ops, or something close to it. The first shiver of real fear trickled a clammy path through the sweat on Toria's back. "You seem to have become lost in your search. Will you kindly allow me to escort you out of Limani territory?"

Octavian stepped forward. Another few feet and he'd be able to snag Greenstar's reins. "What a noble offer from a woman of such status. Whatever have I done to warrant the regard of the daughter of the Master of the City?"

Toria bit her tongue against a litany of curses. Only one way he knew her identity. "You have my friends."

Octavian took another step toward Greenstar. "The vampire Asaron and the warrior-mage Kane Nalamas are with the Eighth Legion, yes. It would be my honor to have Toria Connor join them."

"What the hell have you done with them?"

"They are our honored guests." Octavian's smile, while attempting to be disarming, made Toria's skin crawl. "To have a true warrior-mage pair grace our camp on the eve of battle would be a pleasure."

Confirmation of the worst threw her for a loop. "Eve of battle—?"

Octavian had anticipated her moment of distraction. He dashed forward, under her aim, and wrapped strong fingers around her arm. With a jerk, he wrenched her limb back and pulled her from the saddle. Her weapon fell from her grip and she reacted on instinct—

Pain clouded her vision. She lay dazed on the hard path, unsure when she'd landed. Instead of writhing on the ground from an electric shock conducted through her shields, Octavian leaned above her. She swung her elbow, aiming for a fierce blow to his jaw.

But he snagged her arms and pinned them to the ground. With practiced ease, he transferred her wrists to one large grip, digging her hands into the grass. He straddled her chest, dropping his weight to force air from her lungs in a wheeze. Octavian's free hand circled her neck. His fingers tightened, and she froze.

Larger, stronger, more experienced. Time to reconsider her strategy.

He lessened his grip when her struggles ceased. "Good girl." But his fingers remained loosely circled around her neck, ready to tighten again. "Here's what you're going to do."

Toria might not be able to fight, but she'd never give in so easy. "Bite me." She itched to shock him through her shields, but didn't need a repeat of the previous backfire.

Octavian loomed closer, putting his mouth to her ear. "Don't tempt me, girl."

His breath tickled her cheek as he chuckled, and she twisted her face away. She clenched her teeth to prevent them from chattering in fear. She couldn't move, and she almost couldn't breathe. Not good.

Octavian pulled back. "Paying attention now? Good." Strands of blond hair had loosened from the small club at the base of his neck, and he blew them away out of the corner of his mouth. An incongruous gesture in an otherwise threatening pose. "Technically, we are in Limani territory. Which limits my preferred options."

"Unicorn hunting?" His hand twitched around her throat. She got the hint.

With his other hand, he pressed her wrists deeper into the ground and dug blunted nails into her skin. "Unicorns wouldn't come within a hundred feet of me."

She bit down another retort. Though he kept the grip on her wrists firm, his other hand left her neck to run down her body in parody of a gentle caress. Toria forced herself not to flinch away from his disturbing touch. With lips parted, he clutched her breast with a sharp twist.

Toria yelped, but the pain was secondary to her anger. "Do whatever you're going to do to me and get the hell out of here."

When first discussing her potential future with the Mercenary Guild, Victory hadn't sugarcoated the risks and realities of female mercenary life with her daughter. But if Octavian tried anything, Toria would risk the most painful headache in the universe to incinerate him where he knelt.

He smirked, tongue darting out to moisten his lips. "I could take what I wanted from you, right here, right now." He drew closer again, and this time she did not turn away. "What makes you think I haven't used your partner yet? Limani lands do not protect him."

"What happened to 'honored guests'?"

"Everything's relative, you impertinent brat." The harsh grip on her breast loosened, but his hand remained where it was. "But I need you for a different purpose today. Messenger. Tell the vampire Victory that the Emperor has decreed an expansion to his colonial borders. And Limani stands in our way."

Mama was right. The new Roman ruler was an idiot. Words spilled out despite her precarious situation. "You do realize the British are on the other side of Limani, right? Even if they don't give a shit about us, they're won't want you right on their border."

A blow stung her cheek, snapping her face to the side. Too far, Toria.

"Careful, girl," Octavian said. "Wouldn't want me to take out my frustration on your friends. Leave your partner with a few of the more degenerate men in my ranks. Forget to bring Asaron in come dawn."

He brought his mouth close to her own, and her heartbeat thrashed in her ears. She could deal with him molesting her through her clothes. A kiss might break the wall holding tears at bay.

But he stopped before contact. "Are you capable of delivering such a message? Or do I need to beat more sense into you?"

Toria clenched her teeth and jerked her chin down.

"Good." Octavian breathed deep, as if savoring the moment. "Perhaps Asaron won't get that suntan after all."

He plucked her pistol from where it lay abandoned in the nearby dirt, gripping it by the short barrel. Toria tensed as his arm came down, and this time the crack of pain that echoed through her skull was purely physical.

Slime dripped on her face, prompting Toria back to consciousness through the haze of pain. Greenstar's chocolate-brown gaze, drool dripping from her muzzle, met her own when she pried her eyes open.

Toria wiped gunk from her cheek and brought away a hand damp with saliva and blood. "Damned horse. At least you didn't run off and leave me this time." With cautious fingers, she found the tender spot on her temple where Octavian struck her. But aside from the now-familiar pain—she hoped she didn't have a concussion on top of everything else—no other injury became evident. Nothing like the other night's blinding agony, despite Octavian's strike.

Make that Centurion Octavian, or perhaps Prefect. Why did a legion commander wander Limani's forests? Maybe he didn't trust his own scouts. Maybe he was bored.

But he was not her current priority. Toria raised herself on her elbows. Greenstar had wandered away to munch at the vegetation on the side of the path. She hoped the mare hadn't gorged herself.

She tried to check her watch, remembered the previous soldiers stole it days ago, and instead peered into the sky. The sun had coasted over noon and almost dropped into evening. Another whole day wasted. At least Greenstar hadn't abandoned her for home again.

Toria climbed to her feet and the solo tap dance multiplied to a full ensemble. She hadn't expected Octavian to leave her pistol, but she groaned at the lack of weight at her side. Two lost swords in two days. Had to be some sort of record.

To be fair, it was a nice saber.

But he'd left Greenstar alone, and Toria dug her canteen and a granola bar out of her pack. Back to square one. No weapons, no magic, and dashed hopes of a grand rescue.

"Damn it." Toria ignored the ear Greenstar swiveled toward her.

Octavian's order for her to play messenger had left her with no other options. She would return home by sunset and report her encounter—or at least an edited version of it—to Victory. Then her mother had to assist in a rescue attempt, now that Octavian threatened Kane and Asaron with real harm.

She hauled herself into the saddle. "Let's go home, Greenstar. Time to call the cavalry." Toria snorted. Talking to the horse again. "Maybe this time they'll answer."

The manor house sat farther south than the Guildhall, so Toria rode for home and arrived as the sun touched the horizon. She looped Greenstar's reins around the porch railing and charged inside. "Mama! Mom!"

Toria burst into the third-floor suite Victory shared with Mikelos after a perfunctory knock. She squinted into the drape-shrouded room.

Her mother sat in the large four-poster bed, a study in confusion as she swept back her tangled mass of hair. She switched on the bedside lamp. "Are you okay?" Then, eyes narrowing: "You've been out."

Fresh dirt stained her jeans after the tussle with Octavian. "The Romans are invading."

"Right now?"

"No, but they're planning on it."

Victory rubbed the palms of her hands over her face. "Okay, love. Clean up, let me get dressed, and we'll talk in the kitchen."

Toria backed out of the room and headed for her own. That was as much as she'd get out of Victory with no immediate threat. She threw on clean clothes and visited the bathroom to wash the grime from her face. The sensory ghost of Octavian's hands brushed her skin, and his nails had gouged marks into her wrists. No time to scour away the memories with a scalding shower. In the mirror, her swollen temple blossomed in spectacular shades of purple.

She beat Victory to the kitchen and exorcised her nervous energy preparing coffee. Victory accepted the steaming mug and sat at the kitchen table, enveloped in a plush robe and wet hair constrained to a tight braid. When her mother pointed across from her, Toria dropped into the empty seat, ready for the inevitable.

Victory sipped her coffee in silence, as if this were any other relaxing summer evening. When she set the empty mug on the table, she said, "Tell me what happened. Then, convince me why I shouldn't be angry."

Toria forced her spine straight. She was an adult, able to defend her decisions to the woman who'd always trusted her to think for herself. "I attempted a rescue operation."

"Yes, I am aware. Skip to the part where you tangled with the Romans."

"One Roman." She conveyed the rest of the events of her day in the abbreviated manner of a military report, surprised at the briefness of her encounter with Octavian during the retelling. Fear stretched moments into an eternity. "We're pretty much screwed, huh?"

One of Victory's eyebrows twitched into an arch. Then she rose to prepare a second cup of coffee without a word, letting her daughter stew in the oppressive silence.

Even if Limani wasn't screwed, Toria was. Victory's anger had a long fuse, but Toria had managed to ignite it more than once in her life. She recognized this calm before the storm.

Victory returned to her seat but ignored her mug as she leveled her steady gaze on her daughter. Toria met her eyes, but the prickle at her nape that screamed *Prey!* under a vampire's stare forced her to turn away. She stared at the table instead while Victory drank her second coffee.

Finally, her mother spoke, breaking the tension. "Clean up here, then return your mount to the Guildhall stables. Go directly to the hospital and keep your father company for a few hours, then return here." She pinched her lips for a brief moment, then continued. "I need to prepare for tonight. Max and Sethri are arriving soon. You are not coming with us. You will not follow us. And I hope to gods you haven't ruined our efforts to save the city."

Victory drained the second mug of coffee as the admonishment rang in Toria's ears, then deposited her empty mug in the sink and exited the kitchen. Toria jumped up from her own chair, but held herself back from running after her mother.

Be a good little girl. Run to Daddy. Leave the grown-up stuff to the adults.

The urge to run after her mother and scream overwhelmed her. Scream that while they played around with diplomatic nonsense, Kane and Asaron could be killed. Remind Victory what Octavian threatened to do. Remind Victory what Octavian could have done to her.

But all at once, her anger deflated and she sagged against the kitchen island.

Victory's daywalker was in the hospital. Her sire and foster son had been kidnapped. And her daughter was an idiot. Toria should count herself lucky Victory hadn't locked her in her bedroom.

She'd take the ordered shower, to wash the memory of Octavian's hands away. Then return Greenstar and visit Dad.

Victory might not have a place for her in tonight's diplomatic mission, but Toria would be ready for action when they returned.

"I do not know what to do with that girl."

Victory paced as far away from her nightstand as the bedroom phone cord would allow, clutching the handset like a lifeline. She needed to dress before Max arrived, but she and Mikelos needed to be on the same page regarding their hot-headed daughter before she arrived at the hospital. Maybe he could talk sense into the girl if she wouldn't listen to her own mother, the one with centuries' worth of experience. Despite her usual disregard for temperature and the warmth of her robe, she shivered in a combination of anger and—fear? Yes, fear, for what could have happened to her beloved girl. The twit.

"It's okay, love." Mikelos already sounded so much better than when she'd left him that morning. "I'll keep her occupied tonight. And give her a piece of my own mind."

"Toria's a smart girl. What the hell was she thinking, staging a rescue on her own? She could have gotten killed!" Victory sank to the edge of her bed. "She's already cursed!"

"How rational are you when I'm in danger? Kane is even more a part of Toria than I am of you. How can you fault her for doing everything in her power to get him back?"

Trust her daywalker to be the voice of reason. "I can't fault that. But I can fault her for being an idiot about it."

"Then after you find out what's going on tonight, make Toria a part of the plans. She's already accomplished this much. You're going into this tonight with the certain knowledge that the Romans want the city. She deserves some credit."

"Doesn't mean I have to like her methods."

"No, her methods need work. But experience comes with time. For all her power and knowledge, she's still a kid," Mikelos said. "At least Kane has Asaron to keep him sane. Though between the two of them, this Octavian might throw them at you tonight as not worth the effort."

As always, he found the humor in any situation. "I'll keep my fingers crossed," she said.

Muffled voices came from Mikelos' end of the phone, and when he spoke again, he said, "I have to go, the nurse is being adamant about dinner. When should I expect to see Toria?"

"She has to return the horse, then drive to the hospital. If she's not there by eight o'clock, send out the search parties."

"I promise." The unfamiliar voice on his end of the line grew insistent, and Mikelos said, "I love you. Take care tonight. Don't let Max do anything stupid."

"I love you, too. See you soon." She hung up the phone, then stared unseeing at the painting on her wall as thoughts tumbled through her brain. Toria's warning had put a hitch in the night's plans. She picked up the handset again and dialed the number to Max's personal line with a prayer that he hadn't left the Guildhall yet. "Max? It's me. We need to meet with the others before we leave tonight. I have news."

The manor house library, which held plenty of seating to accommodate the second ad hoc council meeting in two nights, didn't have the space for everyone's hot air. Victory shoved the drapes away from the window and raised the glass.

Distraction complete, she confronted the room again. And had no desire to jump back into the fray. Instead, she drifted toward the back corner, where the human head of Limani's council had tucked himself out of the way in Mikelos' favorite reading chair. "Mind if I hide out here with you?" She flinched when the pitch of Genevieve's voice hit high soprano as she argued her current point.

Alexander Sethri patted her hand on the arm of the oversized chair. He had claimed the room's far corner upon realizing who attended this informal meeting. "You don't need the plausible deniability, my dear," he said. "Good thing Max never warned me what I was walking into."

"I should confess I'm the one who summoned them all here."

"Then far be it from me to hoard your wisdom for myself." As if Sethri hadn't made his gentle rebuke clear enough, he added, "They need it."

She stole one more moment to brace herself, then slipped between the bookshelf-lined wall and couch holding Lena, Daliana, and Genevieve. Victory reclaimed her perch on the edge of her desk next to Max and attempted to imitate his stony calm.

Tristan radiated frustration from his position in the center of the library, fists balled at his side and a golden sheen sliding across his eyes. "We're wasting time again. I should pull my pack from the search for Fabbri. We need to activate Limani's mercenary force and march on the Romans. Tonight."

Bethany laughed, harsh and unamused. "Isn't that what I've said this whole time? Now the pup listens."

An eerie imitation of a growl emerged from low in Lorus' throat. "I didn't bring you here to add to this foolishness, woman. You're being an idiot, Tristan."

Tristan snarled. "I didn't hear you come up with anything better, fish."

Victory might not have the wisdom Sethri claimed, but she had no desire to see her library become ground zero for civil war. When Lorus made to rise, she snapped, "Gentlemen!" Her cutting voice drew glares, but at least silence answered her.

Lowering her voice, Victory spoke again. "Gentlemen. This is not the time to charge ahead with ill-thought-out plans. Lorus, do you have a better suggestion?"

When Lorus remained silent, Victory transferred her stare to the other aggressor. "Tristan?"

He dropped into the empty seat next to Genevieve in lieu of an answer.

And finally, in an attempt to deflect future antagonism. "Bethany?"

The werebadger flicked her fingers in sudden disinterest. "What do I know? Not all of us have your fancy military training."

As if sensing Victory's tension next to him, Max took over. "Sorry to say, but that's what it's come down to. A military operation. We can't dick around with the Romans like we can with the Humanists. The Humanists might be violent, but even they don't want Limani wiped off the map." Max rolled a glass paperweight from Victory's desk between his hands. "Based on Toria Connor's report, the Romans might not have such compunctions."

Victory plucked the paperweight from Max's hand and returned it to her stack of mail. "I hesitate to believe any of us are safe when the Romans invade."

"'When?' What's this 'when' stuff?" Bethany sat straight. "You haven't even talked to the Romans yet. Your daughter got attacked when she went against your wishes. How do we know she didn't make all this up to get us to do what she wanted?"

"The girl might be impetuous," Lena said, "but she's not manipulative."

"Toria knows reporting the truth is imperative under these circumstances," Max said. "Lying, or even exaggerating, provides false information that could lead to unnecessary deaths."

"If a Roman invasion is imminent," Daliana said, "how strong of a force can we muster against them?"

Max patted the desk and Victory retrieved a notepad from a drawer and passed it to him. "Can we count on you and Toria?"

Victory handed him a pen. Her, of course. But Toria? Operating under the assumed immortality of youth, her daughter would never forgive her if left out of the action. But remembering Mikelos' advice and praying she wouldn't regret it later, Victory said, "Yes."

Max made a notation on his sheet. "Tristan, Genevieve, and Lorus, how many fighters can you call from your clans?"

Without hesitation, Tristan said, "Worked that one out two nights ago. I had over fifty volunteers, and I would count on thirty-seven."

Bethany snorted. "Thirty-seven? You think the others wouldn't step up?"

Tristan leveled his golden gaze at her. "I think the others are either too old or too inexperienced, but volunteered anyway."

"My clan also met last night," Genevieve said. "We can add twenty-three hunters. I weeded out my own fair share of overeager kittens."

"Lorus?" Max asked.

"Long as this fight isn't happening within the next few hours," Lorus said, "I'll have time to call in Tersuigel's pack from the bush. That would put us at nineteen or twenty, depending on whether she deems her youngest kit ready."

"The hyenas?" Genevieve sniffed in disdain. "Scavengers."

"Scavengers will overcome live foes when provoked," Lorus said. "Tersuigel herself is a trained mercenary. Including me, we'll play it safe and say twenty."

"Twenty-one," Bethany said, her voice low.

Lorus scoffed. "Oh, don't fret. I assumed you'd want in."

Victory could make nothing of Max's chicken scratches, but when he finished his calculations, he cleared his throat. "With the Guild members who are currently local, ninety-seven."

Genevieve stood. "Victory, can I borrow your phone to call in my clan?"

"And I need to call in Tersuigel," Lorus said.

"Wait," Victory said, before the group scattered. "Are Max and I still escorting Sethri to the Romans tonight?"

"We can't afford to lose you," Tristan said. "The most experienced military personnel we have, not to mention the official political leader of the city."

Max shoved the scrap of notepaper in his pocket. "While I should blush at being compared to the esteemed Victory, where I'm concerned, the plan hasn't changed."

Moving forward into the circle of conversation, Sethri settled himself on the couch arm next to Daliana. "I'll second that."

"I thought we were taking the threats against your friends seriously," Bethany said. "You want to burn like your sire, Victory?"

Max grabbed Victory's arm before she snapped. He dug his fingers into her skin until she relaxed. "Nobody is going to burn," he said. "We will ride in and ask to meet with this Octavian that Toria encountered. No one kills three people alone on a diplomatic mission."

"I still disagree that this is the best option," Tristan said.

"Enough!" Victory had reached the end of her rope. "Disagree all you want. This is a council session, right? We put it to a vote. Second?"

"I'll second," Lena said.

"Then all in favor of a preliminary diplomatic mission to the Romans, say aye."

Toria returned Greenstar to the Mercenary Guildhall stables, apologized profusely to Senac, retrieved her vehicle from the high school parking lot, and drove to the hospital. As ordered. But her thoughts remained with those meeting in the manor library at this very moment. She should be there, giving her input. Sharing information as the one person to have direct contact with any of the Romans.

She loved her father with all her heart, but she did not want to be stuck with him this evening.

From where he lay on his hospital bed, Mikelos said, "I can hear you brooding from here. You sound like your mother."

"Brooding doesn't make noise, Dad."

"Do me a favor, will you?" Mikelos lifted his head from the pillow, but Toria darted to his side so he could relax again.

"Of course, Dad, what do you need?" She was supposed to be there for him to supervise her and make sure she didn't do anything else stupid. Instead, she prevented him from getting his much-needed rest. Too bad Mama didn't see her side.

"Food here is terrible," he said. "Run to the cafeteria and grab a sandwich for me? And salad?"

"Sure, whatever you want." She pressed a quick kiss to her father's cheek and left on the errand. Anything to distract her from this forced inactivity.

The bright cafeteria bustled with evening business—worried relatives and tired doctors who nonetheless had the energy to demand their sandwich be crafted just-so. The harried cashier took her sweet time puzzling over how to bill the ham-egg-tomato-mushroom sandwich Toria ordered for her father. Two nurses conversed behind her in line.

"—Can't wait until the doc discharges that girl," one said. "Been a thorn in my side ever since she got here."

"The poor dear's been through a lot." The second nurse picked through the selection of cookies next to the register. "Hasn't even had anyone to visit her."

"Just that vampire-woman who got thrown out—"

The cashier thrust her hand under Toria's nose. "Seven dollars and thirty-five cents!"

Toria fumbled in her wallet for the correct amount, then grabbed the bag and her coffee and escaped the cafeteria. After she dropped the sandwich off with Mikelos, he sent her to room 302 with the salad. She knocked on the semi-open door.

"What, a knock? I'm bloody honored." The sarcasm jarred the otherwise melodic feminine voice.

Assuming permission, Toria entered. "Hey, my dad asked me to bring you this salad." The hospital bed held a familiar elven girl. "I've seen you at the Mists. Syri, right?"

"I am. You're Victory's daughter?"

Toria handed over the boxed salad and scrounged for utensils on the untouched meal tray. Even she'd prefer a salad over the congealing pasta. "The same. Torialanthas Connor, Toria."

"Syrisinia, Syri."

Informal introductions were so much simpler. Despite her increased energy, Toria had no patience for formal elven mental aerobics.

Syri dug into the greens with gusto. "Have a seat. Your mother owed me food in exchange for talking to her last night. Got kicked out before she could bring it to me."

Toria froze in mid-reach for the proffered chair. "Am I gonna get in trouble for being here, too? I can't afford that now."

"Nah, you'll be fine." Syri waved a dismissive hand, and Toria dragged the chair closer to the bed. "Besides, I'm feeling much better. You can help me sneak out tonight." She waggled her corn silk eyebrows.

Toria huffed into her coffee. "No. No way. If the hospital staff doesn't kill me, my mother will."

"Nobody is going to kill you. Besides, I can help you find Kane." Syri shoved another mouthful of spinach in her mouth, as if she hadn't dangled Toria's greatest wish in front of her.

Toria almost bolted out of the chair. "What are you talking about?"

"Kane is your partner's name, yes?"

"How do you know he's missing?"

Syri waved her fork toward the window. "There's mayhem about to explode in the world outside, and you're here without him. And since you haven't told me the bitch responsible for my current condition has been found, I assume she must still be on the loose."

"Yeah, pretty much. Why would you be willing to help me?"

Syri's impishness vanished. "All the fucking mayhem, remember? We may not know each other well, but I know we're on the same side. And I know we need you and Kane as a working pair to defeat what's to come with these damn Humanists. Where is he?"

Toria feared to burst the girl's gung-ho bubble. "You haven't heard about the Romans?"

"Imperial industrialists fucking up good land and chasing the elves out?" Syri shrugged. "What about them?"

"They've declared war on us."

The expected torrent of curses didn't come. Instead, Syri let the salad box drop to her lap. "What?"

Toria set her coffee on the nightstand. "Let me tell you what you've missed."

"There's blood on my shirt. I can't wear this."

Toria peered through the cracked-open door. "Turn it inside out. No one will notice." The dinner rush had ended an hour before. All the patients in this ward were tucked away in their rooms for the night. Two nurses manned the station in the middle of the hall, both absorbed in paperwork. No visitors roamed the hall. And as a spot of luck, Syri's room sat next to the stairwell.

No better time to make their escape than now. Toria pulled back into the dark room. "Ready?" No sign of the elven girl. "Where did you go?"

A sudden shimmer of motion in the shadows, then Syri stepped into view. "Ready as I'll ever be."

"Neat trick," Toria said. "Teach me?"

"If you're good," Syri said. "But it won't work in that bloody over-lit hallway, so don't count on it." A wave of pain darkened her face when she stuck one arm in her leather jacket.

"Careful," Toria said, remembering her companion's injuries. "It's warm out, you don't need a coat." Toria wasn't tall, and Syri's head barely cleared her chin. The elven girl resembled a punked-out china doll.

"I always need it," Syri said. "Shield us, and we'll make a break for it."

"No magic, remember?"

Syri had sympathized with Toria's current dilemma, as only another magic user could. But now, the girl gave her a hard look. "I've got to do everything myself tonight, don't I?"

The beginnings of a beautiful working relationship. Kane would tolerate her better—he put up with Toria, after all. But if this girl helped Toria find Kane, she could put up with anything, even sassy elves old enough to have a better attitude. She held still while Syri gave her another hard look and swept her hands through the outer layers of Toria's shielding. Her lips moved, but no sound emerged to give Toria a hint about the magic Syri used.

"Now we're ready." Syri brushed past Toria and strolled into the hallway.

Toria flinched, but no cries of dismay sounded from the nurses' station. Trusting the girl, she followed Syri around the corner. They slipped into the stairwell without incident.

One floor down, Toria left Syri tucked on the landing while she darted into her father's room. With Mikelos asleep, it was easy to leave him a note without guilt. She propped it against the vase of flowers on the bedside table: *Syri got discharged and needed a ride home. I promise she'll keep me out of trouble.*

Back in the stairwell to collect Syri, then down to the ground floor. Toria paused at the two doorways that presented themselves. "We should go outside and around the building."

"That'll look more suspicious. We should go out the front door." Syri reached for the interior door, but Toria grabbed her sleeve.

"They'll see us."

"They'll see you. Trust me, warrior-mage." Syri shrugged Toria off and led her through. On the ground floor of the hospital, past the cafeteria, administrative offices and gift shop. Past nurses, doctors, and even one security guard, none of whom gave them a second look. Out the front door, and all the way to Toria's car.

Once settled in the vehicle, Toria let the tension drain from her shoulders. "Better drop the spell now."

"It's not a spell. Why?"

"I've already had one run-in with the cops this week. Probably not a good idea for the car to look like it's driving itself."

"You have a point there." Syri buckled her seatbelt, then said, "We can go now."

"I don't feel any different."

"Because it's not really a spell." Syri fluttered her hands. "There, it's gone. Or do you want me to recite a bloody limerick, too?"

Toria bit her lip against a retort as she backed the car out of its parking space. She craved Kane's stalwart presence, with his solid support that needed no words to accompany action. Silence reigned until Toria stopped at a red light and her curiosity won out. "I had an elven mage tutor. That wasn't elven magic."

Syri held herself stiff against the movement of the vehicle, one arm curled around her torso for extra support. She kept her head turned toward the passenger window, refusing to meet Toria's sideways glances. "You want me to help find Kane or not?"

Victory shut the door behind the departing councilmembers, wishing she also closed the door on the trouble that had invaded her city. But the night was young.

"Time for action?"

She twisted the deadbolt home, resisting the urge to rest against the wall. Max's broad shoulders made the foyer look small. Behind him, Sethri picked an invisible piece of lint from his suit sleeve. Victory threw up her hands for lack of a better way to banish her frustration. "For productivity instead of endless talking in circles? Please, anything."

"At least we got them to agree with us," Max said.

"It was too close."

Sethri tugged his sleeve straight. "But they came through."

"Time to hit the road, then," Max said. "My gear's in my truck. You need time to get ready?"

"Five minutes to change and grab my pack," Victory said. "And leave a note for Toria. Help yourself to anything in the kitchen while you wait."

Max fetched glasses of water for him and Sethri while Victory chewed the end of a pen between her teeth at the kitchen island. How to convey everything she wanted to tell her daughter in a few simple words? Conflict with her daughter never sat well with her, and she had to assume Toria's anger continued. The girl could be headstrong and impulsive, but she was also one of the bravest women Victory had ever met. Pride blossomed whenever she thought she might be the influence.

Toria,

Leaving with Max and Sethri now. Goal is to be home by dawn, so I'll see you in the morning. Hope you've had some good ideas of how to deal with all this, because I want to hear them. Love you.

She resisted the urge to add "Be good" to the end of the note, then attached it to the refrigerator with a handmade magnet. Tracing a finger over the glazed blue and purple clay an eight-year-old Toria had claimed was a cat, she steeled herself for what was to come.

She meant to change right afterward, but once out of the kitchen, Victory bypassed the staircase for Mikelos' studio. He had yet to ask after the fate of his destroyed instrument. She brushed the curve of the antique violin displayed alongside the matching cello in the far corner. Two of the few remnants Mikelos had of his life before her. Connor had given him the broken violin as well, but it had been a mere practice instrument. This piece was his pride and joy. He played it once a year. She always listened from the library, giving him space while letting him know he wasn't alone.

Every once in a while, she found herself jealous of his music. Jealous of the history it meant and the peace it gave him. Her own history bled violence and warfare.

She clung to her life in Limani. She had finally found her own peace in Mikelos and Toria. And Kane, Max, Daliana—a long list of cherished and loved friends.

An upstart emperor on another continent would not ruin that.

"We're ready!" Max's voice from the kitchen jolted her from her reverie.

"Be right there!" With one last caress of the violin's smooth wood, Victory left the studio for her bedroom.

This would be no repeat of the misadventure of Asaron's rescue. She donned proper gear and secured her hair in a thick braid, then returned downstairs to the training room. Her bastard sword slid home in its sheath with the comforting weight of centuries. To the opposite hip, she added a pistol from the locked cabinet.

Footsteps in the hall. She drew her sword in one smooth motion and fell into a defensive stance. She'd wielded this blade for almost five hundred years. As an extension of herself, she knew where every inch of the blade was at all times. This was how she made music.

"You're dropping your point."

Flashing forward in an attack at vampiric speed, Victory whirled the weapon to a point a hairsbreadth from Max's throat. "Still could kill you."

Max didn't flinch. "Then you'll never collect on all the beer I owe you."

Victory hid a grin as she returned her sword to her hip. "And that would be a true shame." She accepted her long split coat from Max and followed him out of the training room.

Sethri awaited them beyond the double doors, briefcase at his side. "Are you threatening to kill my Guildmaster, Victory?"

Max led them out the front door to where he'd left his truck on the circular front drive. "That's nothing new." He dug his keys out of a pocket and dangled them in front of Victory, who gave them a halfhearted swipe. "No, you can't drive my truck. You never let me drive your convertible."

Victory gestured for Sethri to take the front passenger seat and climbed into the back. "The last time I let anyone drive it, they crashed it."

Max settled behind the wheel. "I'm a much better driver than Toria, I'm sure."

"Is the entire trip going to be like this?" Sethri cast Victory a withering expression over his shoulder.

"Yes," Max said, at the same time Victory declared, "No." Sethri didn't hang out with mercs enough. She and Max understood each other.

"Oh, dear," Sethri said.

Max shoved a disc into the dashboard stereo. He pulled off the manor drive and onto the main road while strains of music flowed around them. Mikelos would be able to identify each of the instruments, but Victory merely enjoyed it, letting the breeze from the open windows rustle loose strands of her hair.

She drifted to the music and motion of the truck during the half-hour drive. Time to clear her mind of everything the world had dumped on her in so short a time. There would be more trouble to come when they met the Romans, but right now Victory savored the peace.

The last time trouble of this magnitude came to Limani, she and Max faced down a dozen werepanthers with no backup. And Toria killed a vampire to protect Mikelos and Kane.

No way would she let her daughter be in such danger again. Not that Toria would ever give her the choice.

"You awake, Victory?"

When she opened her eyes, pitch black forest surrounded the vehicle broken only by the truck's headlights. "We're slowing down?"

"I want to check out the point where the Romans attacked Asaron and the kids. We'll head for the bridge downriver if we don't find a welcoming party." As he spoke, Max pulled the truck to the side of the road and cut the engine and headlights.

The world blackened for a split second before her sensitive sight adjusted to the moon's scant illumination. "You asking me to look around?"

"One of us should stay with Sethri."

"I'm more than capable of taking care of myself—"

Max waved off Sethri's protest. "Humor us. We know what we're doing."

"Sure, send out the immortal. Cover me." Victory stepped out of the truck, twitching her coat clear before lifting the outside handle and easing the door shut.

"You got it."

Victory circled the truck to peer into the dense forest. Dappled moonlight cast shadows on the ground between the trees, but the night remained still. Too many convenient places to hide a scout.

Or a sniper.

No heartbeats beside the two in the truck. Not even a breeze across the water ruffled the omnipresent heat.

Victory prowled to the opposite side of the vehicle and surveyed the open area between the trees and the river. Nothing. They might have to visit the bridge and leave Limani territory to find the Romans after all. Not her favorite idea in the world, but she trusted Max's plan. He might not be so old or experienced, but the merc had seen his share of combat.

At the river's edge, she spun in a slow circle. Still no hint of company. Her experience dictated leaving a guard at the river's ford point. Invaders would press whatever advantage they had. On the other side of the river, this road led straight to the Romans' encampment. The dark forest across the water taunted her—the glow of moonlight off the water prevented her sharp eyesight from piercing the darkness, just as the gurgling flow blocked auditory signs.

The tide had washed away any signs of fighting left on this side of the river, though according to Toria, her daughter hadn't had the chance to make many. Victory knelt next to a few old horseshoe tracks leading to the water but found no clues to provide new information.

She returned to the truck. "No one's here."

Max slapped the steering wheel with his open palm and growled a curse. "I'd have preferred to meet them here rather than the bridge."

Victory slid into her seat. "You know how it works. Hope for the best, plan for the worst." When her seatbelt clicked into place, Max flipped on the headlights. The world shrank into the area lit by the harsh yellow beams.

Sethri drummed his fingers on his briefcase. "What if they're not there, either?"

"Then I will be very, very confused," Victory said.

Max pulled the truck off the verge and reversed direction on the packed dirt road. They rode in silence for about a mile, then he turned onto the cutoff toward the bridge.

Max's grip on the steering wheel had turned his knuckles white. "This worries me."

Victory toyed with the end of her braid, then forced her hands back to her lap. "Me, too."

"How so?" Sethri asked.

"Because they're not worried," Victory said. "If they expected Limani to launch an offensive, they'd have left the river ford crawling with soldiers."

"They must know we're in no position for such an attack," Max said. "Or—"

"Or they outnumber us to the point they don't need to be worried." Victory hated to acknowledge the words she spoke aloud. This wasn't her first time outmanned and outgunned. Didn't mean she liked it.

Victory tuned out the world once more on the ride to the bridge. Let Max have his plans about what to do when they met the Romans. She needed to figure out what to do if they didn't.

If the Romans weren't camping on their border, how had Fabbri learned of the potential invasion? And if the other councilmembers were right, with the Humanists' timing too much of a coincidence, what did Fabbri stand to gain from all this?

Victory berated herself for her complacency. The Greeks founded Limani on peace, though they fell to the Romans on the mainland soon thereafter. The colony might continue to thrive two and a half centuries later, but Limani forgot they always risked the same fate that befell their founders.

No one bothered with such a small territory during the Last War. For the past fifty years, the Roman Emperor had lived by the tenets of free commerce and open borders. His heir stirred up trouble for no reason.

"What's that?"

Sethri's question broke Victory from her musings. She scooted forward on her seat, peering out the front windshield. "What's what?"

Max slowed the truck. "Flash of light," he said. "Like a lantern being put out after we turned the curve."

"Someone's up there," Victory said. "I'll give you two guesses who."

"Just need the one." Max finished the old joke offhand as he slowed the truck to a crawl.

Now came the hard part. This had better not be an ambush—she wasn't in the mood. She strained to see past the truck's headlights. Nothing except the road and more trees.

"Shit!" Max jerked the steering wheel to the left, throwing them all hard against their seatbelts. Max hit the brakes before the truck careened into the shallow ditch along the path. A lone soldier remained where he'd stepped into the middle of the road.

One by one, Victory released her fingers from their death grip on Max's seat. Even she hadn't seen the soldier until he appeared right in front of them.

Max rolled down the passenger window and called past Sethri. "What the hell is wrong with you, kid? I could have killed you!"

Oh, Max. What a way to make an entrance. With the truck engine silenced, she picked out heartbeats around them. This kid had backup.

The young soldier sported the standard Roman foot soldier's uniform, not the more extensive gear Toria had described on Octavian. Though barely old enough to shave, Max's rebuke caused him no appearance of intimidation. "Please step out of the truck, sir."

With a gentle nudge, Sethri moved Max out of his personal space so he could speak with the soldier. "Good evening," he said, his tone calmer. "I am Alexander Sethri, of Limani's city council. My escorts are Maximilian Asher and Victory, also members of the council. We're here to initiate diplomatic relations with Julius Octavian."

At his words, five more soldiers stepped out of the surrounding woods. Each of them aimed a longbow at the truck.

The first soldier drew his own short sword. "Step out of the vehicle. Now."

Where is that stupid thing? Toria dug through another kitchen drawer. This curse issue took some getting used to. She hadn't needed anything other than her mind to light a candle since middle school. But one of Kane's ex-boyfriends had smoked—part of the reason he was an ex—and left cheap lighters everywhere. She remembered tossing one in a drawer somewhere.

"Ah ha!" Toria found it from under a pile of old take-out menus. She shoved the drawer closed with her hip and turned around. Syri stood in the middle of the living room half of the apartment's main room, out of place among the homey clutter. "What's wrong?" Toria asked.

Syri shook herself out of her apparent daze. "Nothing. Admiring the décor. Do you even have a proper workroom?"

"You're standing on it. We roll the carpet back." Toria tossed a box of chalk from the counter to Syri, who caught it with one deft hand. "The circle and cardinal points are painted on the floor and already enchanted. Do whatever else you need to do. How many candles did you need?"

Syri examined the box. "Chalk. How quaint." She set it on the ottoman, unopened. "Five candles, please. No specific type or colors necessary." She knelt to lift a corner of carpet, revealing the lines on the hardwood floors. "Wow, you are never getting your security deposit back."

"We lost it the first time I set the kitchen on fire. Kane's primary is earth. He'll restore the wood before we move out."

While Toria propped the rolled-up carpet in a corner, Syri drew glyphs on the floor with lines of white light from her fingertip. Toria itched for a notepad to record the symbols, but soon Syri had her busy placing and lighting candles. Finally, she sat in the center of the glowing circle on her living room floor, facing Syri to the northeast. Faint light from the streetlamps shone through the apartment's skylights, but the rest of the room's warm glow came from the candle Toria held and the four others situated at the main cardinal points of the circle. The halfway points between the main cardinals glowed with unfamiliar sigils. None of this resembled the magic she'd been trained in.

"Do you know what happens when a warrior-mage pair gets separated?" Syri matched Toria's cross-legged pose, shimmering hands resting on her knees.

Toria did not respond, fighting a chill in the warm room at the uncanny echo of Zerandan's rhetorical question the night before.

Syri's eyes caught Toria's and held them, her cat-slit pupils large in the flickering flames. "For too long, I mean."

"The elf Zerandan didn't know." If he didn't know, there wasn't an ice cube's chance in summer Syri did.

"Zerandan's my great-great-uncle. You were in good hands with him. And it's true. Nobody knows. I don't imagine you're in any hurry to find out."

"But you can get me in contact with Kane?" His absence caused an aching wound in her mind. Only that she was certain to sense his death kept her from succumbing to true panic.

"I'm damned well going to try." Syri raised her glowing hands from her knees and placed them flat on the ground in front of her within the circle. "Deep breath. Relax. Leave the hard stuff to me."

Like Toria could argue. Even the shields for this depended on Syri. Despite Zerandan's claims that shields were passive magic, she was pretty sure attempting to mesh shields with not one, but possibly two, unfamiliar magic systems qualified as active. A splitting headache would put a hitch in Syri's plans and might ruin them altogether.

Syri remained motionless, hands braced against the floor. The room around them lightened, cut through with curtains of glimmering translucence. It followed the lines of the circle around them, arching into a dome. The four candle stubs around the circle gleamed brighter, and the unfamiliar glyphs followed suit. The one to Toria's left drew her, and she admired the glitter of unfamiliar magic. The scientist in her stirred, and she listed questions for Syri on a mental clipboard.

Her voice a harsh whisper, Syri said, "Either look at me or look at your candle. I know what I'm doing."

"Sorry."

"Don't care. Just don't fucking move."

Toria froze, thumb and forefinger from each hand wrapped around the base of the new taper of purple wax resting on the ground in front of her. A trickle of strange power wound its way around her spine, and she repressed the urge to meet the power with a tendril of her own, investigating it and how it worked. Instead, she stared into the small flame before her.

The tendril traced her neck and scalp, making the roots of her hair tingle and stand on end. Now Syri was in her brain. Where Zerandan's link had felt like an archaeologist sifting individual grains of sand, Syri unwound a tangled skein of silken threads.

Syri picked at every knot until she learned what it was—Toria's skill with a sword here, her experience horseback riding there. Even knowledge gleaned from her recent history class.

Then Syri found her magic. Toria's crafted physical shields rose around her, fluctuated larger and smaller, and dropped again, as if Toria's own hand moved without her control.

Syri couldn't contact Kane on her own. By herself, Syri had no way to sense Kane from here to the Roman encampment, not without Toria's intimate familiarity with Kane's magical signature.

Thus, Syri used Toria's magic to find Kane instead. A sneaky way of getting around the curse, but it worked. Toria opened her mind even more, letting Syri explore what it meant to be a warrior-mage. Elven magic was so dissimilar from human magic it could barely be compared on the same spectrum. Double-edged blade. A nudge in one direction, and Syri had access to every iota of talent and knowledge Toria possessed. A slip in the other direction, and Syri could crush Toria's mind, overwhelming it with her own power.

Or Syri could fall all the way in, leaving her body an empty husk while Toria gained an unwilling second personality.

No wonder Syri had snapped at her to remain still. Toria wouldn't want to share a brain with herself either.

Max grabbed Sethri's arm, preventing him from opening the truck door at the soldier's order. "Tell Octavian that Toria Connor sent us to parlay," he said.

One longbowman traded startled looks with another, but the initial man held his gladius steady. "The Prefect told us to expect tricks."

Victory bit her tongue. What tricks? They were the ones who stole her sire and foster son. They were the ones who hurt her daughter.

With his smooth voice made even more soothing, Sethri tried again. "My name is Alexander Sethri. I represent Limani's ruling council. We have come to discuss recent events in hopes of coming to a diplomatic solution. I can assure you we travel alone, armed only for personal defense."

Left to Victory and Max alone, the mayhem would have already begun. She appreciated Sethri's steady presence.

The gladius lowered a handful of inches. "We'll have to disarm you if you want to talk to the Prefect."

"Understood," Max said.

At a hand signal, one soldier lowered his bow and jogged away through the darkness. Then, the leader repeated, "Please step out of the vehicle. We will escort you across the bridge."

Max looked over his shoulder. Now he wanted Victory to decide? "Might as well," she said, voice lowered for her companion's ears alone. "How else are we going to talk to Octavian?"

She slid across the bench seat to the passenger side, then switched the lock and pushed the truck door open. Best for her to emerge first. If they changed their minds and attacked, she had a greater chance of surviving than the two human men. She exited the truck with hands raised. Two more soldiers lowered their bows—a good sign. When one approached her, she said, "Sword at one hip and pistol at the other." She would neglect to warn them of the ankle dagger unless they attempted a physical search.

One soldier extended her empty hands. "May we have those?" Good, they planned for the polite route. She unbuckled her belt and handed it over with no more than a slight hesitation. Unlike Toria's magical attachment to her rapier, Asaron taught Victory to treat her sword like a tool, nothing more. But centuries of use created a certain amount of fondness. She hoped she would see it again.

If things went to hell, she would need it.

Max also stepped out of the truck to relinquish his own small arsenal to the waiting soldiers, saying, "Careful now," when he handed over his own belt.

"We know how to handle weapons." The soldier looped the leather around his arm and gripped the bottom of Asaron's sword for balance. "We are trained soldiers, mercenary."

Victory waited for the inevitable retort. Max might be a laid-back guy most of the time, but he held strong opinions regarding the value of mercenary work versus formal soldiering.

Sethri muttered a warning. "Max..." The soldiers around them tensed, and hands drifted once again toward weapons.

But Max laughed, clapping the soldier in front of him on the shoulder. "That you are, kid. But one free piece of advice—next time a potential foe hands over his weapons, step away so he can't snatch them right back."

The soldier ducked from under Max's hand to follow his suggestion, and the surrounding soldiers chuckled at their fellow's expense. Weapons no longer pointed their way. Things would be fine. With any luck, they would avert this whole mess.

Once unarmed, Max and Victory braced Sethri to either side. He did not attempt to step forward and take a position of leadership. Smart man, to stay in the realm of their protection. Even sans physical weapons, they were still lethal. Sethri took his briefcase after it was searched as if accepting a glass of champagne at a party, the picture of perfect aplomb between his escort's bridled tension.

The runner returned, emerging from the darkness behind the bobbing beam of a flashlight. "The Prefect has agreed to see you. If the three of you will follow me?"

Victory placed her hand into the crook of Sethri's elbow, claiming responsibility for the civilian. Max stepped behind the soldier and gestured for him to lead the way.

The remaining force fell in loose formation around them. They turned a bend in the road, and the river spread in front of them. Wider and deeper here, with a stronger current. A metal and concrete bridge spanned the river, remnant of the time before the Last War. The sole physical link between Limani and Roman territory.

And they planned to use it for their invasion.

A soldier next to her broke the silence. "Are you *that* Victory?"

The man behind them shushed him, but Victory said, "Yes, I imagine I am."

"My great-grandfather fought with you in Castille during the Battle of the Straits." He gave her a lopsided shrug. "He would always end the story by telling us how beautiful you were. He is right."

Max responded before Victory found an appropriate response. "Oh yes, she's lovely with a sword in her hand. It's the dresses you have to watch out for."

Victory snorted at his attempt at wit. "Says the man who brings his own sword on more dates than he does women." Muffled laughter met her repartee.

The features of the soldier who'd spoken first marked heritage from the southern portion of Hispania, where Asaron had once found her amidst the wreckage of a brigand attack. The pale skin that marked her vampirism had washed out any olive her skin once held.

The Castilians lost the Battle of the Straits, almost a hundred years ago. It led to the eventual absorption of both it and northern Aragonia into the Roman Empire. It was a miracle this soldier had a great-grandfather alive to tell such stories after the battle. Had she been human, she would have died any number of times in that long siege.

When they approached the bridge, more armed Romans stationed around its base came into view. She wouldn't be surprised if they had also wired it with explosives. That was how the Romans fought. Octavian proved things hadn't changed when he attacked Toria this afternoon.

Victory brushed those thoughts from her mind when they stepped from packed dirt onto cracked concrete. No time to concern herself with past bloodshed. And while Octavian threatened Toria and prevented her from following him, he'd done no lasting harm. Perhaps the curse she seemed to be suffering under was nothing more than a side effect of her separation from Kane. Nobody knew the full extent of how the warrior-mage bond worked, least of all her.

She crossed the bridge holding her head high. From this vantage point, numerous campfires spread through the woods on the opposite side of the river. Those trees held the missing members of her family.

"Hey." She touched the soldier next to her on the arm, capturing his full attention. "Maybe you can help me out."

He glanced behind him, at the soldier who was obviously his superior, before responding. "Depends on what it is."

"Two of my friends are being held here. We're worried about them."

"Yeah, the kid and the other vampire. I saw them yesterday."

"And?"

The soldier stepped closer to her as they walked. "I didn't get to talk to them or anything, but they looked okay. Quiet, mostly."

Victory covered the misstep that accompanied her relief by lengthening her stride. Before she could thank the solider, he pulled away. No matter. She had the information she needed.

A handful of floodlights came on all at once as they reached the opposite side of the bridge, lighting the area with fluorescent brilliance. These Romans moved fast. Military efficiency had improved over the past hundred years. Soldiers scurried about, setting tables and chairs under an open-sided pavilion at the tree line.

The party stopped and waited until preparations were complete. On an unspoken signal, the setup crew faded into the trees, and the soldiers escorted them forward to the pavilion. Sethri claimed the middle seat of the three arrayed on one side of the long table. Victory placed herself on Sethri's left, flipping aside her long coat, as Max settled into the opposite chair.

With little fanfare, an older soldier approached the pavilion, emerging from the dark trees flanked by two bodyguards. He wore a fancier uniform than the various styles of fatigues and forest garb his subordinates sported. The uniform featured little in the way of medals or ribbons aside from a single sign of rank: the small bronze eagles pinned to his collar. A prefect, the leader of this force of warriors. His blond hair silvered at his temples, though he wasn't the youngest of his rank Victory had ever encountered.

This man had assaulted and threatened her daughter. She wasn't impressed.

Sethri stood as Octavian approached, though neither she nor Max followed suit. Both men clasped hands over the table.

"Welcome. I'm Prefect Julius Octavian. Please, have a seat." Both men did so, and another officer sat next to Octavian.

"A pleasure to meet you," Sethri said. "I'm Councilman Alexander Sethri, representing the interests of the city Limani and its citizens. With me are Mercenary Guildmaster Maximilian Asher and Master of the City Victory."

Though she and Asaron traded the pointless title with little fanfare, Sethri had pulled out the big guns tonight. She would let Sethri play at making friends. She occupied herself with a fantasy of lunging across the table and ripping Octavian's throat out.

Octavian signaled for an aide to fetch beverages from the service prepared at a side table. "It is an honor to be in the presence of such famed warriors. Your reputations precede you."

"Yes, we are fond of our more famous residents," Sethri said. "But they've accompanied me tonight as fellow councilmembers. I believe we have much to discuss."

"I agree," Octavian said. "For instance, the attack against my men two nights ago."

Victory tensed, but Sethri accepted his glass of water as if Octavian commented on the weather. "Are you referring to the incident in which your men took two Limani citizens prisoner?"

"I am." Octavian read a slip of paper his aide passed to him. "Asaron and Nalamas trespassed on Roman territory. They are responsible for killing one of my men and injuring two more."

Pride surged in Victory. Toria hadn't been aware of how much damage they caused, but her guys hadn't gone down without a fight.

"Since when has crossing the Agios River constituted trespass?" Sethri lifted his briefcase onto the table and withdrew a sheaf of papers. "According to trade agreements, passage between territories is unrestricted to travelers by foot, horseback, or small vehicle with no goods intended for sale. I've marked the passage here."

He slid the papers across the table, but Octavian didn't move to accept them. "Thank you. We have our own copies."

"Then what has changed?" Sethri asked. "And what can we do to mediate a peaceful solution to whatever problem there is?"

Activity from the nearby encampment did not penetrate the veneer of civility around the table. Octavian sipped his water. "You are aware of the change in command in Roma?"

"Yes," Sethri said. "Though we heard the new Emperor is not one the senators would have chosen without…outside influence."

Now Asaron's inside information would come in handy. Victory awaited Octavian's response. They would see where the man fell in the political spectrum, and then they would have more influence over the situation. Sethri might be the expert, but she'd played this game a long time.

"The new Emperor is the old one's nephew," Octavian said. "Benedictus is… an interesting character." Considering the Emperor was the official leader of the Roman military, it made sense for Octavian not to speak out against him. But the Prefect did not jump to his immediate defense.

"Tell me, one old soldier to another," Victory said. "How much military experience does this Benedictus have, anyway?"

Octavian's aide replied, "He is a decorated admiral in the Roman Navy. Graduated from the Venetian Military Academy at the top of his class."

"We all know the royals get commissions once they're out of diapers," Max said. "Titles and medals tell us nothing."

"The new Emperor is twenty-five years old," Octavian said, ignoring his aide's pained expression. "To my knowledge, his stints aboard a warship have been nothing more than pleasure cruises."

This progress pleased Victory. "Military experience is not a prerequisite for emperorship like it is for the prime minister position in Britannia."

"But this still doesn't explain his desire to claim Limani," Sethri said.

Now Octavian clammed up. Stalemate.

Victory's turn again. "The latest rumors from Fort Caroline"—once again compliments of Asaron's report—"said your new Emperor needs to prove his worth and make a name for himself."

Octavian maintained his aloof attitude. "The Emperor merely has plans for expansion."

"Have you consulted the British with these plans?" Sethri asked. "One of the major clauses of the Revised Parisii Treaty insists Limani remain an independent city-state."

"Telling us what the Romans have ceded to the British in return for our lands is only fair," Max said.

"The Empire of Roma has ceded nothing," Octavian said. "To my knowledge, my superiors have not consulted the British."

Ugh, time for Victory to dredge up her familiarity with Roman political structure. "What does the Senate have to say about the Emperor's actions? Don't they still approve all major military offensives?"

For the first time, Octavian hesitated before responding. "The Senate has approved the Emperor's current plans."

More than anything else she had encountered or heard in the past few days, his statement chilled Victory. A truism of the centuries claimed that if you wanted a good plan to be destroyed without bloodshed, give it to the Roman Senate to pick over.

If the Senate hadn't even wanted this Emperor, why let him ride roughshod over established treaties and policies? While she was usually happy that an ocean separated the New Continent from Europa, now she lamented the fact. Her earlier conversation with the unnamed soldier had prompted memories of a war long lost. It would be child's play to travel to Roma from Castille or Aragonia or even Rus to find out what the hell was going on. But now they knew next to nothing, with no time to send an operative overseas to remedy their lack of information.

Through it all, Sethri seemed unfazed. "I hope you will not find it amiss if I inform the British of your plans? In fact, any information you can give me regarding those plans, such as a tentative timeline, would be appreciated."

"Impossible, I'm afraid," Octavian said.

"Fair enough," Sethri said. "We understand such plans might still be in the fluid stage."

Victory's skin crawled at the Prefect's bland expression. She hated these conversations where men in power discussed warfare like chess moves, as if people didn't die as a result of their strategizing.

Sethri drew another sheet of paper from his briefcase. "Returning to the subject of your prisoners. What sort of ransom do you expect?"

"Ransom?" Octavian settled back in his chair. "I believe you are mistaken."

"You hold a vampire of master Mercenary Guild rank and almost two thousand years' worth of combat experience. And a warrior-mage, ranked as a journeyman mercenary and master mage in his own right," Sethri said. "We are prepared to offer a substantial sum for their returns."

Whatever it was, Victory would pay it without question.

Octavian said, "While your offer is both heartfelt and expected, I'm afraid I cannot negotiate their return. Their presence would be more advantageous to you at this time than your money would be to us."

"As the Guildmaster for Limani," Max said, "I must remind you that a refusal to accept ransom for Guildmembers can incur the Roman military and its local leadership a substantial fine."

Slamming a hand on his pile of papers, the aide said, "The Roman military does not hire mercenaries. We employ honest soldiers."

The Mercenary Guild of the New Continent had stricter policies than did the old-fashioned Guild system still used in Europa. Victory had seen the best and worst the occupation had to offer over the centuries. "No one is disputing the integrity of your forces," she said. "But the men you hold are not enemy soldiers. Whether you like it or not, if you're going to fight Limani, you're going to have to deal with mercenaries."

"Which requires that you abide by Guild rules," Sethri said. Out came another set of papers. The man was nothing if not prepared. "Here are the Guild's ransom protocols to be used when the opposing sides are political entities, instead of individuals or business organizations." He handed the sheaf across the table to the aide, who plucked them from Sethri's hand as if expecting the pages to bite him.

Octavian accepted the packet and scanned the first page. "While I'm familiar with the established procedures for such situations, I'm still afraid I can't ransom my prisoners." He placed the pages on the table.

Stalemate, once again. This was going nowhere, fast. Victory's fingers itched for a weapon, but she settled for another attempt at diplomacy. "You leave us with few options, sir."

"Yes."

"Tell us this," Max said. "Is Rome planning to invade Limani?"

Victory suppressed a smile. When diplomacy failed, it never hurt to be direct.

Ignoring his aide's intentional throat-clearing, Octavian said, "Yes."

Their cue to get the hell out while the going was good. Victory and Max stood as one. "We thank you for your hospitality," she said. "Sethri?"

Securing his briefcase, Sethri rose to his feet. The aide laughed, saying, "You think we're going to let you three walk out of here? Guards!"

Octavian remained in his seat. "Belay that summons. They came in peace. We will let them leave in peace." He gestured to the guards the aide had summoned. "Please escort our guests to their vehicle and return their weapons."

Victory exchanged bemused looks with Max. And here she'd expected to fight their way out. They might stand a chance of getting home yet. Once again, they bracketed Sethri on the return trip to the bridge. But she checked over her shoulder once before the pavilion fell out of sight.

Octavian watched them leave. She caught his eyes, forcing him to turn away.

Stillness reigned in the apartment. The candle flames held a hint of flicker, and the magical sigils burned with steady light.

Syri's exploratory presence in Toria's mind stabilized. Her brain no longer felt like a ransacked room, but instead the subject of a scientific and methodical search. If she hadn't spent the last ten years of her life preparing for long workings like this one, Toria's back and rear end would be screaming in agony. Instead, she compartmentalized the discomfort in an area Syri had already passed over, dismissing it from her mind.

But while she could ignore the physical discomfort, her impatience and anticipation were another story. She understood the necessity of Syri getting this right. Didn't mean she could stay calm about it. When would she get to talk to Kane?

Soon. Syri's lips didn't move, but she followed Toria's thoughts and responded to them. *Wait, never mind. Now.*

With little ceremony, the room around Toria winked out of existence. Blackness engulfed her. Before she had time to panic, the image of a different location altogether swam into view. But now she saw with another's sight.

The world lay tilted. The inside of a canvas structure from the perspective of one lying on their side. Backlit silhouettes patterned the canvas of a small, enclosed pavilion. A second pallet sat on the other side of the tiny space, this one empty.

More silhouettes passed outside the tent, human-sized ones. Now volume faded in, the distinct sounds that accompanied an encampment of military personnel with no immediate plans and under no direct threat.

The head shifted, the body rolling on its side to crumple a blanket in its arms and rest its face in the crook of an elbow. Even from this perspective, she recognized that sprawl anywhere. *Kane?*

The body jerked, and a wave of seasickness passed through Toria's own body when Kane surged to his feet, giving every corner of the pavilion a wild survey. *Stop. Slow is good. Please.*

"Toria?"

Kane's frantic searching halted, and her stomach calmed. In a lower voice, he repeated, "Toria?" He sat with a thump. *You're in my head?*

It would seem so.

How?

Syrisinia. Elven girl. She sent a mental image of Syri as Kane might recognize her, sinuous movements on the Twilight Mists dance floor.

Waves of love and worry and happiness and sorrow crashed over her, and she sagged under the weight. *It's okay. Calm down, love.*

Sorry. Been a tough few days.

Are you hurt? Where's Asaron?

Silence. The room blacked out again, and Toria worried she'd lost connection. But another wave of love rolled over her. When Kane opened his eyes again, he stared at his bare hands. No, his left wrist, encircled by the loose fingers of his other hand and resting on his crossed legs. Strips of pale cloth bound his wrist, contrasting with his dark skin. Even in the dim light, obvious red stained the bandaging.

They won't give him anything other than pig's blood, or cow's blood. He can't survive like that. But we're doing the best we can.

Millennia ago, vampires evolved to be humanity's natural predator. For all their versatility, they remained a specific breed of creature. They could exist on the blood of another animal in a pinch, but not for long. Human blood alone contained all the essential nutrients needed to make a happy vampire.

Brilliant, in a twisted way. The Romans kept the vampire underfed, who kept the mage weak.

Where is he now?

They let him outside for a few hours during the night. They do the same for me every morning.

A flash of unfamiliar memory unfolded through the link. Kane crouched in the center of the ring, protecting his head and face from a hailstorm of twigs and small stones. Now Toria noticed the secondary injuries on her partner's arms, a mess of small bruises and cuts.

If I try to escape, they kill Asaron. If he tries to escape, they kill me. If he tries to eat anyone, they'll cut off all blood and he'll have only me to feed from. If I try to use magic…Asaron isn't brought inside at dawn.

Despite the even tone in which Kane recited the rules he now lived under, the horror of their situation dawned on Toria. She cursed Max for not helping her. She could have saved them from this nightmare.

Don't be mad at Max.

Why the hell not? I wouldn't have failed today if he'd come with me.

Why? What happened today?

With another transfer of memory, Toria imparted all she had experienced since their separation. Waking by the river to discover her partner gone, Zerandan's diagnosis, her second failed rescue attempt, and her meeting with Octavian. She glossed over the more difficult parts, but she never could hide anything from Kane.

He fixated on the mental image of Octavian over Toria, grabbing her, touching her. Threatening Kane, in worse ways than he faced now. *I'll fucking kill him. He checks on us once a day. I can take him out.* He'd always had the more vivid imagination. The images of a broken and bloodied Octavian lying at Kane's feet scared her, despite her longing to exact the same form of vengeance.

I hate to be the voice of reason, but what about Asaron? You said he'd die if you used magic. Kane's frustration leaked through their connection. Despite the jolts it gave her insides, she did not complain when he stood to pace the length of the pavilion. *Mama and Max and the head of the council should be there now. They went to meet with Octavian to try and get you guys out.*

Too bad they won't surrender us.

You're both members of the Guild. The Romans have to let Mama ransom you.

But we know too much.

What, the location of the camp? We already know it. Numbers? Armaments? Those aren't good excuses to deny ransom. She shouldn't be reminding Kane of these facts. He'd always paid better attention to Max's lectures unless they involved direct combat.

A shadowy image overlaid Kane's immediate surroundings. *This.*

A cylindrical object perhaps half the length of their town-car and as wide around as the trunk of a horse lay on the canvas flooring. Despite the fuzziness of its details, Toria noted the metallic shimmer of its surface and the small keypad and computer screen set in the top.

Clearer image? All of his other memories had been picture-perfect.

Best I can do. They hooded me before they brought me to wherever it's being kept. But it radiates power. Awful, disgusting power. Nauseating. So much I could see through the fabric.

Magic?

I don't know what it is. Not any type of magic I've ever felt before. But I'm the naturalist. You're the tech junkie.

Why did they bring you to it?

Octavian wanted me to see whether I felt anything. I didn't tell the truth. Just that I felt warmth on my skin from its direction. The truth, but not all of it.

That's why he said you could never leave?

That he couldn't risk it, yes.

Kane's memory of nauseating discomfort grew the longer he maintained the image, so she studied it hard. The object's fuzziness didn't help much, but she memorized every possible detail. Was that striping on the metal? No, a series of numbers or letters printed along one side. One of the cylindrical ends rounded to a point, while the other remained cut off at the edge. She couldn't make out the keypad's symbols.

Movement on the screen? Despite the straining of her mental vision, it never resolved itself. But she did detect the faint hint of constant change coming from the screen. Like someone typing at a regular rate. Or a...

No. Oh, no. It can't be. They can't. In the real world, her stomach twisted even more than it had during Kane's pacing.

What?

The question came in unison, from both her physical and mental companions. Her fear and tension must pour through the double link with Syri like a waterfall.

In high school, she'd made it her mission to catalog all the books in the manor's library. Jarimis died before she was born, but she felt like she knew the man based on the books he'd collected and researched. History was his passion, and once upon a time, she'd been determined to follow in his footsteps. She'd read all sorts of obscure things.

Such as books called *Weapons of the Last War*, and tech manuals for things like nuclear missiles. Toria conjured a mental schematic, as much as she could remember, and compared it to Kane's hazy memories.

You really think I saw a nuclear weapon, Tor?

What else could it be? I read a mage treatise on nuclear power plants a few years ago, and what you experienced matches everything she recorded about her experience with radioactive materials. The heat, the nausea.

This isn't good. This is worse than not good. Because I don't think Octavian knows what he has.

Ice gripped Toria's heart, but Syri asked the obvious question. *What the hell do you mean?*

He thinks it's a regular missile. His pet mage isn't too powerful, which is why they brought me to it.

If they use it to hit Limani— Syri's mental voice came to an abrupt halt, replaced with seeping horror.

They won't be destroying the city so they can claim the territory. Toria forced out the next words, despite her unwillingness to accept them as truth. *They'll be ruining it. For a long time, longer than anyone except Dad and Mama have. Limani will be gone forever.*

"Admit it—that could have gone worse."

Victory did not respond to Sethri's attempt at positivity. And the rattling of the window at every rut in the road did nothing for her headache. Perhaps she should remove her skull from its current resting place against the pane of glass. Too much effort. "Whatever you say."

Sethri continued, "They did not take us prisoner, at least."

Not a total failure, but a failure nonetheless. Now Victory rolled her neck to the side and rested against the backseat headrest. Better, but not by much.

Finally, Max spoke his first words since they began the return journey to Limani. "We'll rescue them, Victory."

She closed her eyes against meeting Max's in the rearview mirror. "Whatever you say, Max."

"We'll either rescue them," he said, as if repetition made the words true, "or they'll bust out on their own. They're not helpless."

"If they could escape, why would they not have already?" Sethri asked.

Perhaps if she pretended that they didn't discuss her sire and foster son, Victory could hold a conversation about the topic. "Any number of reasons, beginning and ending with the fact that the Romans aren't idiots. Vampires have long been part of Roman society and power structures. And they've got as many mages as any other country. The military knows how to keep such power contained."

Though she did hope their methods had improved over the past centuries. She'd worked with the Roman military often enough in her long mercenary career, as had Asaron. She'd been a Roman citizen in the mortal life she could not remember, and she'd wandered in and out of the upper echelons of power in Roma over the years. Until Limani claimed Victory as one of her own, as she had so many others. Today, Limani herself was a city-state of immigrants, with more descendants of Roman and British expatriates than the original Greek settlers.

A week ago, the Romans were amicable neighbors and trade partners. Now their government had gone to hell, they insisted on dragging Limani down with them, and the British were nowhere to be seen.

Which reminded her. "Sethri, when we get back, we need to send word—" She slammed against the seatbelt, speech cut off, when Max jerked the steering wheel to the side.

Then, with a muttered oath, Max hit the brakes, flinging Victory forward. The seatbelt waistband caught her across the hips, and Max must have braced himself. But Sethri flew forward in the truck cabin, and his skull met glass in a blow that fractured the windshield.

Then, a second crack, as a bullet pierced the windshield and whizzed past her shoulder. She threw herself to the side even as Max yelled, "Incoming!"

She wasted precious seconds unbuckling herself as Max returned fire through the windshield, then hurled himself out of the truck. Finally, she snapped the socket loose and kicked open her own door.

It hit a solid object as it opened. Victory drew her sword the moment her feet touched ground.

Her door had hit a man with a large branch, still staggering from the impact. Max wrestled a second unknown assailant to the ground, two pistols discarded nearby.

She brought her sword to bear when the man with the branch regained his balance and charged. He halted at the end of her blade, dropping the makeshift weapon and raising his hands, before acquiring a second mouth below the chin.

Max gained the upper hand as she heard more than saw him lay out his adversary with a solid blow. The man lay limp, and Max hauled himself to his feet. Victory kept her attention on the man in front of her as Max collected both firearms.

She didn't have Toria's innate ability to read people through magical means. But physical cues provided plenty of information. Heartbeat, so no vampire. He emanated none of the wild scents she associated with werecreatures, and his buzzed hair did nothing to disguise round ears.

Human. She assumed the same of his unconscious friend. Which raised the question—

Max aimed his pistol at the man. The adrenaline of the fight coursed through his body, his blood humming in Victory's ears. "Who the hell are you?"

Victory had to deflect Max's rage before he squeezed the trigger. "Check on Sethri. I'll handle this guy."

No response. Finally, with a grunt of frustration, Max lowered his weapon and sprinted to the truck.

Her show now. "Answer the question."

He didn't move, but his pulse sped up in counterpart to his silence.

The man wouldn't need much encouragement. Victory pressed the tip of her sword to his throat. "Talk. Now."

"We're stopping you."

"Congratulations. Stopping us from what?" Why couldn't she hear Sethri reassuring Max he was okay? Why couldn't she hear Sethri at all?

"From contacting the Romans."

She lowered her sword, ignoring the drop of blood that welled from his neck. "Did you not notice we are driving *back* to Limani?"

He swallowed once, and a thin red line coursed down the line of his throat. "We're preventing you from bringing news to your false council."

Two random idiots with an antique firearm and a big stick against two trained mercenaries. "You're Humanists."

As if her acknowledgement equaled praise, the man squared his shoulders. "Yes, vampire."

Except Victory had bigger problems than this ineffectual operative. The men's presence meant a leak in their impromptu council. Victory assumed none of her fellows had aligned with the Humanists, but she couldn't speak for every elf, every werecreature.

More pieces settled into place. The Humanists had contact with the invading army, explaining Fabbri's knowledge of the Roman approach before Victory shared Asaron's news with the council.

And the timing of this encounter meant the leak of their diplomatic plans occurred after this evening's meeting, not before, narrowing the field of suspects further.

This man might be a useful source of information, but the middle of the woods was neither the time nor the place. Victory caught his gaze and ordered, "Sleep." Any mental faculties he possessed were no match for her power, and he crumpled.

Behind her, Max's footsteps crunched on the dirt road. "Is Sethri okay?" she asked.

Silence.

She turned, and sought his face against the stars. "Max?"

"Sethri's dead."

Impossible. She'd heard the first shot miss, and these morons hadn't gotten anywhere near the truck after it stopped.

But humans were such fragile creatures.

Max settled his hands on her shoulders. "Victory, did you hear me?"

"You're joking." Even as she spoke, she found no heartbeat other than Max's in the surrounding darkness.

"His head hit the windshield. Hard."

Victory shrugged off Max's touch and approached the truck. Sethri's door stood open, and Max had laid him back against the seat. No obvious point of injury, but blood painted half his face.

Max followed. "Can't you—?"

The obvious question. Victory steadied herself. "No. That's not how it works." Perhaps if they hadn't wasted precious time subduing their attackers. Victory collected one of Sethri's hands in her own. It retained its warmth against her skin. "He's already dead. To turn someone, you don't kill them. You—" The explanation caught in her throat; now Sethri's residual warmth burned. She dropped his hand. "You bring them to the brink of death. If I drained him now, there would be no point."

She backed away from the truck. "We need to get out of here. We don't know if more are coming."

"We need to take those two," Max said. "I've got rope in the back."

Time to mourn later. Victory arranged the unconscious men as Max retrieved a coil of thin cord. They trussed the two up in a fashion guaranteed to make them miserable upon waking.

Victory couldn't kill the men indirectly responsible for Sethri's death, but she could make them pay in her own fashion.

In silent agreement, they didn't move Sethri to the backseat. Speed was of the essence, and logic must prevailed over sentiment. A curtain of surrealism descended over Victory when they climbed into the truck. She stared out the side window, avoiding Sethri's body, propped like a macabre doll in the front seat.

How had things gotten so much worse in the span of so little time?

After a reluctant farewell to Kane, Syri cut the connection. When the girl sagged to the side with a groan of pain, Toria helped Syri to a seat on the sofa and fetched water and painkillers. A major magical working, plus the time on the floor, hadn't done Syri's injuries any favors.

Syri swallowed the two pills dry before a long sip of water. "Thanks. Stop hovering."

Toria sat next to Syri, her own body complaining at the earlier unfair treatment. "You going to be okay?"

"Are you?" Syri's measured stare cut deep. "You haven't had the best couple days yourself."

If Toria hadn't been sure Syri closed the link between them, she'd almost be convinced the girl read her mind. "I'll be fine. I wasn't the one hospitalized."

Syri's dismissive gesture spoke volumes. "My own damned fault, as your mother so kindly informed me."

"Dad told me to bring you dinner. I didn't know Mama hunted you down, too."

"She wasn't that bad." Syri finished her water. "What's next, boss?"

"Wait, why am I in charge now?"

"Because we've done the easy part, getting in contact with Kane."

"Oh, once it gets complicated, I have to make the decisions?" Toria ignored the strained catch in her voice.

Syri set her empty glass on the side table and gathered both of Toria's hands in her own. In the gentlest tones Toria had heard from her yet, Syri said, "For the immediate future, Kane is safe. That is a huge load lifted from your shoulders. When your mother returns home, we'll tell her about the weapon. What can we do in the meantime?"

Kane. Kane was safe. Not happy, not healthy, but safe. The strength of their link pulsed within her. The urge to send her love to him almost overwhelmed her, but she resisted in time to save herself from the blinding pain. "The Humanists. The council needs to deal with the big problem, the one that might kill the whole city."

"Which won't matter if the fucking Humanists make it self-destruct from within." The old Syri was back. "What about that bitch on the council? She still at large?"

"Far as I know. You want a snack? I'm always starved after a long working."

"You cook, we'll talk."

Laughing, Toria rose from the couch and headed for the kitchen area to poke around in her cupboards. "Do you know anything about Emily Fabbri?"

"Probably not much more than you. She just got elected. She was behind me getting kicked out of the Twilight Mists the other night with your dad. You?"

While she grated cheese over a plate of corn crisps, Toria related her own experiences at Fabbri's restaurant. The plate went into the oven while she shared what she knew of Victory's encounter with the woman. She wound down the story as the timer dinged. "She hates me on a bunch of levels," Toria said, removing the hot plate with a dishtowel and setting it in front of Syri. "Because I'm a mage, because I'm a vampire's daughter, and because I probably pissed her off a lot when I called her out on her own territory." Three days ago? Time dragged when life kicked you in the ass.

"Her influence is corrupting the city," Syri said. "Like a fucking plague. If we find the source, we can prevent further spread."

They dug into the snack, spending a few blissful minutes over hot melted cheese rather than stress about the task ahead of them. When at last they'd scraped the plate clean and licked the last bits of salt from their fingers, they could face the world again.

Syri pushed the plate closer to Toria. "We're going to hunt Fabbri?"

"Aren't the elves and werecreatures already doing that?" Toria left the dirty plate in the sink rather than wash it. She'd deal with real life later.

"I can find out where the elves have already searched, but I imagine they'll tell me to stay home like a good little girl. If they don't freak out and drag me back to the hospital for 'further observation.'" Even Syri's air quotes were sarcastic.

"I didn't realize your community was so small."

"Sucks being the youngest."

Toria related. Youngest full mage in Limani, youngest journeyman in Limani's Mercenary Guild, youngest in her own family. "Yeah, it does. We're on our own."

"Seems like."

"Café Lizzette closed at least an hour ago," Toria said. "I'm sure it's been searched, but doesn't hurt to check there for information. Some hint of where Fabbri might be hiding."

"Let's go."

Toria had never much considered the cloak and dagger side of combat, subterfuge and guerilla tactics. She was a member of the Mercenary Guild, trained in the arts of warfare. Growing up, she'd imagined throwing lightning across a battlefield while Kane evacuated the wounded. Or confronting an enemy one-on-one with crossed blades.

Instead, Toria and Syri stood in the shadows across the street from Café Lizzette's, contemplating the quiet building. Darkness hid the menacing sign in the front window, but Toria itched for drastic measures. Like punching through the glass and ripping the notice to shreds. She would settle for kidnapping the sign's creator and handing the woman over to her mother.

"You think anyone's in there?"

Toria squinted through the night into the darkened restaurant windows. "Can you, I don't know, sense anyone?"

"Not from this distance."

The women stalked across the deserted street. This late at night, not even the fluorescent store signs brightened the area.

Picking the front lock to Fabbri's restaurant proved simple, and Toria gave a silent thanks for Asaron's patient lessons. But when she tried to turn the knob, it stuck. "Damn." Her fingertips prickled when she touched the knob again, and she jerked her hand away.

"Let me see." Syri traded positions with Toria, crouching while Toria kept watch on the silent street. "It's unlocked. But the place is warded."

"Warded how?" Magic could create any number of shields and alerts.

"To keep out grumpy people like us, I imagine," Syri said. "It's not elven work, though. Got a metallic mage tinge to it."

"Can you get through it?"

"I can try. Might need to pull power from you."

Though she continued to scan the street around them, Toria braced herself against the wall. "Feel free. Not doing me much good right now."

Syri threaded her fingers through Toria's. What a sorry sight. The injured elven teenager and the journeyman warrior-mage with no magic.

The emanating power of Syri's manipulations tickled the nape of Toria's neck, a sensation like spiders along her spine. Syri listed to the side as she worked. Converting human power must tire Syri out more than she let on, consuming her own energy and resources.

Let this night end soon.

"Got it." Syri twisted the doorknob open as she used Toria's arm to haul herself to her feet.

The door swung open, and Toria stepped inside first. The dark eatery appeared much different than she last remembered, with the chairs atop the tables and lack of kitschy music to match the décor. But no one came running, and she sensed no alarm other than the small flash of blue light that announced her presence as something other than fully human. Good signs so far. "No second floor to this place. We should check the back."

Syri brushed by Toria. "And the basement."

Not bothering to ask how Syri even knew about a basement, Toria drew her pistol as she caught up to the girl. The dagger might be better for close combat, but Toria wasn't in a hurry to let anyone get near enough for that. Syri was in no shape for a fight.

Toria pushed open the kitchen door and performed a sweep of the room. Dark and deserted like the front, save for the emergency light above a back exit. Stepping aside to let Syri in, she said, "You mentioned a basement?"

"Right. This way."

Toria followed her to the left, toward three doors at the side of the kitchen. "Storage" in stenciled letters marked the first, and the center door stood open to reveal a cluttered management office. They paused outside the remaining door, listening.

Nothing, and no light from around the edges.

Syri gestured for her to go first. After the briefest hesitation, Toria tried the knob. It turned in her hand without resistance, not even the tingling presence of another ward.

It swung out, and now a dim glow rose from the bottom of the stairs, beyond the blind landing of a switchback in the stairs. Toria crept down with Syri at her heels. Conscious of the blind turn, she kept her weapon ready.

Toria peered around the corner, ready to make a break for it. Boxes and crates spread before her, filling the majority of the basement. The light emanated from a lamp in the far corner. There, stacked boxes partitioned off a small area, and the edge of a mattress poked out between them.

She froze, and in the silence, a snore hitched from the corner.

Breathing into Toria's ear, Syri said, "It's Fabbri. Pretty smart. She must have returned after this place had been cleared."

Toria kept her own voice low, trusting in the sensitivity of elven ears. "You sure?"

"I'm sure. Let me handle this."

Syri would think her an idiot, but she needed to ask anyway. Toria repeated, "You sure?"

The girl patted her on the shoulder and drifted past Toria, making Toria's earlier stealth sound like a stampede.

Toria covered her as she ghosted through the maze of stored goods. A trickle of magic rose from the corner, evaporating as soon as Toria sensed it.

Then, "Got her!"

Now, Toria descended the final flight of stairs and wound her way through the basement. Clad in modest pajamas, Fabbri lay on a quilt-covered air mattress at Syri's feet. The snores had stopped.

"What did you do?" Toria asked.

"Put her into a deeper sleep. She won't wake for ages. Now we bring her to your mother or whoever can take charge of her."

Toria studied the prone body and holstered the pistol at her back. "It can't be this easy, but I'm not about to complain after everything else we've been through. I doubt my mom's back yet. You think Daliana is home?"

Syri dropped the hand she'd held braced against her ribs. "You get her shoulders."

After a silent moment of shock, Daliana collected Fabbri's unconscious body when Toria and Syri arrived at her back steps. "The luck of youth, I suppose," she said, directing the floating body with small finger gestures. It preceded the three women into the house and settled onto a couch.

Fabbri never stirred, not even when her leg fell from the couch and landed flat on the hardwood floor with a thud.

Toria collapsed onto the recliner next to the couch. "I'm not going to complain about it." Syri dropped to the floor at her feet, stretching all the way out on the rug with a purr of contentment.

Daliana replaced Fabbri's leg and covered her with a quilt. "Neither am I, when you two accomplished in one night what twenty of us attempted for days. You do realize your mother will be outraged, right?"

"She'll be pleased I took the initiative," Toria said. She hoped. The clock on the mantle read half past three in the morning. Time flew during forced entry and kidnapping. No wonder exhaustion tugged at her eyelids.

Daliana stood above them, arms crossed over her floral robe. "You disobeyed every single one of her orders. I have half a mind—" The doorbell interrupted her, and Daliana retreated with a sigh.

Rather than give into sleep, Toria shifted in the plush recliner and studied Fabbri. "How long is she supposed to be out?"

"Until I say so," Syri said, not moving from her spot on the floor. "Unless I misjudged, using your power instead of mine."

Oh dear. But Toria lacked the necessary energy when she tried to summon concern. "Hope you didn't give her brain damage or anything."

"Give who brain damage?"

At her Guildmaster's question, Toria shot out of the recliner. She collected herself while Syri struggled to her own feet. "Good evening, Max." Her nonchalance sounded false even to her own ears.

Her mentor filled the doorway, gaze flipping between Toria and the body on the couch. "Guess one thing went right tonight, at least." Max entered the room and stole Toria's seat. "Your mom's in the front room with Dal."

Toria had more pressing concerns despite that exciting bit of news. "Where's Kane?"

"Octavian wouldn't release him to us."

"What?" Toria's nails dug into her palms in a stranglehold on composure. "Do you have any idea what they're doing to them?"

"We were assured of their safety," Max said. "But being a prisoner of war is no vacation."

Toria forced her hands loose before she drew blood. "They're starving Asaron," she said. "Forcing him to keep Kane drained so neither of them has the strength to escape."

"I feared that might be the case." Before Toria could react to her mother's presence, Victory strode into the room and wrapped Toria in her cool arms.

She buried her face in the crook of Victory's neck, inhaling the familiar vanilla of her mother's shampoo. "I'm sorry, Mama."

"Don't be sorry, love. Daliana filled me in. I'm so proud of you."

Despite her urge to stay in the safety of her mother's grasp, Toria wasn't a child anymore. Mama couldn't fix everything now. She stepped away and asked, "Even though I didn't stay at the hospital with Dad?"

"It might be cliché, but what's good isn't always right. I understand when it's easier to ask forgiveness than permission."

"Spoken like a true mercenary," Max said. "She's not the only proud one, girl."

With that load lifted from Toria's shoulders, time to break the bad news. "Syri managed to get me in contact with Kane."

"At least we know for sure they're alive," Victory said. "Octavian wasn't even willing to discuss a ransom. We'll get them soon, though."

"When we spoke to Kane, he said—"

Daliana brushed past Toria and Victory to stand by Fabbri. "The rest are on their way." She placed two fingertips on the unconscious woman's forehead and nodded to herself.

Victory stepped away from Toria. "I'll arrange the front room while you put coffee on. Let Max rest."

Without opening his eyes from the recliner, Max said, "Bless you."

Damn it, this couldn't wait. "Mother!"

Victory froze in the midst of following Daliana from the room. Both women turned back and Max shot upright. "Yes, Toria?" Impatience infused her question.

"Have you ever heard of a nuclear weapon?"

"And that, ladies and gentlemen, is where we stand." Max finished his speech and resumed his seat on the piano bench in Daliana's formal sitting room. Victory scooted a few more inches to make room for him. Despite the close quarters, they needed to provide a united front for what was to come, and hope the other members of their ad hoc council didn't turn on them.

"Where is Sethri's body?" Tristan asked, pain creeping through the werewolf's natural stoicism.

"The hospital," Max said. "I called Mason, the physician under contract with the Mercenary Guild, to take care of the body. We didn't think it prudent to make public the death of a councilmember quite yet."

"And the two men who—" Lorus halted, as if unable to voice the words.

"Locked in my basement," Daliana said.

Victory brushed a finger over the wood covering the piano keys. Despite washing her hands, a light scent trace of Sethri's blood remained. His murderers would get a fair trial once the city's more immediate problems were solved.

"Any other questions before we move on to the next stage of planning?" Max asked.

From her spot on the floor, Genevieve raised a tentative hand. "One, sort of. I don't even know what a nuclear weapon is. You said it's a big bomb, right? So they might take out City Hall or something?"

Victory gaped at her, along with Max and Daliana, and Tristan added his embarrassed agreement. But Victory couldn't blame them for their ignorance. Not all of them had lived for centuries, as she and Daliana had, or studied military history, like Max and Lorus.

"The settlers at the edge of the Wasteland barely eke out a living," Daliana said, as if apropos of nothing. "The center of this continent used to be lush farmland around a major river. The river's gone. Not much grows there now, and not well. Because of dozens, if not hundreds, of nuclear and hydrogen weapons launched during the Last War."

"Then one single weapon used against Limani," Tristan said, his words laced with dawning horror, "could destroy everything?"

"Every living thing," Victory said. "Every building. Ruin this land for millennia to come." She had barely escaped based on a timely warning from intelligence forces, and she'd been on the edge of the targeted area. So many others had not been so lucky.

"The devastation was brutal," Daliana said. "I treated refugees from the area. No one knows when, or if, the Wasteland will ever become viable again."

"But I suspect something," Max said, "based on the information Toria received during contact with her partner. The Roman leadership might not exactly know what they have."

"What makes you think that?" Daliana asked.

"Octavian's pet mage turned to Kane to study the thing," Max said. "Chances are the Romans found it in a bunker somewhere, missed in the global disarmament and forgotten."

"Until now," Victory said. Fear tingled at her fingertips. "Not only is it a weapon of incredible destructive power no one knows how to use, it's an old and unstable weapon." From what she read of their visible reactions, her fellow councilmembers had shifted from uncertainty to fear. Good for them to be worried, but they could not initiate a citywide panic. "This information cannot leave this room."

Tristan scoffed. "We have a duty to protect our people. They deserve to know what we're facing."

"And cause a full-scale riot?" Max asked.

"You've already asked us to hide a murder in Limani's leadership structure," Bethany said, knitting needles flashing in echo of her outrage. "And there's been no official confirmation of the Roman presence. Half my friends think its troop exercises and aren't concerned in the slightest. How far will we go 'protect' our people? If we fail, we leave them even more defenseless."

"And you'd prefer panic in the streets?" Lena asked.

"We don't have the resources to police the city and deal with the Romans," Max said. "Time to make the hard choices. The head of the government is dead. We don't have time to hold elections, even internal ones. We don't know who to trust among the human councilmembers, or they'd be here with us." He paused to survey the room. "Victory and I have discussed a temporary solution."

It had been less of a discussion and more semi-panicked brainstorming in the truck between the hospital and Daliana's house. But no need to share that bit. Victory stood. "Martial law. Or close enough. We take charge and deal with the Romans on our own terms, without having to balance Humanist politics." It didn't solve the problem of a leak within this group, but it simplified many other issues.

"But Limani's military is its Mercenary Guild," Bethany said. "Does that mean Max is in charge?"

"No," Max said. "Not just me. Everyone in this room. We just happen to have the two most experienced military personnel in the city."

"What about all of the weres we've recruited?" Tristan said. "Loyalty to the city does mean they'll be happy to be drafted."

"Anyone willing will receive a battlefield commission," Max said. "We won't force anyone to fight, but a solid command structure is necessary."

"I know we're all scared," Victory said, not hesitating to include herself in the statement. "But we have to remain calm. This makes it easier to deal with the Romans and the Humanist issue."

"How does imposing martial law deal with the Humanists?" Lena asked.

Victory could always count on the teacher in her longtime friend to make sure people followed through. "The one way you might have a real problem with." Even she had a problem with it, angry with the prejudiced idiots as she was. "We declare the Humanist movement illegal." She awaited the outcry.

It didn't come. "That's the first good idea you've had," Bethany said. Words of assent met her from around the crowded room.

"I bet we'd find a plausible excuse if we dug into the city's constitution," Lena said. "If not, it's long past time we added it."

"While it's a shame we should have to enforce the ideals of our city's founding," Tristan said. "The world has changed since Limani's founding."

Max raised his hand. "All in favor of the proposals?"

Victory followed suit, Lena and Bethany close behind. She wasn't about to remind Bethany that she didn't have voting power, since she appreciated the support. Soon every hand in the room raised.

"Congratulations, Guildmaster," Tristan said. "You're in charge. What's the first move?"

When Max immediately looked to Victory for support, she shook her head. "Despite my age, Guild law says you outrank me. What are your orders, General?"

Victory paced her kitchen while Toria worked through a full breakfast of oatmeal, bacon, juice, and coffee. Her daughter needed her strength for the upcoming day, and Victory had readied a meal with all the care of a mother sending her lone offspring into battle.

"Mama, now you're making me nervous."

Victory forced herself to sit at the kitchen table. "Will the gladius work out okay?"

"It'll have to do, with nothing else light enough."

"I love you, sweetheart," Victory said, "and I have every confidence in your abilities. But I'm pleased Max placed you in the reserve guard."

"I'm glad you have confidence. I feel pretty close to worthless. Can't even do the job I'm trained to do."

"Not without reliable magic and not without Kane." Victory hooked her ankles around her chair legs to keep herself from standing to pace again. "And not carrying a blade you're not comfortable with."

Toria pursed her lips. "Thanks for the reminder."

Victory would give anything in the world to trade places with her daughter. But Max had planned this sortie for late morning, unhindered by darkness. Not all of the regular mercenary force had heightened senses.

After draining her coffee, Toria said, "Better go see whether Syri is ready for me." She snagged an apple before leaving the room. Victory hoped she intended to pawn it off on Syri. The elven girl needed her strength to heal.

The doorbell rang. Max was early. Toria let him in on her way to the stairs, directing him toward the kitchen. Victory readied another mug of coffee.

Max accepted the drink and slid into Toria's vacant seat. "Exactly what I needed. We have good troops, but organizing them to include the werecreatures is like herding cats. Sometimes literally."

"Did you get any sleep?" The circles under his eyes did not bode well.

"I caught a nap in my office. I'll be fine." Victory's silence spoke volumes, because after sipping his coffee, Max added, "Toria will be fine, too."

Victory hated this unfamiliar sensation of helplessness. "I wish I could be at your side." She'd spent far too long being the master of her own destiny, fighting either alongside Asaron or with her sword as her single ally. Political life did not infer weakness, but it was tough to bow to Max's wishes instead of demanding he push the plan to sundown.

"Trust me, I wish you could, too."

Max's frankness reassured her far more than any platitudes he might have offered. "Thanks, hon."

"I'm serious. I've got plenty of seasoned warriors, but Toria's not the only journeyman getting a temporary promotion. Add in all the weres and the elves who aren't used to military discipline, and I'm almost desperate to have you helping me run interference."

"Next time?"

Max slapped the table. "Hell, yes. This is just a preliminary run. Gather info, figure out what we're up against. Damn straight the next fight is going to be at night, with you in the thick of it."

"Damn straight," Victory echoed. "Finish your coffee and raid the fridge. I'll make sure the girls are ready." She stood and crossed to the other side of the table, where she pressed a chaste kiss against Max's cheek. He would keep Toria safe.

Of course, she hoped Toria did the same for him. If anything happened to Max, and with Asaron still languishing in captivity, that left her in charge.

Toria waved out the window of Max's borrowed van. Her mother watched from her bedroom, hidden in the shadows of heavy drapes. When they turned a corner in the long driveway, she pulled her arm inside the window and settled in her seat.

She put on a tough front for everyone around her, including her mother, but she would have given her right arm for Victory to be beside her, also geared for battle.

Max drove into town, toward the Hall—the staging point for the mission slated for noon. Ten in the morning, and already Toria wanted the day to be over.

Syri leaned against Toria's shoulder. That morning, she had once again delved into Toria's mind and activated all of the battle defenses Toria had stored away. Today Syri played Kane's part, wielding magic to protect them while Toria relied on her borrowed sword.

When Max first proposed the plan, Toria had felt it a betrayal of Kane. But this liaison was temporary, and soon she would have her real partner back.

"I have a silly question," Syri said, her voice low.

Toria matched her whisper. "Yeah?"

"Have you ever killed anyone before?"

An easy answer, but Toria hesitated. Three years ago. A long time by human standards, a blink to Syri. "In self-defense." She focused on the passing trees. "A vampire after Mama for killing her sire decades ago."

"During the werepanther crisis," Syri said. "I wasn't in the city, but I heard about it. The ringleader—same vampire?"

"Same vampire."

"I've never killed anyone." Syri replaced her head, and Toria pressed her cheek to elven-soft hair.

"Hopefully neither of you will today," Max said. "You're in charge of all the promoted journeymen, Toria. I expect you to keep them out of trouble."

"Don't worry," Syri said. "We're good at staying out of trouble. Or at least getting ourselves out of it."

Hours later, Toria wasn't laughing. She crept through the underbrush, gladius in hand and Syri close by. Three other former journeymen strung out behind her, also silent in the dim afternoon forest.

She paused before they entered a small clearing, keeping to the shadows of the trees. The others halted in their tracks and stayed low behind her. While she wasn't familiar with many of them beyond sight, name, and perhaps a training session or two, she knew Max had given her the best. "Anything?"

A dark green hood concealed Syri's blond hair except for a few escaped wisps. "Nope. We outran them. There's no sign through here. I think we can risk it."

Toria motioned for the others to follow her forward. Syri walked point, rifle clutched in her hands. They stuck to the tree line, skirting the clearing.

The explosions still rang in Toria's ears. She had been positioned with Syri and the others by the caravan of vehicles that ferried the mercenary force out to the major river crossing. Max nixed the bridge as too frontal of an attack, so they'd returned to the spot of the kidnapping.

She'd itched to join the main body, but Toria remained with her small troop. All seven of them could drive, and they held the responsibility of keeping the precious vehicles safe, whether it meant collecting the mercenaries on a retreat or hightailing it out of there themselves at the first sign of the Romans and going for the backup rendezvous.

"Remind me again what plan C was?" Syri's low voice carried to Toria's ears.

"You mean yell 'oh shit!' and run like hell?" Toria suppressed a manic giggle. What the hell was Max thinking, putting her in charge?

After the main body had departed, Toria called for the perimeter scouts to come in. She and Syri had walked out to meet them.

The loss of the majority of the Guild's long-distance vehicles was devastating enough, but there were worse things to lose. Poor Freya had been the sole casualty of the sabotage. The nurse was the Guild's backup medic—she'd requested the rearguard since her three-month-old son remained at home with her husband. The van housing the mobile medical unit exploded first, followed in a violent chain by the other vehicles. The other three scouts were fine. The blast threw their replacements to the ground, singeing them a bit—Freya never stood a chance.

And now there were five.

Syri drew to a halt at the other side of the clearing, and Toria gathered everyone around her. "Okay, through the woods. We'll get to the secondary meeting point and wait for the others there."

"No way," Ari said. "The Romans bypassed the force already. They're probably on their way to Limani right now. We have to warn the city. Do what we can there."

None of Toria's scouts had seen any sign of the Romans before the explosions. Their position had been secure. Max had ensured that before he led the others out.

"Think, girl," Syri said. "The trucks didn't explode because they were shot at."

Taba, the wereleopard, followed Syri's train of thought. "We were sabotaged?"

Toria ran a hand through her hair to hide its tremor. "They must have been rigged to blow before we even left Limani."

Except for Syri, they all gaped at her. "Impossible," Ari said.

"You have no idea what they've been up to the past few days," Syri said.

To Toria's chagrin, every single one of them focused on her instead of their surroundings. This needed to be finished, fast.

"Care to enlighten us?" Ari said.

Toria ignored her. "The river docks are closer than the city. We'll borrow wheels there and get to the meeting point, secure the location for when the others return."

"We should call while we're there and request another medic from the hospital." Ah, another voice of reason in the group. After the morning's swift introductions, Toria couldn't remember the lanky guy's name. Renan? He was a new city resident, but Max vouched for him.

"Good idea," she said. "You're in charge of that."

A low mutter from the other side of the group caught Toria's ear over the forest sounds around them. "What?"

Ari stepped away from Taba, lifting her chin in defiance. "I said, maybe he should be in charge of everything."

Toria's skin chilled under her thick leather armor in the stifling summer humidity. "What the hell is that supposed to mean?"

"C'mon, we all know you're running this show because you're the Guildmaster's favorite."

She'd always suspected Max preferred Kane, but she bristled at Ari's insinuation all the same. "Maybe Max thought I was the best person for the job."

"You don't even have the respect to call him Master Asher like the rest of us," Ari said.

Syri cut off Toria's retort. "Enough," she said. "Time to move out, not stand around and bicker like schoolchildren. Three Roman scouts are coming this way. We need to move. Now."

While not as harrowing, the jog to the docks was no less stressful than the rest of the trip so far. Ari's stare bore into Toria, but she didn't have the energy or inclination to break her momentum in order to tell the girl off.

At least their passing created a cool breeze. She hesitated to drain the water in her canteen, unsure whether they would make it to the river before the scouts Syri overheard came upon them.

A subtle alteration in the humidity signaled their nearness to the river. Soon the docks would be in sight, and she could beg Master Rhaavi for a truck and the use of the radio.

"Heads up!"

Taba's voice alerted Toria of danger as a breeze passed her cheek, followed by the *thunk* of an arrow piercing a tree to her left. She dove to the ground, rolling to her side and drawing her pistol. After all of her charges hit the ground or scattered behind trees, Toria sighted through the foliage.

Before she called out a request to Syri, her vision layered with magesight. Bless the girl for having experience with combat, however limited, and anticipating her needs. Still no replacement for Kane, but she would do in a pinch.

Crouched in the brush next to her, Taba pulled his sweatshirt off and tossed it aside, then unlaced and removed his boots. "Cover me," he said, the words muddling when his teeth lengthened and the bones in his face shifted. In a handful of heartbeats, a spotted leopard kicked out of a pair of jeans and ghosted away amidst the foliage.

Toria watched his golden shape—in both color and magical aura—slip through the underbrush. The forest, already a myriad of summer-bright greens and browns, overlaid with shadows of color that made reality appear drab by comparison. She dismissed the familiar magical shine of nature, instead concentrating on seeking out any sense of disruption.

There. A few hundred yards away, protected by trees and thick brush. They crouched motionless now, having lost their easy targets. Three simple human auras, shades of putrid orange radiating as much apprehension as her own small crew. One also contained tinges of blue, a valiant attempt at mental shielding by a weak telepath.

She had them in her sights. Any other day, she'd pull power from Kane, call a bolt of power, and blast them into a crater.

Not an option this afternoon. She doubted "Lightning Bolt" was one of the charms Syri had dug out of her brain to set in her own mind.

None of the other journeymen were mages of any sort, and Syri's magical abilities ran more to the mental than the combative. Time to handle this the old-fashioned way. Taba's silent figure crept around the Roman scouts—he would circle behind them.

Ari's soft voice came from behind a nearby tree. "Can they see us?"

"I've got their position. Three hundred yards east, right between those oaks," Toria said. "I think they know we're here, but nothing more. Ari and Renan, circle to the right and left, stay low. I'll go straight. Taba's blocking their retreat. Syri, stay here and watch for any surprises."

"Capture or incapacitate?" Ari was all business now, a fact Toria much appreciated.

"Incapacitate, however necessary," Toria said. "We don't have the time or manpower to deal with prisoners. Ready check?" A chorus of low affirmatives met her question. "All out. Now."

Shifting her weight and rolling onto her knees, Toria drew the gladius at her side and rose to a crouch. Renan and Ari disappeared in her peripheral vision, and she led the stealthy charge.

Field-promoted they might all be, but Toria should never have doubted any of her command's abilities. Max had overseen their training, after all.

The orange auras flared neon at Renan's wordless battle cry. Toria surged forward with the others when the three Romans scattered from their positions, blades drawn and arrow knocked. A feline scream echoed through the trees.

Renan tackled one to the ground, where they sprawled for a second before grappling each other. An invisible force jerked the rearmost scout into the trees, bow bashed from his hands, and Toria glimpsed golden fur and snarling teeth. Then she had no attention to spare for the fight, clashing swords with the leading attacker.

She deflected his gladius aside with a screech of metal, knocking into his chest with her shoulder before rebounding away. Ari stood ready to cross blades with him while Toria collected herself and prepared to attack once more. Wishing for the wicked point of her rapier, Toria thrust her sword toward the scout while his attention was on the other woman.

But Octavian wouldn't send out green troops. With a dodge bordering on elven or vampiric grace, the scout extracted himself from between them. The tip of Toria's sword drew blood at his upper arm, nowhere near the shoulder joint she targeted.

A gunshot rang out, and Ari screamed. Another crack, and the scout in front of her, preparing for a charge, dropped to the ground with half of his face splattered away in a mass of blood and shattered bone.

The day-to-day Toria would feel horror, revulsion, fear. But trained warrior-mage Toria had buried that Toria. In stark contrast to her younger self, who'd impaled a vampire and dropped into immediate panic and shock, now she whirled in search of the next danger.

Ari's scream. The other girl had collapsed to the ground a few feet away, blood gushing from her stomach. Renan's initial target had fallen, unmoving, and now he helped Toria confront the remaining Roman scout.

When Toria spun on him, he dropped the gladius in his hand and drew a small knife with his uninjured off-hand. The closest, Renan dove forward. But the Roman raised his arm in one smooth motion and the knife embedded itself in Renan's chest.

Renan's momentum kept him falling forward, and he crashed to the ground.

Before Toria reacted, another gunshot rang out and a matching bloom of red appeared at the scout's throat. He collapsed, twitching.

With her magesight still active, Toria stared at Renan's and Ari's dark bodies. This was…not how the skirmish was supposed to go. Taba trotted out of the underbrush, his muzzle stained with blood. He sniffed each body, then padded over to lean against Toria's side. His shoulders came above her waist, and she buried her fingers in the fur behind his ears.

Syri emerged from the trees, slinging the rifle across her shoulders. She knelt next to Ari to check the woman's wounds. Toria approached Renan's body and rolled him onto his back. At such close range, the Roman's knife had buried to the hilt in his chest, right where his heart was. Despite the futility of the motion, Toria sought for a pulse in Renan's neck. Nothing. Perhaps that was a blessing. Dirt and dead leaves coated his face.

The reality and terror of this situation would hit her the second she stopped to reflect. But right now, Toria controlled the situation.

"How's Ari?" She rose to her feet and turned to Syri, who'd placed her hands at Ari's chest.

"Too much blood loss, too quickly." Her voice quiet, Syri rose to unsteady feet with Toria's help. "I'm sorry."

"Not your fault," Toria said. "There was nothing we could do."

Syri's skin held an ashen tint. "No, it's still my fault. Renan blocked my shot. I couldn't get the Roman until he fell."

Toria wrapped an arm around the girl's waist. "You did what you could. We all did."

Taba licked at Syri's fingers.

Syri gestured to the scattered bodies. "What do we do with them?"

The reply tore at Toria's stomach. "Right now, nothing. We still have to meet the others. We remember this spot and return for them later. Taba, I'm assuming you're stuck in that form for a bit?" The wereleopard pawed the ground in response, so Toria collected his clothing and shoved them in her pack.

The birds returned on rustling wings, but the gunshots might attract others. "Let's go."

Now they were three.

Fabbri did not wake by dawn. She didn't even wake by mid-morning. Whatever spell Syri used to knock the woman out had proven more powerful than Daliana anticipated, and the elven healer feared to muck around in the human woman's mind further. Instead, she called upon a friend to smuggle Victory safely to her house despite the daytime hour.

Since Victory could worry about her daughter and friends from Daliana's house as easily as from her own, she didn't protest the summons.

Thus, when Fabbri woke in Daliana's curtain-shrouded sitting room, Victory stood over her.

The planned attack had started moments ago. Victory blessed the woman for the distraction even as she presented a stony façade. "You're awake. Finally."

Fabbri pushed herself to a sitting position and stared at Victory, eyebrows furrowed. "Where the hell am I?" Then, the reality of her current situation and pajama-clad form sank in. "You kidnapped me!"

"That seems to be going around," Victory said.

Daliana entered the room bearing a tray with three mugs and a steaming pot of coffee. "Lovely to see you up, my dear. Would you care for a meal to break your fast?"

Fabbri clutched her blanket around her. "You're offering me breakfast? Before you torture me to go along with the kidnapping? The council will hear about this."

"There is no council," Victory said. "We disbanded it when we declared martial law."

"Sethri would never—"

"Sethri's dead. Your people killed him."

Victory expected immediate cries of denial and outrage, perhaps accusations of lies. But Fabbri could not fake her dismay, as she gasped and looked to Daliana for confirmation. After a somber nod, Daliana sat next to Fabbri and placed a hand over where the other woman clutched the blanket. In her shock, Fabbri didn't even recoil from the elven woman's touch.

"They were supposed to follow you," Fabbri said, voice hushed. "Spy on you. After what happened to Mikelos and the others, I didn't want anyone else to get hurt."

"Sounds like you've lost control of your own group," Victory said. "You weren't around when we discussed meeting with the Romans. Someone else on our side of the council is reporting to you. I need to know who."

Fabbri pulled her knees to her chest, as if the blanket and closed-off posture would protect her from Victory's menacing stance. Daliana covered the awkward silence by pouring coffee.

Victory could be patient. Unfortunately, Fabbri refused to meet her gaze. She'd have to do this the old-fashioned way, by reading micro expressions and catching changes in heart rate. "Was it Bethany?" Fabbri did not react to this first guess, but Victory pressed on. "It would make sense. She's been privy to every major meeting since all this started, but she's not a councilmember."

The woman continued to stare at her knees, ignoring the mug Daliana offered her.

"You know I'll figure it out," Victory said. "Why delay the inevitable?" She was more than happy to accept the coffee from Daliana, to savor the warm aroma. She needed this. Midafternoon approached, a time when all good vampires should be in bed. Preferably with their daywalkers snuggled beside them, but a hospital bed still trapped Mikelos. She always forgot how much she counted on his steadying presence until he wasn't next to her.

"So you can torture them for information instead?"

Victory dropped into the armchair across from the couch with an intentional sigh of frustration. "I know you think I'm lower than scum because I'm not human. We anticipated a rational conversation with you about this. But you're awfully hung up on this torture thing, and all we've done is offer you breakfast."

No response.

"I'd much rather cook than scrub blood out of my carpet," Daliana said. Victory appreciated her attempt at levity.

Fabbri plucked at a loose thread on the quilt in lieu of a response.

This wasn't working. They needed to confront this irrational torture fear head-on before the woman worked herself into a catatonic state. Victory tossed back the last of her coffee, wishing it was something much stronger to fuel the memories she was about to share. "I have been starved into a blood rage so fierce that I've killed an innocent child. I've been staked outside to wait for the sun to rise. I've had the skin flayed from my back."

Daliana picked up the thread. "I've had iron spikes driven into my body to watch the skin sear around them," Daliana said, her own voice as devoid of emotion. Then, gentling, she continued, "We have lived a long time, Emily. But there are still lines we will never cross."

Though she didn't lift her head, Fabbri finally spoke. "What happened to the two men who went after you? I don't figure you let them get away after...after what happened to Sethri." Her voice cracked on the words.

"Victory and Max returned to Limani with them," Daliana said. "We're keeping them in my basement, but they're comfortable."

Close enough. Still knocked out, last time Victory checked, tied up and thrown together on an old mattress. Daliana had done some fast-talking to convince Victory and Max not to toss the men through a few windshields of their own.

"Why not hand them over to the police?"

"Because no one knows Sethri is dead," Victory said. "That's a complication we don't need." A significant difference existed between losing the leadership of the local Mercenary Guild, or the symbolic Master of the City, and the nominal head of the local government.

"They will stand a fair trial once the current crisis is addressed," Daliana said. "We've placed the government on temporary hiatus, not exchanged justice for vengeance."

Fabbri nodded once, then reached forward for the last coffee cup.

Taking her action as a willingness to cooperate, Victory returned to her original line of questioning. "Are you ready to tell us who your insider is?"

Fabbri clutched the mug between pale hands. "It was Lorus."

Though he muttered about losing another vehicle to the vampire's mad family, Customs Master Rhaavi handed over keys to a pickup truck without argument. Toria figured it had more to do with their blood-splattered clothing than the way Syri batted her eyelashes. She accepted the keys with assurances to return the truck in one piece, hoping she'd be able to make good on the promise, and didn't stick around for him to change his mind.

Syri climbed in the passenger seat, and Taba, once again in human form, hopped into the bed. They careened along a back road toward the rendezvous site at speeds high enough to make Taba yelp every time Toria jolted over a pothole. No time to waste. They had to make it to Max, warn him of the infiltration of their forces, and break the bad news of the deaths.

After today, Toria swore she'd never again be responsible for anyone other than herself or Kane.

Not that she'd done a stellar job of keeping Kane safe, either.

Despite her best efforts and disregard for traffic laws, they arrived late to the secondary meeting site. Max hobbled to the truck as Toria stepped out of the cab. A red-tinged bandage bound his left calf above an incongruous bare foot. "We found the wrecks," he said without preamble. "And Freya. You guys are okay?"

"No, sir," Toria said. Taba vaulted out of the truck bed behind her, and she stifled a startle reaction when Syri slammed the passenger door. Even surrounded by the mercenary company and warmed by the summer sun, fear gnawed at her chest. "Three scouts ambushed us on the way to the docks. We lost Renan and Ari."

"Damn," Max said. "They're pulling out all the stops. No prisoners?"

Toria gestured to the empty truck. "No survivors. Syri's a good shot."

Max clapped the elven girl on the shoulder. "Good girl. Taba, report to Genevieve. You two, come with me."

They jogged across the clearing to keep pace with Max, despite his injury. "What happened, Max?" Toria said. "Are you okay?"

"Lucky shot grazed my leg and shredded my boot. They were ready for us." A cluster of Max's more experienced mercs crouched on the ground around a map. "Tell me where they ambushed you."

Toria triangulated between the docks and their original position, but Syri beat her to the reveal. She jabbed a spot on the map with one thin finger. "We left the bodies there."

An older merc placed a red sticker on the plastic map at the point Syri indicated. A dozen or so other red marks littered the area of the map between them and the river.

"The main force didn't follow us," Max said. "But you guys ran into one of the trios of the scouts infiltrating our side of the border. We know one thing for sure, though."

"The bastards don't know what's coming?" said one of the older mercenaries, noting map coordinates on a pad of paper.

"A frontal assault isn't going to work for us," Max said. "Time for more unique methods. Your mother's about to get recalled, Toria, whether she likes it or not."

Victory fumbled her empty mug. Lorus had sat pretty low on her list of potential suspects. "Okay, now I'm really confused."

"Lorus never shared his motives with me," Fabbri said. "I just know Bethany was supposed to be the scapegoat."

Unable to restrain her nervous energy, Victory placed her empty mug on the tray and paced to Daliana's fireplace. She drummed her fingers on the mantel, then faced Fabbri. "The scapegoat for what? Inviting the Romans to invade the city? Assaulting Limani citizens?"

The doorbell rang, and after a penetrating look in Victory's direction, Daliana left the room. But Victory had no interest in accosting Fabbri while unsupervised. Now she had a different target.

Fabbri had pushed herself into a corner of the couch. Before Victory could snap that she wasn't going to eat her, Daliana called from the front door. "Here's our chance to find out."

Victory crowded into Daliana's living room with the other councilmembers, who'd arrived after Max sent his force to the Guildhall to rest and recover. Max's injury warranted him a seat on the couch, and she perched next to him, Toria and Syri at their feet. After they arrived, Toria spent almost ten minutes in the bathroom. The red skin on her hands told Victory her daughter had scrubbed them raw.

Having accepted Daliana's offer to borrow proper clothing, Fabbri perched on a kitchen chair in the corner of the room. Lorus stood by her side. He seemed to return every glare aimed in his direction at once, his black eyes absorbing all light in the room.

Though his tone remained steady, the gray cast to his skin gave away his anxiety. "These are serious accusations you level against me."

"Talk to Fabbri," Victory said. "She made them."

"You would have us trust the word of someone we should convict of treason?" Lorus scoffed, as if clearing water from his blowhole.

Fabbri had edged as far away from Lorus as she could and remain in her chair. "I saved the note you sent me to arrange our first meeting."

"As if a piece of paper could implicate me."

"I have a wolf who can verify that," Tristan said. "She can sense the history of objects. We give the note to her, and she can tell us who wrote it."

"Utterly outrageous." Lorus spread his arms wide. "This morning we were fighting the Romans, and now you're trying to make me out to be the villain?"

Daliana rose from the piano bench. "What was your plan, Lorus? Weaken the ruling body of the city, all the while feeding information to the Romans so they'd know when to strike?"

"That was the impression I got," Fabbri said. She shrank under the attention from the room. But when the wereporpoise maintained his moody silence, she squared her shoulders. "He made a deal with the Romans. He'd be the new governor of the city under Roman control."

"How could you?" Bethany asked, her plaintive question giving voice to the room as a whole.

In response, Lorus sneered.

"But you forgot something," Genevieve said, "in all your planning." She stood and crossed her arms.

When a hint of confusion broke through Lorus' stiff façade, Tristan said, "Not a surprise, considering our aquatic brethren don't have much of a sense of smell." He rose to his feet next to Genevieve.

Finally, Lorus asked, "What the hell are you two talking about?"

"It's not that we can smell lies," Victory said. "But pheromones. Body chemistry. Stress hormones. They speak volumes." She also stood to add her support to the show of force.

Following suit, Daliana said, "And you've made them since you came into this house."

Though she appeared half-asleep at Victory's feet, a steel edge resonated in Toria's sleepy voice. "Does this mean we can arrest him and get on with the more important stuff?"

Laughing, Max hauled himself up with Victory's assistance and placed his weight on his uninjured leg. "That we shall, girl. Lorus Gunnar, you are under arrest for treason against the free city-state of Limani."

Though his injury no longer bled, the delicious scent emanated from Max like a tantalizing treat despite the snug bandage. Victory considered herself a bit of an expert on the subject, and her friend was in no shape to return to combat. "Are you sure you don't want me to convince one of the elves to take a look at that?" Victory asked. "Syri's literally right there."

Syri paused in cleaning her rifle from her seat in a corner. "Oh no, you don't want me. I can get Daliana, though."

Max ignored them in favor of the maps spread across the table in the Guildhall's little-used conference room, their ad hoc leadership headquarters. After he repositioned the token representing Tersuigel's werehynenas, he glared at Victory. "I'm not wasting anyone's energy on my little scratch when I've got two people still in critical condition."

Toria poked her head inside the conference room door in time to hear Max's counter-argument, and she shared a look of frustration with Victory. Asaron, Max's former mentor, would have ordered the man, but Victory didn't have that sort of relationship with him. And if Asaron were here, Max wouldn't be injured in the first place, because none of this nonsense would be happening.

"That's what the hospital is for," Toria said. "That's why Saul and Mason are there. To heal people."

"I'm saving them for tonight's casualties," Max said. "Tor, you brought the notebook I wanted?"

Passing over the blue book, Toria said, "Wow, you're optimistic."

"Fine, Max. Suffer," Victory said. "Now, why are we here and not the rest of your officers?"

Victory finally caught some sleep in Daliana's guest room, then booked it to the Mercenary Guildhall as soon as possible after sunset. Toria met her mother with all of her gear, and Victory itched to do something useful with her sword. Time to act, before the Romans regrouped and hit the city with their full force at first light. After this afternoon, they should still be scouring the countryside for the remnants of Max's initial strike. It was a race against time while each force regrouped. Limani had the advantage of home territory and the timing of the next attack—because they would be the ones making it.

"I've already briefed them on tonight's main mission and they're busy coordinating with Tristan and Genevieve's forces," he said. "Not to mention waiting for Tersiguel's pack to arrive. Bloody hyenas."

"Be glad they're here," Victory said. "Tersiguel doesn't work with just anyone."

"Exactly," Max said. "Which is why I've assigned her forces to you. I can't think of a better team to hit the camp from behind while the main force confronts the Romans with the wolves and panthers."

Victory pulled one of Max's maps toward her, pretending to study the area she already knew like the back of her hand. "Did we ever get an official count on the Roman forces?"

"Best estimate from what we've seen so far, both this afternoon and when we met with Octavian, is approximately two thousand men," Max said. "It's likely the vast majority is human and without much combat experience. These are local recruits from the southern colonies, not troops from Europa."

"That leaves you with fewer than two hundred for the frontal attack," Victory said. "Those are ten-to-one odds in their favor, Max."

Max slammed his hand on the table. "Don't you think I know that, Victory?"

Silence rang after his outburst. She didn't bother to apologize. Both of them were tense with battle nerves. "The plan will work," Victory said. "I just haven't led a combat force in centuries." In the Last War, she'd performed operations solo, with maybe a partner or two for backup. Usually Asaron, and they'd fought together for so long they barely needed words. Much as it pained her pride to admit weakness in front of her daughter, Max deserved her true assessment.

"I've heard all the stories," Toria said. "I doubt you've lost your touch to cause mayhem."

"Thanks," Victory said. "I'll try to live up to your grandfather's exaggerations."

"Not exaggeration," Max said. "Asaron and I have spent years discussing tactics, and he's always told me to go straight to you if I want something done that might not fit with my other officers' sense of honor—not that you lack honor yourself."

"No, Asaron's right," Victory said. "It's hard to fight for almost a thousand years and not develop your own ideas on what's fair game. My sire is even more devious than I am."

"Which brings me to the reason the girls have joined us for this little meeting," Max said. He pointed to Toria and Syri. "You two are getting us Asaron's devious mind."

Hope flashed in Toria's eyes. "With Kane, right?"

Luckily, Max knew better than to put Toria in the awkward position of disobeying an order from her commanding officer. "Once you set a pissed-off Asaron loose in the middle of the Roman camp," Max said, "I fully expect you to fetch your partner and get him up to speed on the rest of your goals."

"Which are?" Toria asked.

"You three are finding that nuclear weapon for me. And disarming it."

Victory crouched in a hidden pocket between two trees covered in ivy and brambles, out of sight of the first row of Roman tents. Daliana's shoulder pressed into her back.

The heat of the summer night worked in their favor, though Victory's hair curled out of its tight braid in the oppressive humidity and Daliana proved that elven sweat smelled as bad as human. The army celebrated tonight, declaring themselves the victors in the first sortie against the Limani forces. The unseasoned troops didn't appear to know the difference between "driven off" and "retreated."

Daliana's low whisper echoed like a shout to her strained senses. "Sounds like all the celebration is happening farther in. These tents are filled with sleeping bodies, judging by the heat signatures I can see through the canvas. Haven't spotted any wanderers."

Matching the other woman's soft tones and blessing how elven hearing equaled vampiric, Victory said, "Support staff. These guys probably weren't involved in the combat today." She gave the trees another pass. Moonlight filtering through branches lit the woods like a bright stage. "The sentry we skirted is repeating his pattern. Haven't seen anyone else."

"Sneaking through here is our best bet." A hint of question marked the end of Daliana's words, bowing to Victory's experience.

"Agreed. Support staff means supplies. Lots of supplies. Look for ammunitions wagons or trucks, and we've got our first target."

Victory gripped the bark of the tree next to her, prepared to pull herself out of her stiff crouch, when a nearby explosion shattered the world. She covered her ears and suppressed a scream, lowering her auditory sensitivity too late to save the ringing in her skull.

Fingers touched her temples out of the darkness—when had she closed her eyes?—and the pain receded to a manageable level. Echoes of leaving the Mists after a night of dancing versus remembered days of aerial bombardment in Castille. She shoved those memories aside.

Daliana's face hovered inches from her own. "Better?"

"Yes. You?"

"Shields are good for some things," Daliana said. "Like preserving eardrums. But we need to move."

Victory once more expanded her senses to the world around her. Men boiled out of the tents, officers screamed orders, and lamps on tent poles filled the forest with light. "Someone did not follow orders." Victory and Daliana's explosion was supposed to cue the rest of the teams.

"They might have needed their own distraction," Daliana said, her gentle tones more forgiving.

"Right now we need to take advantage of this one. Let's go."

No matter who screwed up, it might work in their favor. This section of camp had emptied, and checking over her shoulder, even the sentry they'd evaded had abandoned his post.

Both women remained in the black shadows of the trees until the last possible second. Now screams drifted across the Roman encampment, echoed by the sharp reports of gunfire.

Victory drew her sword. Daliana already had her pistol in hand. Brief regret washed through Victory. The elven woman was a healer by nature if not in true power. Never a warrior. She damned the Romans for dragging her into Victory's repressed, if not forgotten, world.

They dashed into the now-deserted section of camp. Victory halted next to an officer's empty pavilion and pointed to two trucks hitched with large cargo containers. "There."

"They blow up our trucks, we'll disable theirs," Daliana said.

"Keep watch." Not waiting for Daliana's assent, Victory darted through the empty space. She slipped to her knees between the truck cabs, trusting the mechanical beasts to keep her hidden from view.

She drew a small package from her pack. One of Max's mercenaries moonlighted as Limani's resident demolitions expert, and it amazed her how fast the man had managed to throw these nasty surprises together. That he had such materials on hand bothered her civilian side a bit, but the mercenary in her trilled with glee. He'd even included simple step-by-step and color-coded instructions.

Another explosion from a different section of camp rocked the night. "Madness and mayhem" should be the official slogan of Limani's Mercenary Guild.

Victory squirmed underneath the truck, peering into the engine's unfamiliar workings. She'd never had a major interest in the mechanics of modern transportation, despite her attraction to fast, shiny cars in the days when more vehicles ran on gasoline than electricity. The instructions indicated she should shove the small block wrapped in bright red plastic anywhere it would stay, so she wedged it between the front right wheel and axle.

A thought wormed its way through her battle-focused mind. The first explosion was Toria's cue. Somewhere in the camp, Asaron sated his hunger. And her children searched for an ancient nuclear device.

Place the clip on one of the blue wires to the red part of the plastic casing. Attach the other end of the wire to the metal protrusion from the small cylinder of black plastic the size of two of her fingers. Press the green button on the other end of the cylinder. Sixty seconds to gain some distance.

She shoved herself out from under the truck and ran.

Daliana met her as the two women dove through the rows of tents back to their original shelter, pressing themselves to the ground on the opposite side of the trees.

Thirty seconds of tense waiting. It occurred to Victory that she should remind her partner to remove any pieces of wood that impaled her torso should the trees protecting them shatter. Daliana would be fine with her bulletproof vest, but Victory didn't want an inconvenient branch to incapacitate her for too long.

"Dal—"

Explosion number three cut her off. The trees didn't shatter at this distance, but a wave of heated air blew past. Victory tensed for a wall of flame, much more fatal to her than a sliver of wood. A heap of tent canvas crashed to her left.

Deafening silence followed the blast. Then the screams of men flowed toward them.

Victory recovered first, launching herself to her feet. She grabbed Daliana's arm, hauling the elven woman to her feet with little effort. "Our work here is done. The rest of the Guild should be on their way in. Time for you to get out of here and regroup with Tersuigel."

"Right, let's go." Daliana paused when Victory didn't follow. "Coming?"

"Can't." She shooed Daliana away. "Go on, I've got stuff to do."

"Like what?" Frustration leaked into Daliana's voice. "The plan's gone to hell. We should get out before we're spotted."

Words Asaron spent years beating into her spilled out by rote. "No plan ever survives first contact with the enemy. Now I've got—"

A shout halted her midsentence. They dove for the forest floor again, and a crossbow bolt struck the tree trunk they'd spent far too long arguing next to.

Orienting herself, Victory drew the pistol at her hip. The damned sentry had returned, waving his crossbow around and screaming for them not to move. She aimed, but a bloom of red appeared at the soldier's throat before she squeezed the trigger.

Lying next to her, Daliana had beaten her to the punch. "You're welcome. Now get out of here before any more come. I'll make it fine on my own. Go find Asaron." She bounded to her feet and disappeared among the trees.

Victory peered into the camp. But with the soldier down, the immediate area was again deserted.

Aim for the screams, where Asaron likely exacted his own vengeance against his former captors.

She stalked out of the comforting darkness and into the camp. Every inch of her tingled with battle-awareness and a rising bloodlust. Crimson tinged her surroundings, and her fangs almost ached with the primal urge to sink them into a Roman neck.

Victory knew her sire well. He would go straight to the top.

She would make sure to reserve Octavian's neck for him.

Three more explosions followed Victory's stealthy progress across the camp, along with a trail of bodies.

She knocked out the soldiers she surprised with mental commands to sleep. Those she didn't surprise often surrendered at the first sight of the blood-splattered warrior. Those slept, too.

She drank from those who fought back.

Despite her ability to survive most mortal wounds, they still hurt even as fresh blood sped along the healing process. The stab to her thigh and through-and-through bullet wound in her left shoulder did nothing to improve her mood.

Now, she crouched in the shadows between two pavilions. Across from her sat a single tent separated from the rest. The prisoner's tent sat empty.

The center of camp lay a short distance away, filled with higher-quality tents and larger pavilions. Officers' quarters, and the command center. Soldiers, officers, and aides ran to and fro in a blur of activity, coordinating the defense against Limani's forces.

She sensed mild panic in the air, amidst the smoke drifting through the camp. Max had given them more of a fight than they expected.

No sign of Asaron so far, though she had come across an officer lying dead, his throat ripped open. He might not have been the cause—the werecreatures stalked their own prey.

No sightings of her daughter, either. But if Kane was free, Toria was sure to stay close by after days of separation from her partner. Despite the urgings of her heart to find her children and protect them, she had to trust in their proven abilities to protect themselves.

She continued her study of the command center. Octavian would be there, coordinating the furious activity and directing the defense. Too many men, and too much light, prevented her from a more subtle assassination.

But an option remained, her crazy idea of last resort that wouldn't work in a million years had Octavian not proven during their previous encounter that he was a man of education and class. She rose to her feet, squaring her shoulders and ignoring the itch of blood drying around the scrape on her cheek. With empty hands held outstretched from her sides, she approached the command center.

An aide spotted her first. He called a warning to a passing soldier, who nocked an arrow to his longbow and ordered her to halt.

Victory stopped and spread her empty hands wide. "I request a meeting with Prefect Octavian. I invoke the rights of Roman Article Seventeen!"

The aide jerked in surprise at her words, then bolted through the tents, leaving the longbowman to cover her.

Contact made. This would all be over soon. Assuming the soldier didn't have twitchy fingers and shoot her by accident.

After all, enemies didn't stroll into the center of camp and declare themselves members of an ancient Roman house every day.

Tension permeated the small tent as they awaited their cue. Toria gripped Kane's hands in her own, stroking his palm with her thumb. The fabric of his improvised bandages brushed her bare arms, pushing her anger ever closer to the surface. What was taking so long? Had they infiltrated the Roman camp so much faster than it had seemed? She tried not to imagine the Romans capturing her mother, too.

Kane's gentle voice dragged her from the land of maybes. "I can feel your nerves vibrating from here."

She rested against his warm shoulder. "I'm okay."

In unison, Asaron and Syri said, "No, you're not," then shared a chuckle at Toria's expense.

"Thanks for the votes of confidence," Toria said. "I've got—"

A flash of light and rolling wave of sound announced the awaited explosion. Toria bolted to her feet as screams erupted outside, officers shouting conflicting orders and soldiers damning the Limani mercenaries.

Asaron crouched by the tent entrance, peering out at the camp. "Toria, a shield?" He jerked his head in her direction when she did not respond right away. "Damn, I forgot."

She'd explained her situation when they'd settled in to wait. Now helplessness struck her when she couldn't fulfill Asaron's request. A short-term external shield was a combat mage's standard work, and Kane had no energy for anything unnecessary to his own immediate survival.

"I've got it." Syri placed a light hand on Asaron's biceps, and a shimmer covered his features, making it hard to look right at him. "Be careful."

After a brief, "Stay with them," to Syri, Asaron vanished into the night before Toria could defend her remaining capabilities. They all flinched at a nearby scream of pain.

"Time to go," Syri said. "Can you find the bomb again, Kane?"

Kane accepted the knife Toria handed him. "I've got a decent idea of its location. Toria, need I remind you of the quick and dirty way to remove a curse?" He replaced Syri at the front of the tent and peeked outside.

Fighting for your life was one thing. What Kane implied belonged to another category entirely. "I'd been trying not to think about that," Toria said.

At her own hesitancy, Kane's voice softened. "This is war, love. The mage is an enemy soldier. It wouldn't be murder."

A week ago, those words would never have come from her partner's mouth. Events had altered him as much as they'd forced their changes on her. But he spoke the truth. Finding no sufficient denial, Toria said, "Let's get out of here. Syri, you've got point."

She prodded Kane out of the tent behind Syri. The elven girl dashed across the path as Toria and Kane followed on her heels, ready for any possible trouble. But aside from stumbling over a single pale corpse, all the action centered elsewhere. The soldiers had cleared the area, racing toward the more immediate attack.

As they ducked between two empty tents and checked for a clear direction, a second explosion ripped through the camp. Now the Romans' attentions would be divided.

Toria pitied Octavian. Limani had destroyed the Prefect's detailed strategy for the morning, and he would be facing her mother. But at the memory of his hands roaming her body, sympathy turned to satisfaction. Mama would vent her fury, and the man would be lucky to bargain for his life.

Kane pointed toward another corner of the camp, away from the explosions. "Octavian's pet mage ordered a temporary building to hold the bomb, and he's camped outside it."

"You can sense it?" Toria asked.

"I can sense the absence of it. Mages have it shielded so tight that the earth itself is invisible to me."

She trusted her partner's impression. Earth sense was his elemental gift, just as she could trace intricate circuitry. "Come on."

The trio wove through the Roman camp in the direction Kane indicated, staying between tents and vehicles, keeping out of sight of the scurrying troops. Two more explosions shattered the night, and they passed one pocket of fighting. Syri halted and drew two long knives.

Toria grabbed her arm before the girl could dive into the fray. "We can't, Syri."

"They're my cousins!" But the two elves who fought back-to-back appeared to need no assistance, flying blades keeping the Roman soldiers at bay.

Kane grabbed Syri's other arm when she would have taken another step forward. "We have a job to do."

One of the elves let out a jubilant battle cry when he dispatched a soldier, and Syri stopped pulling toward them. "Ugh. Right."

They encountered more pockets of combat as they progressed. Werewolf howls and feline cries echoed through the night. An unfamiliar scream halted them again, feral and haunting, followed by yet another explosion.

"Tersiguel," Toria said, "or one of her pack." They ducked past the ruins of two trucks and between another row of tents.

"Whoa!" Kane snatched Syri back before she could step into the open. "Shield. We're there."

They paused by an empty tent, half-collapsed from its inhabitant's mad dash to join the fight. A wide clearing surrounded a neat wooden hut and two large pavilions, nicer than most of the officers' quarters they'd passed. Lanterns lit one of the tents from within, the red one with obnoxious yellow and blue trim. The light remained steady though, with no indication of who or how many people the tent contained.

But she couldn't sense this shield. A new bolt of frustration raged through her.

Kane jumped as if shocked. "Calm, love."

Their link still worked at least. If anything, it must be more open now that Toria had no way to control any emotions leaking through to her partner. "Sorry."

He knew better than to patronize her with a response. Instead, he said, "The area in the shield is a dead zone to me. I can't tell what we're up against in there. Syri?"

"One human mage," she answered without hesitation. "Who did not take nonhuman magic into account when he crafted this overpowered beast. They think they're setting a trap. He's got two others—nonmagical—with him in the dark tent. The red one's empty."

"A trap ready to spring once anyone comes along," Toria said. "I doubt our armor is good enough for concentrated blasts against whatever distance weapons they've got in there, not while we're also fending off magical attacks."

While the sounds of fighting in half of the camp continued strong, the other half had died down. They needed to make their move, and make it soon.

Kane wasn't going to like this. "I've got an idea," Toria said. She wore the belt holding her magical aids out of habit, but now they might come in handy. She dug out her quartz crystal focus and held it out to Kane.

He cradled it in the palm of his hand. "Yes?"

"Can either of you tell whether the shield is self-contained?"

Warrior-mage and elf examined the invisible structure with their inner sight while she waited with impatience. She would never get used to not being able to do such simple tasks herself. She needed her magic back.

"Looks like it to me," Syri said. Kane nodded agreement.

Perfect. Now for the next step. "And the shack is shielded separately?"

"Yep," Syri said. "Gonna share with the class?"

"Improvised flash-bomb," Toria said. "Disrupt their defenses. I may not be able to manipulate energy, but I've still got all my passive shielding. Kane, leech that power from me and channel it into the crystal. We throw it at the tent, and—"

"Poof," Kane said. "Leaving you defenseless. Absolutely not."

"But it makes me less of a target," she said, "if I look like a regular fighter." If Toria still had her full abilities—still been *whole*—she'd have sensed Kane's hesitancy and fear cascade through their link. Instead, standing next to her, he may as well have been a million miles away.

Kane clenched his teeth, hissing in frustration. "I hate it, but we're running out of time." He gripped the quartz in one hand and placed the fingers of his other on her cheek.

The world dropped out from beneath her feet, and Syri grabbed her arms from behind before she jerked away from the pressure building in her skull. A few seconds merged with eternity, and for the briefest moment, she sensed Kane. Mingled pain and love surged through her core—

Then nothing. An internal "pop" relieved the tightness in her head, amidst the detached sensation of the world around her. Kane removed his hand from her face. The airiness around her body intensified, and she resisted the urge to check that she still wore clothing.

That was it. No more magic. She had nothing left to convince herself life would return to normal. Now she was a regular fighter. And Kane became the only warrior-mage in Limani.

A different type of pressure built, but Toria forced down her tears. "Did it work?"

Kane unclenched his fingers, and the crystal he held vibrated with sparkling amethyst light. "It tingles." Without further ado, he hurtled the stone toward the dark tent. It shot through the air like a miniature shooting star, hitting the top of the pavilion with a burst of sparks and crack of lightning. A second loud shock followed the first, as the electricity found the metal tent poles and sent power surging through the structure.

Silence followed the short fireworks show. The odor of singed fabric drifted across the clearing.

"The bomb saturated the tent," Kane said. "I can't tell anything with my magesight."

Toria drew her sword. "I'll go check." Before either could stop her, Toria crept forward from their hiding spot.

She met no resistance passing the area where the shield's edge should be. She kept a steady pace to the pavilion entrance. Still no evidence of movement from within, so she tugged aside a corner of the blue fabric with a finger.

She found the interior spare—a camp cot and a few chests lined the edges, not a lavish display of creature comforts. The bodies of the two soldiers sprawled unmoving in the center of the tent. Loaded crossbows lay within reach of their lifeless fingers, reaffirming Toria's decision not to charge right in.

Fingers snapped once, and a putrid green light illuminated the corner. A gaunt young man wearing battered khaki cargo shorts that rode low on his hips lounged on pillows in the corner. He appeared at ease despite the dead bodies at his feet in the oppressive, unmoving air. Spiraling tattoos decorated his naked torso. One intricate knot on his lower abdomen emitted a fiery orange glow.

"She keeps coming for me," the mage said, a touch of legitimate surprise in his voice. "How charming."

Toria stepped into the tent and pointed the tip of her sword at the mage. "Who the hell are you?"

"Your puppet master." He snapped his fingers a second time.

Every muscle in Toria's body tensed beyond her control. The sword hilt dug into her tight grip, and she had no idea whether blood or sweat slicked her skin. Pain ran through every joint in her body, and her teeth ached with the pressure of her jaw clamping together.

Her rage at this man, the mage who'd cursed her, overwhelmed the agony. The mage retained his casual pose, but strain corded the muscles under his skin. She leaned into the pain, loosening her muscles as much as possible, but every limb screamed with cramps. Despite her best efforts, a high-pitched whimper escaped her gritted teeth.

After a second whimper, as she desperately wished for her shields, the pressure eased. She gasped air into her aching lungs, but remained unable to control her limbs.

The mage's eyes narrowed. "Someone else has been draining your power. Not what I'd intended. But you've some use in you, yet."

An alien urge to call out for Kane bubbled up from within. To plead for help, for rescue. For him to save her. She'd have laughed at the idea if she had any control over her body. The mage's eyes flickered silver as she fought his compulsion.

She refused to be used to lure her partner into a trap. There had to be a way to turn this to their advantage. The mage wanted her to summon Kane. He had no idea about Syri. And with the slightest bit of freedom he'd afforded her to call out, she managed to slip out a single warning. "Syri! Blast the fucker!"

Every muscle in her body seized.

Feet pounded across the clearing toward the tent, Kane's boots followed by Syri's lighter steps. Her teeth snapped shut again, and she curled in on herself, the weight of the pain pushing her to the ground.

The tent flap snapped open behind her, but she had no way to caution them further. The mage lunged to his feet, baring a mocking smile around crooked teeth.

Toria might not be able to sense him magically, but she needed no form of psychic link to recognize Kane's warm presence at her back. Relief, physical and mental, spread through her as Kane drew the pistol holstered at her lower back.

The mage's rictus grin transformed to horror, and a pistol cracked inches from Toria's head. The orange tattoo disappeared in a spread of crimson when the bullet buried itself in his stomach and disrupted the magical energy with his own blood.

He collapsed onto the pillows with a howl, clamping both hands over the wound. All pressure eased from Toria, and she lifted her sword with a sore arm now under her own control. Magesight flooded her vision as her magic poured into her, turning the dark tent into a miasma of corruption.

Kane, keeping the pistol squared toward the mage, stalked across the tent toward him. "I should kill you. But you're the one tied to the bomb."

Syri followed at his heels, twisting her twin blades. "Then I guess he lives. For now." She sheathed her blades and accepted the pistol from Kane to cover the mage. With complete disregard for his injury, he hauled the mage up by his arm.

Toria should have assisted them, but they hadn't just been metaphorically blinded by returning abilities. She caught the loop of power Kane flung her way even has he wrangled the mage and used it to rebuild a base-level shield. Her magesight dimmed from a chaotic roar to a useful trickle of information, and clean violet tongues of energy licked at one of the chests along the wall. She followed the siren call of her own energy and heaved open the lid. The mage had tossed her rapier among a tumble of other ritual paraphernalia, as if the blade was no more important than a spare candle.

She sheathed her replacement sword and clutched her rapier. The blade might be new and untouched by her magic, but the hilt of the sword contained years of her imbued magical signature. Things had to get better from here on out. With partner and sword, she was whole again.

No one was around to notice the three of them escort a bloodied, staggering mage out of his pavilion and to the small structure next door. Explosions no longer rang through the night, but the sounds of combat, screams of rage and cries of the wounded, still emerged from the other side of the encampment. Giddy with power flowing through her veins once again, Toria pointed to the padlocked door and blew it open with a targeted bolt of energy. They didn't need the mage to disarm this nuclear warhead. She could take anything—

"Steady, girl." Syri's fingers intertwined with her own, reeling her back before she became drunk on her reborn power.

Instead, Toria cast a simple cantrip, and a floating orb of light escaped her fingers and hovered above their heads. The shack was empty except for one thing. Upon the bare dirt ground sat a metal cradle holding the cylindrical object she recalled from Kane's memories. It had loomed large in his thoughts, but altogether the weapon wasn't even as long as she was tall. But Kane hadn't exaggerated the nauseous aura it produced, waves of roiling ochre contained by a gunmetal shield the same color as the Roman mage's.

The electronic keypad lay dead. No ticking numbers marked how much time they had left to prevent the utter devastation of her beloved home. Toria whirled on the mage collapsed at Kane's feet. "You wired it to yourself."

No immediate answer, until Syri nudged his knee with her foot. "The power itself was easier to work with, so I bypassed the control system." When the mage gasped in pain, showing bloodstained teeth, Kane ripped a strip from his already tattered shirt. He wadded the cloth and pressed it to the gunshot wound, folding the mage's hands over it.

Toria's scientific tendencies overtook her hatred of the man for the briefest moment. "Idiot. You could have killed yourself. There's a good chance you would have died anyway when it blew if you tied it to yourself too deeply."

"I had no choice."

Syri drew one of her long knives and twisted her wrist so that the orb of light glinted off the blade. "You do now. Tell us which of your little tattoos is tied to the bomb, or I'll start cutting them out at random."

Before the mage could begin gibbering or Kane could protest, Toria said, "No need." His shorts had ridden up when he'd hit the floor, revealing a tattoo on his thigh glimmering with the same swirling mass enveloping the bomb. She slid the pant leg a few more inches with the tip of her sword. "That one."

A newer tattoo compared to the more faded ink work on his torso and arms. A delicate spiral above his knee, overlaid by a heavier star. It glowed in the same fashion as the tattoo that had stolen her power, the one now hidden behind a bloody bundle of cotton.

"At least knock me out first," the mage said. His lack of fight almost disappointed Toria. "Make sure I don't bleed to death after you do it."

"You're helpful all of a sudden," Syri said. "Why the fuck should we even let you live?"

"Because of all the military secrets I hold?" The mage returned her feral grin. "I doubt you three are authorized to let such a source escape your hands."

"Bargain all you want," Toria said. With a sweeping gesture, she invited Syri to do her worst.

The elven girl placed a hand on the mage's forehead. Light flowed from her fingers into his skull, and the mage slumped to the side. If she'd pulled the same trick as on Fabbri, he wouldn't wake for anything.

Kane's turn, but shooting a man from a distance was one thing. Her partner was not so bloodthirsty that he'd enjoy slicing up a defenseless man. Toria offered Kane the small knife from her boot, and Kane sucked in a breath before placing the blade to the side of the tattoo. He sliced through the skin, peeling away the layer holding magic anchored with ink. Blood dripped through his fingers, staining the pounded dirt floor.

The shield around the bomb shattered and faded while Kane cut, the ochre magic flowing through the air and reabsorbing into the mage's skin. It dispersed throughout his body, soothing a few of the lines on the mage's face.

No wonder he'd put a link on Toria's magic after tying so much of himself into the weapon. Her energy had supplemented his own. She ruthlessly suppressed any dash of sympathy, but a promise was a promise. She ripped the hem of her own shirt to have a new bandage ready once Kane finished.

The last of the magical aura drained from the bomb into the mage, until it lay inert. No magic, no electrical power, just a dull undertone of violence that should never have seen the light of day again. "It's done," Toria said.

Kane removed the knife, sagging to the ground next to the mage. Syri replaced him at once, wrapping the makeshift bandage around the mage's leg with deft fingers. "Now what do we do with him?" Kane asked. With the threat gone, all of their adrenaline seemed to have drained in unison. His tired voice matched Toria's aching body.

Toria dialed back her magesight. Now her partners weren't glowing vessels of power so much as worn-out people. "Grab him and run like hell before any Romans get the bright idea to check on their precious pet." Not sure whether she meant the mage or the bomb. She couldn't wait to rebuild her shields. After about a hundred years of sleep.

"There's a truck on the other side of the mages' pavilions," Syri said. "I almost feel obligated to steal it."

Bless Syri for proving some levity remained in the world. "I'm totally fine with taking their toys," Toria said. The sounds of fighting continued outside. But they'd completed their mission.

Time to go home.

Article Seventeen of the Roman Constitution contained a tricky bit of language. A holdover from the old Imperialate, before Emperor Gordian IX created the Roman Parliament three centuries ago. With the caste system demolished, official houses of nobility had been tainted to the point of unrecognizability to anyone without expertise in genealogy and heraldry.

But five hundred and thirty-seven years ago, Victory married into the House of Galerius. The marriage lasted six months before she left Leto for his womanizing and gambling, but Octavian didn't need those details.

The law required the Roman soldiers to escort Lady Victory Galerius into Octavian's presence for an audience. Access was all she needed.

Despite the fighting nearby, she cooled her heels under two soldier's watchful gazes. She still owned property in the Roman Empire, and Mikelos retained many financial interests from his days of musical fame. However, her own past as a lady of the nobility seemed a much more impressive way to demand a face-to-face meeting with the Prefect. Calling on Article Seventeen had occurred to her as a possibility for getting within range of Octavian the day before, but she'd never solidified the plan. She could wing it. That was her specialty.

The aide came scurrying, three more soldiers trailing behind. He gave her a low bow; the soldiers followed suit after brief hesitation.

This might work after all.

Rising, the aide fumbled in a pocket and withdrew a green handkerchief. "I apologize for the wait, your ladyship. Prefect Octavian is willing to see you. He offers this token in return for your firearms. You are more than welcome to retain your blades."

She wouldn't quibble over trivialities, though Article Seventeen gave her the complete right to her arms. They were at war, after all. A point to Octavian for not being stupid. In silence, she dangled the pistol from her pinky for the soldier on her right to retrieve, then stood with her hands held a few inches from her sides.

Reassured that she wasn't about to replace the pistol with a knife, the aide approached with the handkerchief and offered it to Victory with another bow. An embroidered herald decorated one corner, and she assumed the small coat of arms belonged to Octavian. Presenting it for her keeping implied she remained under his protection during the audience. "Thank you."

The soldiers fell into an honor guard formation, escorting Victory and the aide through the camp's command center. Shouting officers who coordinated with other areas of the camp via runner fell silent when they passed, staring at the scruffy vampire being given the deference due any Roman lady of birth. Rumors must already spread, wildfire-like.

Spotlights lit a cluster of tables near the largest pavilions. Prefect Octavian stood ready to greet her. His support staff froze when Victory halted a few feet from Octavian. The officers saluted as one, and Octavian bowed, holding the position at the angle decreed for a high-ranking military official to give a member of the lesser nobility. He did the political dance well, even dressed in fatigues and dirt-scuffed boots.

Victory dipped her chin when he rose. "Thank you for the chance to parlay. If there is any question of my use of Article Seventeen, I assure you I can be found on record in the seventh dynasty House Galerius, as Leto Galerius' second wife."

"Thank you," Octavian said, "but verification will not be necessary."

Convenient, since such a check would be impossible in their current situation. She folded his handkerchief into a small square before tucking it away in a pocket. She withdrew the white satin glove wrapped around her belt and tossed it to the dirt between them.

Octavian stared at the glove, then traded bemused looks with the officer next to him. "You can't be serious."

Victory kept her gaze level, resisting the urge to laugh. "Deathly serious, as it were." The situation had indeed shifted from the strange to the downright absurd.

"Didn't your little town outlaw dueling?"

"Luckily, you camped a few miles outside our border," she said. "Are we going to get on with this, or do I need to insult your manhood or something equally juvenile?"

"I see I have no choice but to accept," Octavian said. "Dare I ask the reason for this little stunt?"

Victory said. "If I win, I have effectively decapitated your army and left them no choice but to turn around and go home."

"If I win, I've killed an obnoxious vampire whose forces will fight all the harder. I'd hardly call that fair."

Victory maintained her composure in the face of such a bizarre conversation, as mild as if they discussed the weather. Asaron would be proud. "You already accepted the challenge. Your choice of weapon, sir."

"I will confer with my officers," Octavian said, a note of stiffness appearing in his voice. He was not as amused, evidently.

She'd surprised him. Now, how long could she drag this little drama out? "Take all the time you need."

The minutes stretched while a huddle of men surrounded Octavian, with runners dispatched with messages and directions for other areas of the command center. The battle did not halt for her, after all. Victory studied the officers around her, all of whom stared at her with blatant curiosity until she acknowledged their attention. Then they returned to work, pretending they'd never had a moment to spare for her, nor that they'd found themselves unable to meet her direct gaze.

"I've made my decision." Octavian's announcement jerked her attention to the man in front of her. Subordinates flanked him, resolve emanating from the entire group. "The weapon shall be pistols. My second shall be Commander Tiberius Ibrahim." Octavian made a slight gesture with one hand, and yet another aide ducked into one of the pavilions behind them.

"Excuse me, sir," Ibrahim said. "But the lady has no second herself, leaving the requirements for a formal duel unfulfilled." His voice dripped with satisfaction as he probed for any hole in Victory's farce to exploit.

A soldier's shout of warning rang out behind Victory, and rifles all around the command center sprang to attention. These must be the elite guard, to be outfitted all with firearms. She turned on her heel, keeping her hand from her own sword lest Octavian decide she had broken their terms of truce.

A lone man, battered and blood-splattered, emerged from the shadows between two of the grander pavilions. He pushed messy red hair out of his face, leaving behind another bronze streak. The loveliest sight Victory had seen in days. He'd probably waited to make such a dramatic entrance.

Asaron marched across the silent clearing to stand at Victory's left. "I'll be her second. Almost wish she'd chicken out so I could face you myself, but my girl would never do such a thing. Let's get on with this."

Octavian had sent two soldiers running during Asaron's speech, but the elder vampire laughed while the men passed by. "The kid is long gone, too."

"It seems I no longer have control over my own encampment," the Prefect said, a growl entering his voice.

The aide returned from the pavilion and presented a wooden box to Octavian. The general opened it to reveal a brace of ceremonial pistols. With a curt acceptance, he directed the aide toward Victory.

The young officer approached with hesitant steps and stopped, forcing Asaron forward to give the pistols a proper inspection. He wiped his hands on his battered leather trousers before handling the fancy weapons. He checked the chambers, popping out the single bullets and reloading them with deft fingers. Asaron gave a double thumbs-up to Octavian before returning to Victory's side.

While Octavian had his aides mark out the official twenty paces that would separate the duelists, Asaron said to Victory, "You sure about this, love?"

"I can handle one bullet. Make sure that's all they get the chance for, okay?"

He captured one of her hands in his larger ones, pressing her fingers to his lips. "Mikelos will haunt me to the end of time if I let something happen to you."

"I know," Victory said.

"Are you going to kill him?"

Before she answered, Octavian called out from across the command center. "If you're ready."

Asaron joined Ibrahim to the side, the two seconds creating an incongruous pair. Victory stood where another soldier indicated, accepting her weapon with a simple thanks. The soldier ignored her politeness.

She hefted the pistol. Down the line, Octavian posed with military precision. Victory cocked the gun and leveled it at Octavian, signaling her own readiness.

"I hereby revoke my protection of the Lady Victory Galerius," Octavian said. "You may proceed, Commander."

"Yes, sir," Ibrahim said. "On my mark, sir, your ladyship." He raised an arm to the dark sky.

Victory drilled holes in Octavian with her eyes, but he avoided her direct gaze. His own attention aimed at her heart.

"Mark."

She wasted no precious time before squeezing the trigger. She kept her arm steady as she shifted the rest of her body, side-stepping with a short burst of vampiric speed. A bloom of red appeared over Octavian's stomach at the same instant a searing heat shot through Victory's right shoulder.

Chaos broke out across the command center. But most importantly, the bullet missed her heart, one of the few vulnerable spots to a vampire her age. She remained on her feet.

Judging by the shock on Octavian's face as he clutched his stomach, he hadn't expected her to still be standing.

Two of Octavian's officers ran toward her with swords drawn, past their wounded Prefect already being tended by Ibrahim and a medic. Asaron slammed into one of them from the side, tackling him to the ground and distracting the other long enough for Victory to wrestle her sword from its sheath.

Strength flowed out of her shoulder along with her blood, but she swung her sword underneath the soldier's guard and caught him between his pants and bulletproof vest. The tip of the blade pierced his skin, and she flung him aside, twisting the sword out of him with the flick of her wrist. He landed with a howl, blood pumping from his stomach.

Victory didn't give him a second look. She stalked toward Octavian where the soldiers had lowered him to the ground, and Asaron joined her side, wiping fresh blood from his mouth. The medic had pressed bandaging over the prefect's wound, trying to stem the flow of blood. Victory smelled the rotten stench of guts and bile. Even if they managed to seal the wound, the true risk lay in infection. Ibrahim drew his sidearm and stood to face them.

He cocked the pistol and aimed it between the vampires, unsure of who posed the greater threat. "You got what you wanted. Now get out of here before I have both of you killed."

Victory exchanged glances with Asaron. They couldn't stop now. Not so close to cutting out the heart of this fruitless invasion. The chaos of combat had ceased around the camp, though shouts and cries of pain remained. Having no idea who had emerged the victor of this sortie, she couldn't take any chances.

Asaron drew the knife tucked into his belt and let it fly at Ibrahim where it stuck in the commander's neck. The man dropped his gun and clutched at this throat. The medic bolted to his feet and ran as Ibrahim collapsed over Octavian's legs.

In another burst of speed, Victory stood over Octavian, placing the tip of her sword against his throat. Soldiers all around the clearing aimed rifles, poised to fire.

Octavian gasped in pain. "If you kill me, you won't make it out of here alive."

"Good thing I'm already dead," Victory said. "This is what you get for attacking Limani. This is the message your men will bring to the Emperor."

"I am glad to die for my—"

Already, too much black blood soaked Victory's leather vest. She leaned forward, using her own body weight to push the sword point through Octavian's throat. The tip glanced off his spine, leaving a jagged, spurting gash.

A roar spread through the spectators, and Asaron dragged Victory to the ground with him. Bullets whizzed overhead before a second shout called off the soldiers' hasty actions.

Victory gritted her teeth against a gasp of pain. "Let's get the hell out of here, shall we?" Asaron had most of his weight on her injured shoulder, but she wasn't going to complain about him saving her skin.

They grabbed hands and rolled to their feet, balancing their weight against each other for momentum. Black wounds also stained Asaron at multiple points—he hadn't reached her side unscathed. "Run!"

Drawing on final reserves of strength, the two vampires dashed from the camp. She wasn't sure who hauled who most of the way in the blind blur as soldiers and tents gave way to trees and brush. Soon, dark woods surrounded them. Starlight brightened where the path split the trees a little farther ahead.

When they reached it, Asaron collapsed onto the side of the road. "We're good."

Victory sank to her knees next to him. "We're both going to bleed out before we make it home." Her shoulder screamed. The bullet in her body prevented any healing, draining her by inches. Asaron had too many injuries to count, moving only due to the amount of Roman blood he'd taken once freed from imprisonment.

Asaron peered along the road. "Hear that?"

A truck appeared, chugging along as if unaware that war raged nearby. A truck with a Roman license plate affixed to the front fender. Cursing this sudden bad luck, Victory pushed herself to her feet using her sword for balance. Not that she knew what she would do with a truck full of soldiers bent on revenge.

The vehicle slowed to a halt at Victory's side. She raised her sword with hands that couldn't tell whether they still had fingers attached to them.

The passenger-side window rolled down. "You two need a ride home?" Toria asked.

EPILOGUE

Mikelos slipped his hand into Victory's underneath the council table. While strange to have him by her side in this setting, his presence reassured her after the whirlwind events of the past few days. But he helped to fill a room so empty without Lorus and Fabbri, both in police custody. And Sethri, ready to be buried the next day.

A speakerphone sat in the middle of the conference table, a rare temporary gift from the elves to allow immediate overseas communication. From it emanated the strong voice of the young Roman Emperor, dimmed by the distance of an ocean. The council had nominated Victory to be acting head, due to both her political experience and knowledge of how to deal with temperamental nobility from her days as a professional bodyguard.

"Now that you've ruined my plans to expand my territory on the New Continent," Emperor Benedictus said, "and alerted the entire British Empire to be on guard against future attacks, how do you propose to amend this situation?"

"Need I remind you, sir," Victory said, "that your possession of a nuclear device breaks international treaties, never mind your attempts at expansion. I don't believe Limani owes you any sort of apology."

The rest of the council gaped at her, though Mikelos leaned back with a satisfied smirk. He'd done his share of standing toe-to-toe with nobility stuffed with righteous indignation.

"The British ambassador here in Roma has clamored the palace for apologies since the news broke yesterday of the attack on Limani," Benedictus said. "And we've not even done anything directly to the British."

Here the Emperor showed his true youth, at least in the political arena. The old Emperor might have taught his nephew a bit more before passing away and feeding him to the wolves. "If you'll accept a piece of advice from an old mercenary who has dealt with the British," Victory said, "they don't need an excuse to clamor for anything."

A short chuckle emerged from the speaker. "I'd hate to ask your opinion of the Empire."

He'd lightened up. She could work with this. "While honorable to a fault, your typical Roman citizen believes might makes right."

From her other side, Max stifled a laugh. One of the human members of the council, on the other hand, appeared ready to pass out from embarrassment.

"I thank you, my lady," Benedictus said. "Your honesty is a refreshing change from my ministers here in Roma. I don't suppose I could tempt you with the honor of a state visit? I realize I have much to learn yet about ruling."

"It is tempting," Victory said. "But right now, my place is here in Limani. However, I believe I could offer you a piece of advice?"

"Be my guest."

"Don't apologize to the British. They will be sated by a formal apology to Limani. Which can be offered at a conclave between all three countries designed to revisit the old treaties. It is past time for some much-needed changes. Territorial negotiations can be part of the new meeting."

Silence from the speaker. Everyone in the room on her end of the line tensed, waiting for a response.

"My lady Victory? Are you still there?"

"Yes, sir. I'm not pressuring you to make a decision now, of course. Just offering my opinion on the situation."

"A solid opinion it is," Benedictus said. "Let me first announce here the need for a conclave between the Roman Empire, the British Empire, the free city-state of Limani, and any other countries, in order to discuss global matters in this modern era."

"Thank you," Victory said. "Limani will be glad to attend."

Toria sat with Kane and Syri in the baking trial room, ready to sneak out at the first opportunity. They'd come to support her mother, one of the prime witnesses in Lorus' trial for treason against Limani.

The arduous trial had stretched through the long days of summer. Treason was serious business in Limani, and this was the first trial for such in over seventy-five years. Lorus never claimed innocence, and the city's defense attorney had drawn out evidence of his guilt over the last two months.

Tonight, the room overflowed for the final pronouncement. "Too much, Syri?" Kane asked. A woman in the row ahead of them turned to glare at his interruption of the proceedings.

Syri had returned to the hospital for two weeks after the final battle, after aggravating internal injuries from her original attack. Even now she wasn't at a hundred percent. Kane's attentiveness to the girl amused Toria for the most part. She'd been inseparable from them since her release from the hospital.

Syri waved Kane away. "Hush, I'm fine."

The central tribunal officer stood from the long table at the far front. He cleared his throat. Every little movement in the room ceased and silence descended over the crowd.

"In the city-state of Limani versus Lorus Gunnar," he said, "Gunnar has been found guilty of state treason and sentenced to death by hanging. Based on the defendant's documented confession, no appeals will be granted."

He banged his gavel, and the room exploded. Toria lost sight of her mother in the front row when people around them bounded to their feet. Cheers, jeers, and even various expressions of dismay surrounded them.

"Let's get out of here," Syri said. "It's done."

Fabbri clasped Victory's hand as they stood at the edge of the pier. She would board the Roman cargo ship bound for the British colonies as soon as the deliveries to Limani finished unloading. "Thank you for everything. I'm sorry things turned out the way they did." She lifted one of the packs at her feet. "Though to be fair, banishment is preferable to death."

"I'd agree," Victory said.

Two dock workers approached, ready to bring Fabbri's belongings onboard the transport. "Guess this is it," Fabbri said. "Watch over the city, Victory. And good luck in Roma."

"I will. Good luck yourself." Victory moved away while Fabbri helped the men gather the rest of her bags. Despite the awkwardness, she'd volunteered to escort the woman out of Limani territory following the conclusion of Lorus' trial. Missing the man's daytime execution hadn't pained her in the slightest.

She returned a final wave as Fabbri boarded the ship, then turned toward the customs house where Mikelos waited in the air conditioning with a music text. She sank into the chair next to him in the empty waiting room.

"She off?" Mikelos asked.

"She's gone. The world can return to normal now. At least until the fall."

"You excited to visit Europa?" Mikelos patted her knee before rising to his feet. "See the old stomping grounds?"

"I'm more excited for next week's emergency elections, when I no longer have to act as interim council head." Victory followed Mikelos out of the waiting room. The horn from the cargo ship sounded, and they paused to watch it pull away from the pier. "But yes. The trip will be good. The world needs it."

The surreal situation did not hit Toria until mid-song on the Twilight Mists dance floor. She froze, staring at the other dancers and people lounging on couches or chatting at high-top tables. "What are we even doing here?"

Kane and Syri had been dancing inappropriately next to her, but she assumed it was because Duncan, Kane's ill-fated date from earlier in the summer, stared at them from the bar. They broke away from each other.

"It's Thursday night," Kane said. "Thursday night is half-price drinks and industrial music. I'm here for the drinks and the boys. You're here for the music and the drinks and the boys. Syri's here because she's been attached to us all summer. And possibly for the boys."

"You're the only man for me, darling," Syri said.

Kane laughed. "Still not interested. What's wrong, Tor?"

"This!" Toria waved her arms. "These people! They're acting like nothing happened."

Dismissing his carefree attitude, Kane placed his hands on Toria's shoulders. Concern for her sifted through their link. "Let's take a break from dancing for a few." Without waiting for her agreement, Kane tugged her toward the couch they'd claimed in a far corner. "You want to invite Daliana for dinner tomorrow?"

Toria had seen Daliana in her official capacity as therapist on an irregular basis since high school, and both she and Kane had visited her multiple times over the summer. The elven psychiatrist had been booked solid for weeks as the residents of the city absorbed the recent events, but she'd been amenable to seeing them over meals instead of during office hours as a favor to Victory.

"This isn't some flare-up of my nonexistent posttraumatic stress disorder," Toria said, pulling out of his grasp and veering toward the bar. "This is dehydration."

Once ensconced on their couch, beer acquired, Toria continued. "Nothing is really settled. This won't be over until the conclave in Europa. Which we can't attend. Despite how we are the reason there is still a Limani to attend the conclave."

"Is that what this is about?" Syri said. "Not being able to go next month?"

Kane clinked bottles with Syri across Toria before taking a swig of his beer. "Classes start in two weeks. I'm not missing a semester and delaying our graduation. Sorry, love."

"I could go," Syri said. "I'm finished college."

"You're not going anywhere without us," Kane said. "Not until we figure out how much of your magic is entwined with ours after being in Toria's brain. Zerandan's orders. And Victory's." The mage had been surprisingly willing to explain the curse he'd laid on Toria before being ransomed back to the Romans, but they wanted to take no chances.

A knot loosened inside Toria, and a bit of tension drained out of her tightly wound soul. "So, life can go on as normal, and we can go back to being treated like children?"

"So life can go on as normal," Kane said, "and we can dance. After we finish our beer."

Toria draped her arms over the top of the couch to either side of her, drawing Kane and Syri closer. When Syri rested her head on Toria's shoulder, she asked, "We are stuck with you now, aren't we?"

"You complaining?"

"Not one bit."

The Reluctant Master

The silk gown was a different sort of armor than Victory was accustomed to. She swept down the main staircase of the manor house for an imaginary audience, queen of her own domain, and twirled at the bottom. Never let it be said that a seven-hundred-year-old vampire couldn't still have fun.

Victory entered the library and spun again for Jarimis, enjoying the way the long skirt fluttered around her ankles. She'd traded in her mercenary career for the steadier life her family wanted in Limani, and things like leaving her hair loose and wearing pretty clothes for fun instead of undercover work were still a novelty.

Jarimis leaned back in his fancy office chair. "Different. Nice." Her vampire progeny's black hair spiked at odd angles, a strong indication that he'd rolled out of bed at sunset and gone straight to work. "Ally finally won the battle?"

"She said if I was going to lounge around at the bar, I had to play the part of exotic vampire," Victory said. "Apparently jeans don't count." Though Allesandra managed the bar and nightclub Victory owned, her first loyalty lay with Jarimis. He would always be her priority as his bloodbound daywalker, a human enhanced with increased healing and extended life, and Victory would never begrudge her that faith. However, Ally had stricter ideas than Victory about things like "style" and "propriety," even though Victory had not claimed the formal title of Limani's Master of the City.

She didn't want the responsibility of protecting the humans in the city from outside vampires. She didn't work for free.

Jarimis pushed a piece of scrap paper toward her. "Before you leave, take a look at this."

She plucked it from the desk and read the three names written in Jarimis' neat print. Andersen Hunt. Keely Hunt. Joy Vilece. "Context?"

"Any of those jump out at you?"

She read them again, searching her memory for any hint of familiarity. "Should they?"

"Not necessarily. Mira called me earlier. They passed through Newport Hill a few days ago and dined on a local hunter. When they didn't appear anywhere in the Grand Strand, she figured they must have gone north instead." He twisted a pen around his fingers, reminiscent of the way he used to absently play with his knives.

"I see." No other major settlements sat between Limani and Newport Hill. The vampiric hierarchy in the colonies was a lot less formal than in the mainland Victory had left behind, and usually Mira, the vampire Master of the City of Newport Hill, only called Jarimis to gossip. But if she had passed along specifics, this was important.

"Who knew being in charge was less power and prestige and more herding cats?"

"Not in charge, remember? I just live here."

Jarimis' laughter followed Victory out of the library and all the way to the front door.

Today was going to be different.

Mikelos had hid in this backwater city on the other side of the globe for long enough. As far as the rest of the world knew, the famous concert duo had disappeared from the mainland without a trace years ago. He was now a mild-mannered shop boy called Mike. His vampire Connor was dead.

But it was easy to wake up and determine this slump had gone on long enough. It was harder to stick to the decision in the cold light of day. To decide things needed to change. That he couldn't live out the rest of his natural lifespan hiding from the world and never making another personal connection.

Mikelos shivered in a sudden gust of wind as he locked the music shop's front door for the evening. He'd lived in Limani for a year, but it didn't feel like home.

After checking the latch a final time, he shoved his keys in the pocket of his woolen coat, then pulled on a pair of thick gloves as he rambled in the direction of his apartment.

He hadn't frozen last winter, and he would survive this one as well. Didn't stop him from missing the winter villa in Chora. Right now, he could be lying on the veranda enjoying the warm seaside breeze and drinking delicious local wine—

But those moments were lost forever.

Mikelos stopped at the next intersection. Keep going toward his empty apartment? Warm light spilled from a coffee shop, along with the faint stirrings of live music. The cold air burned his lungs. He could face these memories.

He crossed the street and opened the door to the coffeehouse. The music embraced him, welcoming him like a long-lost friend. Music surrounded him all day at work, but records could not imbue the listener with soul and passion the way a real performance should. The rhythm of the acoustic guitar shivered along his spine as he edged through the crowd. He enjoyed the young woman's voice, loaning vocals to her instrument, while he purchased his espresso.

His fingers danced on the side of his leg, echoing the chords in the music on the neck of an imaginary violin. He shuddered, told himself it was a residual chill from outside, and wrapped both hands around warm ceramic to still them.

He tried not to critique the musician, but old habits die hard. Something sounded off about the guitarist's instrument—a slight rattle underscoring her strumming. At the next break, he pushed himself away from the wall and approached the tiny corner stage.

The worst she could do was turn him away and ignore his advice. But if she was any sort of proper musician, she wouldn't. All musicians, from those playing concert halls to performing in off-beat coffeehouses, knew better than to scoff at care for their instruments.

"Excuse me," he said. He took his cue to continue from the guitarist's friendly, open expression. "Did you know your seam glue is starting to give way?"

Today might be different.

Victory parked in one of the reserved spots behind the Twilight Mists. Once inside the club, a quick scan of the room showed no potential problems. She might be retired, but losing a few centuries worth of mercenary habits took longer than a year.

The number of people in here for a weeknight encouraged her. Business was good.

Allesandra waved from the other end of the bar as Victory approached. She claimed the stool that emptied after Jarimis' daywalker handed a glass to a tiny human woman wearing eye-watering purple. The mixed drink matched her hair. "Hello, darling," Victory said, settling the drape of her skirt. Jarimis had plucked Allesandra out of a seedy bar on the edge of the Wasteland almost a decade ago, and she'd completed their small family ever since.

"You can thank Jarimis for letting you sleep in," Allesandra said as she replaced the vodka on the shelf behind her. "I was all for dragging you out of bed. From now on, every minute you're late comes out of your next paycheck." She wiped her hands on a handy towel. "Want anything?"

"You don't actually pay me. And no, thank you."

"Was Jay still working when you left?"

"Of course. He sends his love."

Allesandra left Victory to her own devices as they met a sudden rush of drink orders. The Twilight Mists fulfilled Allesandra's dream of running her own place, but she would always be most at home pouring drinks and chatting with strangers.

Her family was happy now, settled and content. Jarimis had spent too much of his long life following on the heels of Victory's mercenary career, but he'd never chosen that life. Establishing a home in Limani to found a university fulfilled his dreams, too. At heart, Victory would always be a mercenary. But for now, she could consider Limani home.

Half an hour after approaching the guitarist, Mikelos found himself playing Lydia's second guitar and laughing his way through half-remembered folksongs.

He'd meant to go home afterward, but another hour later, he helped Lydia load her gear. Caught up in her whirlwind energy, he escorted her toward the new club recently opened in a refurbished warehouse.

Neon above the doors named the lounge "Twilight Mists." Inside, the bar curved out from one wall, and intimate seating clusters surrounded the dance floor on two more sides. The stage sat empty tonight, with recorded music piped through hidden speakers—a dance song that had topped the charts on the mainland a few years ago.

The way Lydia's waiting friends embraced him into their midst, sliding him into their circle as if he'd always been there, both surprised and warmed Mikelos. It was a nice reminder of the common bond musicians shared. When the music slowed, the others paired off. But he wasn't ready to leave yet.

A young woman drifted toward the seating, and after a steadying moment to feel the beat of the music, Mikelos approached and gave a formal bow, as if he still wore a tailor-made tuxedo and not battered jeans. "Might I have this dance?"

She gaped at his formality, but recovered in a flash and placed her hand in his. "My pleasure, good sir."

He swept her into a slow waltz. This was…more than different. This was good.

"My friend Liam is coming by to meet me soon," the woman said, tossing hair over her shoulder. The gesture exposed the delicate point of one elven ear, and she stared at Mikelos as if daring him to comment.

But the simple act of dancing with a beautiful woman transported him to the past, and the old Mikelos answered, the one who had charmed nobility and society ladies for almost two centuries. "Then I shall have to ask him for the next dance."

This startled the elven girl into a peal of laughter. "Oh, I like you. My name is Syrisinia, Syri."

"Mikelos."

Now why had he given his real name, instead of the bastardized version he'd used since arriving in Limani? This new take on life was turning out better than he'd expected, but he still needed to be careful.

Syri's friend arrived two songs later, and Mikelos left them to their dancing. He welcomed the break. The coffee earlier had not prepared him for an evening of unexpected exertion, and a drink was in order.

Mikelos ensconced himself at a small table near the end of the dance floor, with a sweeping view of most of the club, and watched Lydia and her friends dance. His attention wandered to the attractive bartender who'd served his beer. She leaned on the bar to converse with a darker-haired woman across from her. The brunette was striking, and the unexpected flash of familiarity intrigued Mikelos.

As she shifted on her barstool, the light caught her delicate glass. The red liquid within absorbed the light and coated the sides of the glass in a way even the best ruby port never did. He didn't know the woman. But he knew that liquid, and he knew the graceful movement of her hands as she talked.

In the course of his research before moving here, Mikelos had learned that Limani counted two vampires in residence. The Master of the City and her male progeny. This must be the Master herself. If anyone in this city might recognize him, it would be her.

He'd try to make his exit before she spotted him.

Victory lounged at the end of the bar. Allesandra had pushed a glass into her hand a few minutes ago, and a tentative sip revealed a smooth blood wine. Allesandra continued to improve upon her version of the drink, and Victory marked this one a success.

Allesandra wandered over and propped a hip against the bar. "I saw the response you left to my note last night. If you're going to ask the werewolf alphas for permission to host their kids for a teen night, we should consider reaching out to the elves as well," she said. "Establishing a neutral meeting ground would benefit all the supernatural groups in Limani."

Victory considered her next words while she sipped her drink. "There's a difference between holding a night at a club and setting myself up in an official capacity as a leader in the community. I am not the Master of the City."

Allesandra stared at her for a few moments. "I hate to break it to you," she said, her words catching on a laugh, "but since you and Jarimis are the only ones who live here, and you're the elder, you already are."

To be fair, the thought had occurred to Victory. But it seemed pretentious to hold such a title when her court consisted of one progeny and his daywalker. Especially since said progeny did what he wished regardless of his sire's political status. "Consider me still in denial."

Allesandra's shoulders shook with repressed giggles. Hell, even her progeny's daywalker didn't give her the respect due such a fancy title.

Victory surveyed the crowd, which had shifted in demographic as the night progressed. As humanity's only natural predator, she read the mood of a crowd and picked out the individuals within. She hadn't hunted for a live meal in ages, but she retained the senses and skill.

She grounded herself in the physical. Feet propped on the rungs of her barstool and right fingers curled around the stem of her glass. She tuned out the distraction of the lights above the dance floor, and the throbbing bass of the music turned into the echoing heartbeat of life all around her.

Humans comprised most of the Twilight Mists' patrons, thanks to their global majority. However, amidst the swirling humans danced two distinct elven figures who moved with a liquid grace. Over in a far corner, a small group sprawled together on couches. They sat closer together than humans would, with lounging postures that almost echoed their furrier forms—younger members of the local werewolf pack. Now that she paid attention, their musk underlined the regular human odors that permeated the Twilight Mists.

A lone man sat near the wolves, nursing a drink and watching the dancers. Human, but he caught Victory's attention where the others didn't. Something tugged at her memory, something that stretched back further than her time in Limani.

Light caught the man's profile as he sipped his beer.

"Daywalker," Victory said.

Allesandra lowered the notepad she used to mark inventory. "What?"

"Not you." Victory left her glass on the bar and stood. She skirted the dance floor, zeroing in on the impossible person sitting in her club.

He'd scrambled to his feet by the time she made her way through the dancers, but he stopped cold at her approach. His eyes flicked past her to the exit, and his muscles tensed. Was he considering making a run for it? Why?

But now that she was closer, the pieces fell into place. Decades had passed, but she recognized the man beneath the coarse exterior of jeans and shaggy brown hair. The last time she had seen him, he'd stood onstage. She'd worn a ballgown then too, but with a dagger strapped to her thigh, irritated that the woman who'd hired her as a bodyguard had insisted on such exposed seats. He had worn a tuxedo, taking a bow with the other featured member of the orchestra. A vampire—Connor. Which meant this was—

"Mikelos?"

Mikelos wasn't fast enough. The vampire stalked through the dancers toward him. He grabbed his coat and lurched out of his chair, but she stopped a few feet away.

Her posture wasn't threatening, and her fingers twisted together, almost in nervousness. And then she said his name. "Mikelos?"

Of all the damned luck. But ingrained habit made being rude to the Master of the City intolerable. After a beat, he dipped his chin. "Yes." His hands ached, and he loosened his grip on the coat.

She inclined her head in return. "My name is Victory. I give greetings to you and your bonded. Might I have the honor of joining you for a drink?"

This was getting worse by the second. "I'm sorry, I was just leaving." His voice cracked, and he knew she could read his radiating distress as easily as he read sheet music.

Surprising him, she dropped the formality, even going so far as to reach for him before aborting the gesture when he stepped back. "Are you okay?"

He didn't want her concern. He wasn't part of that world anymore. "Excuse me," he said, brushing past her on his way toward the exit.

Once outside the Twilight Mists, he pulled on his coat. But his shivering didn't stop in its warm embrace. This is what he got for trying to break himself out of his slump. Everything he lost ended up thrown back in his face.

Today was undeniably different. His secret was out.

Jarimis waited on the porch, backlit by the front door, when Victory drove up to the manor house. Allesandra pulled in right behind her. Victory's mind whirled with thoughts of Mikelos, but the focused expression on her progeny's face drove away her concerns for the musician's hasty exit.

Allesandra bounded up the steps and embraced her bonded as Victory asked, "What's wrong?"

Jarimis held his daywalker tight, but he met Victory's gaze over the petite woman's hair. "We've got trouble. The three I told you about."

They gathered in the kitchen. Jarimis and Victory sat on opposite sides of the table while the daywalker flitted around the room, preparing her bedtime cup of tea. Allesandra's confidence, despite Jarimis' concern, did much to reassure Victory that they weren't in an immediate crisis situation.

"There's not much we can do now, with sunrise so close," Jarimis said. "But three vampires attacked one of the werehyenas out for a late-night hunt. She reported one man and two women, so odds are it's the three Mira called about."

Allesandra leaned against the counter, gripping her mug. "Is she okay?"

"Alive," Jarimis said, "but badly drained. They were out to feed, not kill."

"But a human would be dead," Victory said. "It's probably only luck they found a hyena instead. Thank the gods it wasn't one of the elves. We'd have a war on. I'm guessing the three went to ground?"

"Looks like," Jarimis said. "But the hyenas weren't able to track their vehicle once it hit paved roads."

Victory slumped in her chair. "I suppose I get to deal with this? Being the Master of the City and all?"

Her progeny and his daywalker traded amused looks. "She finally caught on?" Jarimis asked.

"Finally," Allesandra said.

"Cute," Victory said. The vampires would stop travelling as dawn approached, if they hadn't already after such a full meal. "The city will be safe during the day. I'll go with Allesandra to work tomorrow night. Can you join us?"

"I have a meeting with the construction committee," Jarimis said. "But I can meet you afterward."

"Go armed, please," Victory said. He would know it was not a request. "We'll give them one night to come to me and ask permission to be in my city. If they hunt unauthorized again, I'll go after them."

"Three against one?" Allesandra asked.

"They'd have to see me coming," Victory said. "If I can't take them, I retreat and call the Mercenary Guild. I still pay dues for a reason." She tapped her fingers on the table until Jarimis covered her hand.

Allesandra joined them at the table, steaming tea in hand. "Tell Jarimis about Mikelos."

"Who?" Jarimis leaned forward in interest. He did love his gossip. Likely why Mira always called him with the vampire news instead of Victory.

"Remember the string duo we saw on the job with the baroness of Varga?" Victory asked. "The violinist was sitting in the Twilight Mists tonight. Without the cellist."

"The vampire and daywalker?" Jarimis asked. "Why would the daywalker be here without the vampire?"

"I remember serving his drink," Allesandra said. "He looked kind of rough." She slipped her hand into Jarimis' free one, linking the three of them. "Who was his vampire?"

"Connor," Victory said. When the finest musical duo in the world visited a city, even the lowly mercenaries heard the news.

"They were brilliant. I only ever got to see them twice," Jarimis said. "I think they stopped performing a few years ago. Cancelled some shows without notice, then nothing. Such a shame."

"Well, if Connor's not here in Limani, we probably know why." Victory remembered the expression of anguish on the young man's face. But young was a misnomer. Mikelos had to be over two hundred years old. "He's dead."

Time didn't heal all wounds, but Mikelos did feel better in the morning.

He stared at the violin case in his closet, then closed the door. Some things he still wasn't ready for.

Lydia surprised him at work that afternoon, bounding through the rows of new music. He returned her grin with one of his own, surprised by how pleased he was to see her.

"We're going back to the Twilight Mists tonight," she said, fingers picking through a crate of old records next to him. "You ran out on us last night. Everything okay?"

Mikelos continued re-alphabetizing the row in front of him. "Just got tired all of a sudden."

"Don't disappear next time. We were worried," Lydia knocked his hip with hers. "But you'll be there tonight?"

"Sure," he said, the word escaping his lips before thought.

"Great!" Lydia squeezed his arm. "My break's almost over. See you tonight." She disappeared from the music shop as fast as she had appeared.

Mikelos stared after her, fingers stilled on the records.

"You should invite her to dinner."

Connor gestured with his champagne glass across the salon, pointing out a redhead. She caught Mikelos' gaze when he followed Connor's line of sight.

"Look at that dress," Mikelos said, raising his own glass in the human's direction and winking at her. "She's a man-eater." The gold material hugged the woman's curves, leaving nothing to the imagination.

"You need more excitement in your life," Connor said.

Mikelos draped his free arm around the shorter man's shoulders, not caring whether he wrinkled both of their tuxedos. "I have plenty of excitement following you around, brother. Besides, we leave the city tomorrow."

"That's why she's perfect!"

Connor's laughter echoed in Mikelos' mind, and he shook himself all over. The store's only customer, a bespectacled gentleman examining the newer imports, made no secret of the curious look he shot in Mikelos' direction.

Mikelos ignored him and returned to work.

"You should invite her to dinner."

But a date with Lydia didn't interest Mikelos. He wasn't interested in a date with anybody. The sudden desire for simple friendship, however, clawed at his gut. A memory of storm-washed blue eyes flashed in club lighting, and Mikelos knew in an instant who he'd rather talk to.

Though concern about the three strange vampires approaching Limani simmered in the back of Victory's mind, the werehyenas patrolled the borders. They had taken this offense personally with the assurance she would be the first to know if another attack occurred. For now, Victory stepped in to play bartender while Allesandra dealt with administrative tasks in the office, and she would never tire of the way patrons lit up when they realized the mysterious vampire owner of the Twilight Mists could mix drinks. Soon she wouldn't be so mysterious, and that day couldn't come soon enough.

Despite Allesandra's preference for Victory to highlight vampiric elegance when she visited the club, she wasn't about to face potential enemies wearing a sheath skirt. So today she wore casual clothing once more, with her long hair braided to prevent a tangle hazard.

Her sword leaned behind the bar, out of the way.

Two potential problems. Her brain switched between the known daywalker and the unknown vampires. If the strangers were smart, they would come to her first and avoid further problems. Maybe they had assumed the werehyena hunted outside of Limani territory and was fair game?

Too much to hope for, whispered her cynical side. Perhaps she should consider requesting that the younger club-goers leave early? One fewer worry if the vampires were less than friendly if—when—they showed up here.

More patrons poured into the club. Here was something to keep her mind off the strangers. Mikelos was back.

Mikelos ordered his drink from the second bartender, a man with tattoos curling around both arms beneath pushed-up shirtsleeves. He pretended not to notice Victory's attention on him, making sure to stick close to Lydia and her friends while they drank and danced. Now that he was here, the sudden desire to talk to the vampire again had buried itself in a bundle of unexpected nerves.

He'd become a bit more settled in his current life than he'd thought, and the idea of seeking out ties to what he had been before unnerved him.

Ignoring her would be a lot easier if she would stop *watching* him.

He drained his cider and laughed with the others at Lydia's joke. But his mind was not on the conversation around him, and he could put this off no longer. Eventually, someone would notice the vampire's attention on him, and things would get even more awkward.

Mikelos excused himself. This time he approached Victory's side of the bar. She busied herself wiping an already sparkling surface. What, now she wouldn't face him? "Can we talk?"

The damp towel paused, and Mikelos met her eyes square on. Their gazes locked for five heartbeats.

As he expected, she blinked first.

Humans didn't meet a vampire's eyes. The prey instinct was too strong. His ability to stare her down for so long was the best indication of his true age he could give her. A dirty trick, but it would intrigue her.

"Sure," Victory said. She blinked again, as if trying to get his measure anew. "It's quieter upstairs."

She grabbed two bottles of the cider Mikelos had ordered earlier and ducked from behind the bar to join him. With a jerk of her head, she led him to the spiral staircase in the corner. The balcony area was cozier, with scattered couches and intimate café tables. The club's acoustics meant conversation at a normal level despite the music.

Victory dropped into a chair in a secluded corner and handed him a bottle when he settled in the other. The chairs sat at an angle, giving both of them unimpeded views of the balcony area. She leaned back in her seat, as if she thought any perceived form of intimidation would scare him off. But now that he was here, he wasn't scared. He also had no idea what to say.

"So," Victory said. She seemed equally unsure, toying with the end of her long braid.

"So," Mikelos said. He sipped cider to sooth his dry mouth. There was only one real way to begin this conversation. "I'm sorry I ran off last night. I was surprised you recognized me."

A laugh escaped Victory's lips. "I'm not one to stand on ceremony. I promise I was much more startled to see a famous face in my small club on the edge of nowhere."

Contrariness compelled Mikelos to defend his new home. "Limani isn't the edge of nowhere."

"Yes, it is. Or else you wouldn't be here."

She was quick, that was for sure. "Fair enough," Mikelos said.

They sat in silence for another few moments, nursing their drinks and pretending to enjoy the music. Victory broke first. "Mikelos…where is Connor?"

Her voice was gentle, but the words still hit him like a battering ram. He studied the label on his drink without seeing the words. "Dead," he said. "I made a fresh start."

"I'm sorry."

The otherwise useless words contained more empathy than he had expected. "Thank you."

"I could never do it," Victory said. She picked at the edge of the label on her bottle with one fingernail. "Losing Fatima, my first progeny, was bad enough. I don't think I could risk that with a daywalker. You must be very strong."

"Oh? Why do you say that?"

"Fatima's daywalker Santiago committed suicide after she was killed. I still miss both of them."

They lapsed into silence again. This wasn't the conversation Mikelos had planned, but they had to get through the awkward stuff first. The appearance of the other bartender approaching their seats at a brisk clip saved him.

Victory rose, her body tensing. "Nikau. What's wrong?"

"Sorry for interrupting," Nikau said. "Allesandra sent me to find you. She said Jarimis is outside with 'three friends.'"

"Where's Ally now?" Victory asked.

"She left the club."

"Idiot girl. Let's go."

Mikelos stood and grabbed Victory's arm. "Wait. What three friends?"

Victory met his eyes again. This time, Mikelos blinked first. "Vampires." She tore away, Nikau close on her heels.

Great. More of them. Mikelos sighed and followed.

With both Nikau and, to her surprise, Mikelos close behind, Victory hastened downstairs as Allesandra appeared at the club's entrance. Relief washed over her. "What the hell, Ally?"

Allesandra met her at the bar. "Had to check it out for myself. Everything is fine. Jarimis is out there talking to them by their truck."

Victory pointed Nikau toward the front door. The mage shoved his shirtsleeves up farther, and the tattoos shimmered with an eerie glow under the lights of the club as he marched out. He'd keep an eye on the situation while they handled things here. "Did Jarimis have his sword?" She ducked under the bar and grabbed her own as she asked.

The music played on, but a crowd had gathered at the commotion. Allesandra ignored them all, saying, "No, but you know that doesn't mean anything."

True. Her progeny had never warmed to the sword, even carrying an ostentatious rapier in protest. But no vampire was ever defenseless, so she wouldn't panic yet.

"I think we're overreacting," Allesandra said, in counterpoint to her fears.

"Was he wearing his red gloves?" If the sword wasn't his favorite weapon, Victory's progeny seemed born with knives in his hands. The first time she had ever seen him, he'd carried dual daggers poised to eviscerate her during a surprise daylight attack as the human assassin Jarimis had once been. Since vampires didn't need added protection from the winter weather, he wore his custom-made Kwolek gloves, made of nearly bulletproof fabric, to prepare for a fight.

"Shit," Allesandra said. "Yes." She dodged through the crowd toward the DJ, and the music cut off. The dancers let out a shout of dismay and milled around for a moment, then drifted toward the cluster already surrounding the bar.

Victory clambered up on a barstool. After her piercing whistle, all attention was on her. "Sorry to interrupt your evening, ladies and gentlemen, but we've got a bit of a situation on our hands. I'm guessing most of you heard about the vampire attack last night?"

Calls of agreement rippled through the crowd. Limani was a small town, and word spread fast.

"The vampires responsible are outside—" A louder cry arose, but Victory raised her hands and waited for everyone to calm. "—But there is no immediate danger. To the backdoor, please." She pointed, and Allesandra waved at the group from where she'd positioned herself under the stairs.

Her mercenary-in-charge voice still worked, and most of the people filtered out of the club, corralled by the DJ and the human waitstaff. With a word from Allesandra, the werewolves left as guards for the collection of vulnerable humans.

Her werepanther waitress, on the other hand, stayed. As did an elf, along with two mages she knew as Nikau's partners.

And Mikelos.

Victory jumped from the barstool. "What are you all still doing here?"

After escorting the rest of the customers out, Allesandra reentered the club proper with a sawed-off shotgun propped on one shoulder. You could take the girl out of the Wasteland…

Rania bared teeth that had elongated into feline canines. She tugged off her serving apron and dropped it on the bar. "You're the Master of the City. You're a *good* Master of the City, from the stories I've heard of other places. I'm not going to stand by and see you overthrown."

"That's not really how it works," Victory said. She looked to Mikelos for backup. He had to be familiar with the intricacies of vampire politics and hierarchy.

Mikelos laughed, contrary to everything she expected. "This is Limani. It may be the city on the edge of nowhere, but it's my home. And you're the Master we choose."

The words moved her. But not likely in the way the former daywalker meant. Responsibility crushed her shoulders, and what he said was true. She was the Master in name, and now she had to be the Master in deed as well.

The words spilled from Mikelos' mouth, but even after, he stood by his short speech. He knew nothing about this woman, but she had been kind to him. She had evacuated the club instead of letting any humans be caught in the crossfire.

Connor had never backed a Master before. They travelled too much, and all cities opened their arms to welcome the famous musicians.

The front door to the club burst open, and a cold winter wind swirled through the room. Two vampires clutched Nikau the bartender and a dark-skinned man who must be Jarimis, Victory's progeny.

Irritation flashed in Nikau's eyes, though the tattoos on his arms no longer glowed. In contrast, Jarimis stood loose-limbed, without a care in the world.

The third vampire, unburdened by a hostage, stalked across the dance floor. Victory stepped forward to meet him. While the others in the club gathered in a semicircle behind Victory, Mikelos moved next to Allesandra, nearer to the bar. The daywalker kept her focus on Victory.

No, her real focus was on Jarimis. As was Victory's.

Instead of greeting the stranger, Victory's priorities laid elsewhere. "You guys okay?"

Nikau winced as the woman holding his arm tightened her grip further. Jarimis, on the other hand, met Victory's inquiry with an enthusiasm out of proportion to the situation at hand.

"Quite well, thanks. Might I introduce you to Andersen Hunt? I am escorted by his lovely wife Keely Hunt, as is Nikau by their progeny Joy Vilece. They are formerly of Fort Caroline, but felt the need for a change of scenery." Jarimis spoke as if making introductions at a dinner party.

Mikelos liked him. Jarimis reminded him of Connor.

That didn't bring the same flash of pain it might have two days ago.

Finally, Victory turned to the other vampire before her. "I'm sure you already know who I am."

"Victory, Master of the City of Limani," Hunt said. "Your progeny has done me the favor of informing me of your interest in stepping down from the position." His hands clenched and unclenched at his sides, betraying his nerves. Despite the rumpled business suit, he and the two women in cocktail dresses had attempted the formality common amongst most of vampire society.

Victory absorbed the words for a heartbeat. Then she looked to Jarimis again. "You told them *what*?"

"If I may—" Hunt said, but Victory silenced him with the wave of a hand.

"Quiet," she said. "The grownups are talking. Seriously, Jarimis?"

"I knew you weren't actually protesting the job," Jarimis said. "It just seemed the quickest way to get them inside." Jarimis sprang into action as the words left his mouth. One gloved hand disappeared into his jacket and reappeared in a flash. With a smooth movement, he drew the dagger across Keely's throat. It wouldn't kill her, but it would incapacitate for a good while

She dropped to her knees, her hands clutching her neck. Thick blood oozed between her fingers.

Almost simultaneously, light flashed from Nikau's arms, forcing the second female vampire to release him. Joy cried out in pain as the skin of her palms and fingers charred.

Jarimis grabbed Nikau's shoulder and pulled him away, across the dance floor. The mage's hands glowed, and Jarimis held the bloody dagger ready.

Despite her injured hands, Joy made as if to lunge for the escaping pair. She froze when Allesandra racked the slide on her shotgun. The noise echoed through the otherwise silent club. "Try it, bitch," Allesandra said.

Since Allesandra still focused on Joy, Mikelos saw Hunt move before she did. He shoved Allesandra away as Hunt pulled a gun from inside his suit jacket at vampiric speed and pulled the trigger. Pressure and a sharp pain pierced Mikelos' side, and he staggered against the bar. The familiar copper tang of blood filled his nose as it seeped from the wound in his abdomen, staining his shirt.

He lost his grip on the bar and sagged to the ground. Almost two hundred years, and he'd never been shot before. That hadn't been his life.

As the world faded out around him, he found he couldn't recommend the experience.

Victory dove forward the moment she saw Hunt draw the gun, but even with her own enhanced speed, she couldn't reach him before he pulled the trigger. She held her hand-and-a-half bastard sword out of the way as she slammed her shoulder into Hunt's chest. They crashed to the ground in a pile of limbs, and the pistol skittered out of reach.

She shoved herself away from Hunt to find Keely almost atop her. But a shotgun blast rang out through the club, even louder than the previous gunshot, and Keely fell to the floor, a gaping hole in her chest where her heart had been. With the destruction of her heart, true death claimed her.

Hunt screamed beneath her. He writhed his arms free and wrapped his hands around Victory's neck. She spared a moment for confusion at the useless and very human attack. But his goal wasn't suffocation, and the constriction she felt was the slow crush of her windpipe and trachea. Injuries that made drinking difficult were not easy to heal from.

Where Hunt held her head limited her field of vision, but she had a perfect view of Rania and the elven man confronting the third vampire. Despite her burned hands, Joy drew a dagger from somewhere in her tight dress. The elf lunged forward, and she slashed at his face. He drew away with a hiss of pain.

Victory still clutched her sword, so she smashed the cross-guard into Hunt's jaw. With her own supernatural strength behind the blow, the bottom half of the man's face crushed inward with a sickening crunch.

His scream of rage turned into a howl of pain. Hunt released Victory and brought his hands to his jaw, eyes rolling back.

She pushed herself off the still body and surveyed her club.

The elf held a bloody hand to one cheek but didn't seem distressed. Elves were tough. As if feeling the weight of Victory's examination, he pointed to the club's door, hanging half off its hinges.

Joy was gone, as was Rania. Hopefully the werepanther chased her down or out of Limani territory. Either was okay with Victory.

The three mages stood over Keely's body. Nikau nudged her with his boot, but the woman wasn't coming back from that.

Then, the commotion near the bar drew her attention. Jarimis and Allesandra kneeled next to a body. Mikelos' body. Hunt's shot hadn't missed. As she neared, the heady scents of Mikelos' blood and Allesandra's panic reached her.

She dropped to her knees, setting her sword at her side. Allesandra's hands clamped on Mikelos' abdomen, but blood seeped around her fingers. No scent of bodily waste, so not a gut shot. But a kidney and most of his liver must be shredded.

She tuned out the sounds of Jarimis and Allesandra arguing, Nikau and his friends discussing incineration for the vampire bodies, and narrowed in on a slow, irregular heartbeat.

Mikelos was alive.

"I'm not turning him," Jarimis said, his voice raw. "That's not how it works. You don't just do that to somebody."

When Jarimis turned to Victory, she knew what he would say. "You have to do it."

"What?" Allesandra said. "But you just said—"

"Not turn him," Jarimis said. "Daywalker. His body will remember."

No. That was baggage she did not need in her life, even if she never maintained the bond past this one drastic lifesaving action and he reverted to a regular human in three or four months. But the devastation on her progeny's face crushed her. "Jay—"

"He's *Mikelos,*" Jarimis said. "He's one of the best damned musicians in the world. He is not dying on my watch."

But Jarimis couldn't do it. He already had a daywalker, and a strict limit of one per vampire existed. And damn it, her progeny knew Victory couldn't resist him. She'd given him a home in Limani. She had to give him this, too.

Jarimis held his second, clean dagger out to her.

Fuck. Mikelos was dying. As the man's heartbeat grew fainter, Victory snatched the dagger from Jarimis and drew it down her forearm. The blade was sharp enough to delay the pain, but a beat later it lanced across the wound as dark blood welled up from the slash.

She'd never done this before, and for a moment, panic seized her. Mikelos' breath hitched, and this spurred her into action. He wasn't dying on her watch, either. She smeared the blood onto one palm and replaced Allesandra's hands over Mikelos' wound. Jarimis helped guide her forearm over Mikelos' lips, twisting her flesh painfully until more blood dripped into his open mouth.

Mikelos arched off the ground as his body seized once. Then his lips closed over Victory's arm, and he drank of his own accord. Survival instincts kicked in, and Victory tried to pull away from the searing burn of his mouth, but Jarimis held her arm firm.

The pain was worth it. Mikelos would live.

Mikelos woke in an unfamiliar bedroom. Soft lighting emanated from matching bedside lamps with stained-glass shades, and thick floor-length curtains covered the wall across from him. Gradually, the rest of the room came into focus. Antique furnishings surrounded the large bed, dark hardwood pieces that would overwhelm his tiny bedroom. The pale blue sheets beneath him and plush navy duvet covering his legs complemented the silver highlights in the understated wallpaper. A far cry from the bare apartment he'd called home for the past months.

He struggled to sit up, ignoring the jab of pain in his abdomen, but a soothing voice encouraged him to relax. A gentle hand touched his bare shoulder, and electricity rippled under his skin.

He gasped and fell back onto the pillow. The sensation was both distinct and achingly familiar, but either way, he'd never expected to feel its like again.

Mikelos turned his face. But it wasn't Connor who stood next to him. Instead he found Victory.

First things first. Were they still in danger? "What happened to the other vampires?" Then, "What time is it? And where am I?"

Victory answered as if giving a formal debriefing, but her other hand fluttered at her side before she shoved it in her pocket. "It's daytime. Approximately sixteen hours since the attack. Keely Hunt is dead. Joy Vilece ran out while I was saving you and evaded the werecreatures. We thought we'd incapacitated Andersen Hunt, but he also disappeared in the commotion of saving you. We've found no sign of either of them, though they left their truck and the werehyenas patrolled all day. And…you're in one of the guest rooms in my house." She stared at the abstract painting on the opposite wall.

Despite the ruined shirt and wisps of hair escaping her braid, she looked beautiful.

Victory met his eyes and held them. Five seconds. Ten. "You…you bonded to me," Mikelos said. The thing she'd said she could never imagine.

Victory left her hand on his bare shoulder and settled into the plush armchair next to his bed. She'd washed her hands, but a bloody handprint stained one chair arm. She had been with him from the beginning. And it seemed her concern for him overrode her respect for her furniture.

"Here's the thing," she said, but didn't finish the sentence. She studied the curtains with a strange intensity, but she still rested her hand on his skin, and the connection pulsed between them.

The immediacy faded with time, but for now it would be like a drug to Victory. Even though their relationship had not been sexual, Connor hadn't been able to keep his hands off Mikelos for months after they first bonded.

"You got shot," she finally continued. "It was pretty bad. This…it was the only way to save your life. I'm sorry."

He covered Victory's hand on his shoulder with his. He stifled a gasp, echoed by Victory, as the power of their new bond flowed between them. Drawing upon experience he thought he'd never use again, Mikelos tamped down on the connection until it caused less of a distraction. Victory stiffened, but he kept hold of her hand. She'd never created a daywalker. He was the one with experience in this situation.

No wonder she verged on panic. Though she radiated calm, now he could read her like an open book the way no one else in the world could. The way the muscles in her hand twitched under his grip and how her focus alternated between him and everything else in the room.

In a perfect world, the decision to bond with a vampire came after weeks or months of negotiation. Mikelos didn't know about Limani, but in most parts of the world, both parties signed extensive contracts. Victory must be worried about stealing his choice, even to save his life.

Two days ago, fury would have consumed him. Fury that this woman returned to him the one thing he craved, but not the way he wanted. The possibility of immortality was an empty future without Connor by his side. This woman could never complete him the same way. Instead of creating beautiful music, her mercenary hands wielded only death.

But as Limani's Master of the City, maybe she wasn't that mercenary anymore. And maybe he wasn't the same person either.

When Victory met his eyes again, he sensed the relief wash through her body. "It's okay," he said. "Thank you. Come here."

Victory helped Mikelos sit up, shoving extra pillows behind him. With a nervous chuckle, she curled next to him in the bed and allowed him to wrap his arms around her. She avoided the bandaged area, but it was already almost healed.

Victory twitched every time they shifted and the power of their bond zapped through her. "Is that going to keep happening?"

"It'll fade in a few weeks." Mikelos wasn't sure now whether this new closeness was the result of their bond or from the traumatic experience they had just shared. Maybe he just liked her. He didn't really care. "Depends on whether this will be a permanent thing or not." She hadn't wanted a daywalker. The stab of fear in his gut had nothing to do with his wound. Maybe this was just a taste of what he'd had before, and he would lose everything all over again.

His apprehension drained away when Victory smiled at him. "Maybe it can be," she said.

They lapsed into comfortable silence together. Today was different. Mikelos was home.

Limani: A Brief History

An excerpt from *A World Without Dragons: Living as an Émigré Beyond Qin Borders* by Lady Zhinu Zhuanxu-Wallace

The independent city-state of Limani started life as Greek colony. The alliance of Greek city-states in Europa joined in the rush to settle the "New Continent," managing to establish a foothold along the coastline near a major bay along the middle of the eastern coastline. They snagged space between the British colonies to the north and the newly claimed Roman territories to the south.

But while the British settlements were funded by second and third children of the werewolf nobility, and the massive Roman plantations were supported by corporations led by wealthy Roman vampire lines, the Greek colonists embodied the nature of their origins. These disparate colonists, from multiple Greek cities, maintained the ideals of equality and democracy that linked their alliance back in Europa. The major factor in their favor was that a larger proportion than expected of the original group of colonists consisted of mages from every elemental faction. These were mages schooled in the Greek magical academies[1] held in esteem throughout Europa, looking for adventure and new beginnings.

Bolstered by resources pouring in from their new territories in the New Continent, the Roman Empire set its sights on expansion at home once again. In a few short years, the last Greek city-states that had existed for thousands of years fell. Some fought for their independence to the bitter end and ended up in ruins, while others signed treaties with Roma that would ensure certain freedoms for their people.

Suddenly cut off from all support from home, as the city-states had bigger issues to worry about, Limani almost failed as a colony. But the mages, already spread throughout the territory and attempting to establish livelihoods for themselves, helped to keep the farms growing food and the small manufactories creating goods needed for the survival of their home. Those who were more combat-inclined helped the colony defend itself from incursions from the north and south. But every time the British and Roman settlements in the New Continent thought they smelled blood in the water, Limani proved itself more than willing to defend its staunch independence.

After the Last War, the British and Romans established Limani as a neutral zone between their lands.[2] But Limani had better things to do than play politics with great powers across the ocean. Instead, it established trade deals with the nearby Romans and British to become as self-sufficient as possible.

Limani also never forgot its roots, keeping to the ideals of democracy and fair representation. Over the years, a family of werewolves sought sanctuary from their noble families who'd disapproved of a marriage made for love. Other werecreatures drifted in, found a society where they weren't automatically second-class citizens, and made themselves at home.

When two vampires settled in the city soon after the Last War, one of them started a bar and the other announced plans to found a university.[3] Limani tolerated its eccentric immortals, even giving the acknowledged Master of the City a seat on the city council with a partial vote, similar to the positions held by the werewolf alpha and representative of the other werecreatures.

Elves have lived in Limani since shortly after its founding, but more moved in once it had a functioning university, mage school, and Mercenary Guildhall—three of the modern hallmarks of civilization. However, the city is not without its share of drama. The past 20 years have seen both political upheaval and the threat of invasion. The werepanthers fought for, and achieved, equal government representation. And Roman Emperor Benedictus VII attempted an ill-fated incursion into Limani territory, only to be soundly rebuffed by the city's combined forces.

Overall, Limani is a quiet town on a river. At once a microcosm of the greater world and a wholly unique culture in its own right.

---

[1]See "Chapter 7: From Academy to Museum" for more information on the current state of magic.

[2]For a more complete picture of Limani's role in the Last War, refer to Vilece & Brawley, eds. *Innocent Bystanders: The Roles of City-States in the Last War.* Oxenafor University Press.

[3]Learn more about Jarimis University in "Chapter 9: Notable Institutions of Higher Learning" and about Victory in "Appendix C: Masters of the City and Other Alternate Forms of Government."

Photo by Brian Roache

ABOUT THE AUTHOR

By day, J. L. Gribble is a professional medical editor. By night, she does freelance fiction editing in all genres, along with reading, playing video games, and occasionally even writing.

Previously, Gribble studied English at St. Mary's College of Maryland. She received her Master's degree in Writing Popular Fiction from Seton Hill University in Greensburg, Pennsylvania, where her debut novel *Steel Victory* was her thesis for the program.

She lives in Ellicott City, Maryland, with her husband and three vocal Siamese cats. Find her online (www.jlgribble.com), on Facebook (www.facebook.com/jlgribblewriter), and on Twitter and Instagram (@hannaedits). She is currently working on more tales set in the world of Limani.

www.ingramcontent.com/pod-product-compliance
Lightning Source LLC
Chambersburg PA
CBHW020502310726
48979CB00016B/2758/J

* 9 7 8 1 9 4 7 8 7 9 2 2 5 *